The Flaxborough Novels

'Watson's Flaxborough begins to take on
the solidity of Bennett's Five Towns,
with murder, murky past and much acidic
comment added.' H R F KEATING

Broomsticks Over Flaxborough

Naked as on the day she was born, save for a
double-looped string of amber beads and a pair of
harlequin-framed spectacles, Mrs Flora Pentatuke,
of 33 Partney Avenue, Flaxborough, leaped
nimbly over the embers of the fire.

As she danced into the deep darkness beyond,
there arose small yellow flames, stimulated by the
not inconsiderable draught of her passing. Briefly
they were reflected from Mrs Pentatuke's well
developed but still handsome buttocks. They
illuminated too the backs of weighty thighs and
calf muscles. The thighs were dimpled and lacked
the tautness of the calves, which looked as if they
had been hardened by much exercise. As, indeed,
they had; for Mrs Pentatuke was a zestful member
of Flaxborough Ladies' Golf Club.

She pranced towards the edge of the clearing,
swerved and came back for another fire vault. Her
hands moved in gestures of sinuous supplication.
Now and again they would stretch to become rigid
extensions of the strong, white, plump arms. Then
Mrs Pentatuke would halt on tiptoe, shut tight her
eyes behind the bejewelled glasses, and cry in a
rich tenor: 'O mighty spirit! We are thine! Amen
evil from us deliver but!'

The Flaxborough Novels

Whatever's Been Going On At Mumblesby?*
Plaster Sinners*
Blue Murder*
One Man's Meat*
The Naked Nuns*
Broomsticks Over Flaxborough*
The Flaxborough Crab*
Charity Ends at Home*
Lonelyheart 4122*
Hopjoy Was Here*
Bump in the Night*
Coffin Scarcely Used*

* also available in Methuen Paperbacks

COLIN WATSON

*Broomsticks
Over Flaxborough*

A Flaxborough Novel

A Methuen Paperback

A Methuen Paperback

BROOMSTICKS OVER FLAXBOROUGH

First published in Great Britain 1972
by Eyre Methuen Ltd
Copyright © 1972 by Colin Watson
This edition published 1985
and reprinted 1988
by Methuen London Ltd
11 New Fetter Lane, London EC4P 4EE

British Library Cataloguing in Publication Data

Watson, Colin, *1920*–
    Broomsticks over Flaxborough.
    I. Title
    823'.914[F]   PR6073.A86

    ISBN 0 413 51660 1

Printed and bound in Great Britain

To Miles and Margaret

Chapter One

NAKED AS ON THE DAY SHE WAS BORN, SAVE FOR A double-looped string of amber beads and a pair of harlequin-framed spectacles, Mrs Flora Pentatuke, of 33 Partney Avenue, Flaxborough, leaped nimbly over the embers of the fire.

As she danced into the deep darkness beyond, there arose small yellow flames, stimulated by the not inconsiderable draught of her passing. Briefly they were reflected from Mrs Pentatuke's well-developed but still handsome buttocks. They illumined too the backs of weighty thighs and calf muscles. The thighs were dimpled and lacked the tautness of the calves, which looked as if they had been hardened by much exercise. As, indeed, they had; for Mrs Pentatuke was a zestful member of Flaxborough Ladies' Golf Club.

She pranced towards the edge of the clearing, swerved and came back for another fire vault. Her hands moved in gestures of sinuous supplication. Now and again they would stretch to become rigid extensions of the strong, white, plump arms. Then Mrs Pentatuke would halt on tiptoe, shut tight her eyes behind the bejewelled glasses, and cry in a rich tenor: 'O mighty spirit! We are thine! Amen evil from us deliver but!'

Other figures appeared in turn at the fire. Several jumped over it with something of the expertise of Mrs Pentatuke. Some skipped up to it resolutely enough but then seemed to find themselves wrongly footed for take-off. They went into a quick shuffle and leaped with such determination that they were winded on landing. One or two shirked the ordeal altogether by making a last-minute switch of direction and hop-skipping round the perimeter of cold ash. Among these were a portly middle-aged man with a small beard and two women who held hands and occasionally glanced at each other's feet as if to seek reassurance that they had not lost step.

The bearded man wore a mask over the upper part of his face. The mask was made of a soft velvety material neatly hemmed around the contours of nose and cheeks. A bag of the same material was slung under his belly, with the purpose, presumably, of preserving modesty rather than anonymity.

A watcher would not have found it easy to make a tally of the number of people taking part in the ritual. Somewhere in the sky was a third-quarter moon, but rifts in the heavy, slow-moving cloud were thin and infrequent. The street lamps on Orchard Road were at least a hundred yards distant, on the other side of a double row of black poplars and a thorn hedge more than eight feet high. The glow and fitful flaming of what was left of the wood fire showed sometimes three or four, sometimes as many as eight figures at once. The total number of dancers was greater than a dozen but probably fewer than twenty.

Women outnumbered men and seemed less inhibited in their choice of costume. Even so, the example of Mrs Pentatuke's virtually complete nudity was emulated by only two others. Most had retained one or more articles of underclothing. One somewhat diffident-looking participant wore a black one-piece bathing costume, the skirt of which she kept tugging down over errant segments of her bottom.

'O master! Give us the power of thine unlight!' The cry came from a tall, scraggy man in khaki shorts. He had halted so suddenly to make this supplication that those behind bunched up like holiday makers thwarted by the closing of an ice-cream kiosk.

Somewhere in the outer darkness there sounded off the response of Mrs Pentatuke.

'Seven times and seven times and Yah-loo-hally!'

The jam resolved itself and the round went on. Perhaps the tempo had slackened a little. Some feet dragged for a step or two; but then the stubbing of a naked toe against a stone or a root would restore vigour.

Between the dancers and a bank of foliaged shrubbery – possibly laurel or rhododendron – that screened them from the gardens of the nearest house stood a woman who gently beat a drum with one hand while in the other she held a treble recorder. The tune was a somewhat stilted version of Percy Grainger's 'Handkerchief Dance'. The woman's lack of height – she was not much more than four feet tall – was emphasized by her wearing a broad, square-cut cape of thick tweed and, at the end of sturdy, unstockinged legs, a pair of rock climber's shoes. Her hair was mannishly cropped. She was, as nearly as might be judged in the near-darkness, of a stern and chunky countenance, well weathered and inclined to whiskeriness. If ecstasy possessed her, she did not show it. She was quite grotesquely cross-eyed.

Mrs Pentatuke completed two more circuits, then skipped off towards a point where three small, steady lights gleamed. She halted and drew several deep breaths, her head thrown back, her neck taut and throbbing still from the exertion of the dance. Her spectacles had slid a little down her sweat-dewed nose. She pushed them back with two fingers.

The lights were the flames of three candles, each set within a large glass jar to shield it from the night breeze. The wax of the candles appeared to be black. The jars were suspended from a branch overhanging a pair of card tables that had been set up together and spread with a sheet of black polythene.

'Behold that which is and is not and is again!' declared Mrs Pentatuke when she had got her wind back. 'Yah-loo-hally!'

'Nema!' gasped a fat, grey-permed woman in woollen drawers and heavily-armoured brassière who had just arrived at the tables.

'It is almost time,' cried Mrs Pentatuke. 'I feel Him near!'

The fat woman grasped her bosom in both hands, as if to help contain any explosion that its violent heaving might portend, and nodded eagerly. Her face was much flushed.

Mrs Pentatuke selected one of a number of assorted drinking vessels that littered the tables. It was a china mug fashioned in the likeness of a can-can dancer's be-frilled rump and overprinted: *Ooo, la-la! Bottoms Up!* She dipped the mug into a green plastic bucket that was more than half full of a pale amber-coloured fluid – the aggregate, presumably, of the contents of a number of bottles that had been heaped on the ground near by – and drank with a sort of dedicatory ferocity.

'Take me, Abaddon!' called Mrs Pentatuke into the upper air.

'Ashtoreth, strike off my seals!'

She searched among the glasses, cups and mugs until she found a squat jar, the lid of which she unscrewed. With some of the contents of the jar – something oleaginous that smelled not unlike sage and onion stuffing – she anointed her hips and thighs. Then she replaced the lid on the jar and stood it back where it could be seen readily in the light of the candle.

The woman in the woollen drawers was drinking quickly, and with eyes tightly shut, from a goblet that she had filled at the plastic bucket. Her breathing had subsided a little but her face was still dark with blood pressure and pricked with little beads of sweat. Having drained the last of the liquor, she held the goblet a few inches in front of her face, squinted at it critically, and broke wind. 'Baboon blood,' she remarked to Mrs Pentatuke, then dropped the goblet into the bucket, where it sank.

'You ladies enjoying yourselves?'

The inquirer, who had silently manifested himself beside them, was a bald-headed man with inquisitive, restless eyes, an expression of bland solicitude and a church porch voice. He wore scouting stockings rolled down to the tops of a pair of brogues. Round his waist was a string of pennons of the kind collected and displayed on windscreens by motorists anxious to be deemed hardy travellers.

Mrs Pentatuke ignored him. She was listening intently as if to some far distant but immensely significant sound. The other woman made one of her hands into a claw and cackled a little self-consciously.

The man moved nearer to Mrs Pentatuke. She remained preoccupied, her head half-turned away, absolutely still. He leaned forward and sniffed carefully once, twice, three times, then looked at the woman in the woollen drawers and nodded over his shoulder to indicate Mrs Pentatuke.

'Flying tonight, is she?'

The fat woman scowled. 'Don't be sarcastic,' she said. She waddled away towards the fire.

The man shrugged and helped himself to a drink. Mrs Pentatuke remained in an attitude of entranced abstraction. The man raised the family-sized coffee cup in which he had ladled up his liquor.

'Hell fetch the Synod,' he murmured with the rapidity of established habit, then, more feelingly: 'And boil the Unreverend William Harness in cat vomit and give Bertha Pollock the whistling piles!'

'Hush!' whispered Mrs Pentatuke, snatching off her glasses to hear better.

There reached them, above the panting of the fire-leaping celebrants and the flat, monotonous accompaniment of the 'Handkerchief Dance', a strange lowing noise. It was rather like the plaint of a great bull, far off but full of menace.

The sound ceased for several seconds, then came again. This time, seemingly, from a slightly nearer point. It was not quite a bellow, yet more urgent than a moan.

Mrs Pentatuke replaced her spectacles and pressed her hands together.

'The Master!'

Adjudging her now almost cataleptic with expectancy, the man beside her reached out with his free hand and, without interrupting the steady downing of his drink, amiably patted and lifted those parts of her person that seemed to him most deserving of commendation. Mrs Pentatuke offered no objection; but nor did she in the slightest degree respond. After a while, he turned his back on her and took another cupful of liquor. This he drank in large, hurried swallows as if in anticipation of imminent drought. He did not appear to enjoy it much.

Three or four others staggered up to the improvised bar. They leaned hands on knees long enough to regain their breath and then, chattering and giggling in admiration of the novelties among the cups, jugs and goblets, snatched their own choices and filled them at the bucket.

One was a Toby jug in the likeness of a winking clergyman with an enormous strawberry nose. Another represented a huge frog; a third, a lady with one breast too many and a head too few. At the bottom of a fourth there lurked to astound the unaware toper a beautifully executed glazed earthenware dog's turd, very lifelike.

'A hundred and sixty-nine!' Mrs Pentatuke suddenly called out.

'Thirteen and thirteen and thirteen!' cried a man with a pernickety, high-pitched voice. He wore a deep helmet of dark felt, rather like a woman's cloche hat, to which small horns had been stitched. The helmet was pulled down to mask the upper part of his face and was pierced with eye holes.

"And ten thirteens again!" added a bouncy, chinless woman with pince-nez and a habit of good-humouredly emphasizing everything she said by hugging whoever happened to be nearest to hand. Her sole garment, a short fur coat, undulated glossily over several gallons of friendly bosom.

'A coven of covens!'

This neatly expressed summary of their arithmetic was contributed by the woman who had sorted out the pot frog. Whilst not underdressed so radically as her companions, she presented an appearance that in its own special way was much more alarming. Buttoned boots protruded from beneath a black skirt that draped the narrow, bony-looking figure from waist to ankles. The upper part of her body was encased in an archaic black corset, from which the thin, very white shoulders and arms emerged like potato shoots. A black straw toque hat of the kind considered *de rigueur* by Victorian widows, was perched upon her head. Of her face, nothing could be seen, for drawn down all round the toque and knotted beneath the woman's chin was a black veil of so close and opaque a weave that only where it was stretched tightly against the skin could an underlying pallor be discerned. The most curious, and disconcerting, thing about this veil was the woman's election to drink directly *through* it, rather than raise it above her mouth. There resulted the impression of a frog trying to nuzzle its way into a black tent.

Some more dancers arrived for refreshment. There now was a decidedly festive air about the assembly.

A woman with a big, loose straw hat tipped over one eye and a pullover tied about her middle seized the bearded and masked man and charged him round and round in a private, frantic waltz.

Mrs Pentatuke's earlier companion, the woman who had taken amiss the remark about flying, was back again; she and the recorder player, now partly undressed and presumably enjoying an intermission, had the pot of savoury-smelling ointment between them and were rubbing each other vigorously and with squeals of gratification.

A series of painfully ruptured harmonics, repeated persistently, proclaimed that the recorder had fallen into less instructed hands. The drum, too, was being much abused somewhere.

Mrs Pentatuke helped herself to more drink. The level in the bucket had fallen by several inches. She drained the mug in two eager gulps and pushed away the scraggy man in shorts who had blundered into her and was short-sightedly scrutinizing her beads, which he fed through his fingers like ticker-tape.

From much nearer than before and at greater volume came repetition of the bellowing sound.

Mrs Pentatuke stared into the dark and thrust out her arms.

'Master! Apollyon!'

Those near her fell silent. All looked towards the source of the noise, which, a few seconds later, was repeated. It sounded very like a foghorn.

One of the other women called tipsily: 'Coo-ee!'

The bearded man frowned at her and made a quick gesture of prohibition with his hand. Then he got down on his knees.

So did the woman with the squint. She swayed slightly and steadied herself by squatting back on the heels of her thick shoes.

The horn boomed again. Somewhere a woman was weeping and laughing in turns. The dancing had stopped altogether. Every now and then the glow of the fire embers was blotted out as somebody moved cautiously past. Men and women seemed to be feeling their way to form a crescent-shaped assembly with the invisible horn blower at its focal point.

'Asmodeus!' A man's voice, loud but plummily genteel like that of a bank manager playing a robber in amateur dramatics.

'Asmodeus!' 'Asmodeus!' Some of the chorus sounded uncomfortably self-conscious, but others – mostly women – vied in the expression of fervour.

Once more the deep bull-cry welled up from the dark centre of the arc of watchers. It was palpable, a sound that actually had body; they could feel it pushing against their flesh. It repelled, yet summoned. From some of the women escaped whimpers of fright.

Mrs Pentatuke was the first to descry the point of dusky red, no bigger than a firework fuse, that had winked into being in the patch of darkness at which they all had been staring.

She breathed a long, hoarse, ecstatic 'Ahhh!'

Very slowly, the spark grew in size until it looked like the end of a strongly-drawn cigar. It became bigger still and started to elongate. The shape the light assumed was that of a flame, but it was a strangely steady, very red flame, as if it burned in a closed and vitiated room instead of the open air. It was three or four feet above the ground.

As the power of the flame increased, it become more and more angrily crimson. Now there could be seen on each side of it something erect and curved and tapering. And below, limned in red, the lumpish outline of a vast cranium.

What the assembly saw was a beast, or a man masked in the semblance of one, with that sullenly burning candle set between its horns.

The spectacle set off a medley of cries, groans and liturgical recitals, with Mrs Pentatuke's constantly reiterated 'Take me, Master!' beating the others by several decibels.

The name Asmodeus was called out most often, but Apollyon could be heard occasionally, while one discriminating diabolist – a spindly, meek-looking young man who affected the curious sartorial conceit of a brassière worn as buttock-sling – piped 'Angra Mainyu!' whenever he got a chance.

The ex-recorder player sturdily rooted, vide St John the Divine, for 'Abaddon Six Six Six!' It sounded as if she were trying to acquaint the horned figure with her telephone number.

Whoever had taken possession of the drum began now to beat it with steady, businesslike rhythm and the dance was resumed. This time the circle was tighter, with the impassive and sinister bulk of the Master at its centre.

After a round or two, some of the celebrants became afflicted with giddiness and either fell over or staggered out of orbit.

Near the abandoned scene of the fire, someone gave a long, raking cough. Then another coughed, and another. A stench of burning sulphur drifted about the circle. Mrs Pentatuke's eyes were watering. She took no notice. She contrived to pass nearer and nearer the horned man with every circuit.

The ignition of the sulphur had induced a heap of half-charred branches and dry twigs to burst into flame. For several seconds the object of tribute could be clearly seen.

His head, surmounted by the great horns with the red flame between them, was black but gleamed wetly, as if it had just been dredged from ancient and noisome pickle. The face was a fairly even compromise between bovine and human, save that the teeth were characteristic of neither: they were small, needle-like, and bright green. The huge eyes were suggestive of a pair of hard-boiled eggs that had been jammed into raw wounds.

The Master's body seemed small at first, a mere appendage to the great head, but it was actually that of a plump, heavily built man of average or a little over average height. The skirt was of light cinnamon colour and greasy as if it had been rubbed with a cosmetic tanning oil. A pelt, possibly of a goat or a dog, was tied round the lower part of his paunch. His chest hair was black, thick and curly. He was sitting with legs apart in a folding canvas chair of the kind favoured by film directors. There lay on the ground close by his right foot a conical object, presumably the instrument that had produced the bellowing noise.

Before the renewed blaze spent itself, three of the women broke, one after another, from the ring of dancers and rushed up to the Master.

The wearer of the black bathing costume was one; her demeanour was a good deal bolder than it had been earlier, the costume had a long split in one side and a shoulder strap had parted. Kneeling, she shut her eyes and held out her arms unsteadily.

With a swirl of black cloth, there landed like a raven at her side the woman in boots and widow's veil.

The third arrival was the best preserved-looking member of the nude extremists. She made a few sensuous pirouettes, then curled herself neatly into the Asmodean lap and entwined determined fingers in the goatskin.

There were cries of encouragement. Whoever had captured the recorder forced from it a succession of strangled shrieks. The pace of the drumming increased. Those who were still dancing tried at first to keep step, then either switched into spasmodic individual leaps and jigs or surrendered to exhaustion and dropped to the ground.

The veiled woman and the one in the bathing costume moved off in attitudes of mutual commiseration towards what remained of the liquor supply.

The fire flickered and died.

For a while the satanic candle continued to glow. Its rays falling on the limbs of the woman contentedly grappled to the torso of the Master rendered them the colour of pottery. Then, startlingly, the light was snuffed out.

It seemed that a great door of darkness had closed upon the focal drama of the rites. No one moved. The only sound was the intoning, deep in the throat of Mrs Pentatuke, of the Lord's Prayer in reverse.

The orison was correct in form, but her heart was not in it. By the time she got to '... bread daily our day ...' the words were being delivered hastily and without thought. She had not yet reached the beginning when her voice was drowned by another.

'I HAVE CHOSEN!'

The words boomed out with a more than human amplitude.

There were murmurs of excitement, accompanied by some thwacks on the drum. A woman in a nightdress looked about her nervously and then after some hesitation, called out: 'O mighty Pan!' She pronounced it 'Pen'.

Some way off, a car engine started. Headlamp beams swung among trees and disappeared round the end of a driveway. The doors of another car slammed. Small shrieks and giggles were squeezed here and there out of the dark. A bottle splintered musically against stone. In the glimmer of the sole surviving candle, the woman in the bathing costume was dancing dolefully with the empty liquor bucket up-ended over her head.

It was clear that the ceremony, although not yet at an end, had entered the phase of independent interpretation.

Mrs Pentatuke stood alone, statuesque, indifferent to the slight chill borne now in the breeze from the east. She stared at the point in the distance where she knew to be a small grove of ash trees, the trees of the Old Religion whose magic was still respected by those otherwise hard-headed farmers who left them undisturbed even in the middle of ploughland. She waited.

Ten minutes had passed when a pinhead of dusky red appeared exactly in the line of Mrs Pentatuke's steady gaze. Quickly it bloomed to incandescence. Stems and branches of trees stood out in scarlet tracery against the blackness beyond. Up and down and about, the devil's candle moved. A squeal, as of shocked discovery, rose from the grove. Soon another followed, but this second cry was succeeded by a series of short whoops not at all indicative of distress.

The hour bell in the tower of Flaxborough Parish Church began to strike twelve. It was no longer the eve of Saint Walburga, but the morning of May Day.

The red flame in the ash grove waved erratically once or twice, then went out.

Mrs Pentatuke slowly unclenched her hands. Only later did she discover that the strong, carefully manicured nails had engraved in each palm four little blood-filled crescents.

Chapter Two

THE FOLLOWING ACCOUNT APPEARED HALF-WAY DOWN the third column of page five of the *Flaxborough Citizen* dated Friday, 2 May.

FOLK AND FUN: OLD CEREMONIES RECALLED
The quarterly 'Revel' of the Flaxborough, Chalmsbury and Brocklestone Folklore Society attracted a good attendance when it was held on Wednesday in the grounds of Aleister Lodge, by kind permission of Mrs G. Gloss, OBE.

Study subject for the evening was 'The Survival of Roodmas', Roodmas being the ancient festival associated with the last day of April. A number of members brought masks and decorative articles, made by themselves, modelled on traditional examples.

The very successful dance session was led by Mr and Mrs H. Pearce, Mr and Mrs H. Hall, and Mesdames G. Gooding and F. Pentatuke. The caller was Mrs Pentatuke, who also agreed to take charge of the Devotional Half-Hour, in the absence through indisposition of Mrs H. K. Framlington, JP.

Mr G. Gooding was responsible for the erection of a tastefully decorated 'quaffing bench'. Faggot-master was Mr J. Cowdrey.

The music was provided by Miss A. Parkin, who rendered selections on recorder and tabor.

Refreshment organizers: Mrs Pearce and Mr J. Bottomley.

Winner of the President's Maypole Trophy for best living custom demonstration: Miss Edna Hillyard.

The *Flaxborough Citizen* was a weekly newspaper and it went to press on Thursday afternoon. Anything that happened later than lunch time but before tea on a Thursday might, if it were sensational enough, be accommodated by special dispensation of the editor and at the price of great gloom and recrimination in the machine room. Five o'clock, though, was the absolute limit. At five, the last page of metal would be locked with its fellow in their forme and trundled off to the mangle for the matrix to be pressed.

Thus it was that the paper containing the report of Miss Hillyard's success in the Revel competition made no mention of her subsequent disappearance. For although it would not be true to say that no one missed Edna throughout Thursday, she was known to be unpredictable and quite liable to take a trip on impulse or to present herself at the home of a friend, with an off-hand yet perfectly confident request for hospitality. In the offices of her employers, Flaxborough Corporation, her periodic absences were noted with irritation but not alarm. Her landlady in Cheviot Road was used to knocking at Edna's bedroom door without response on two or three mornings a month.

On Thursday evening, however, shortly after six, a discovery was made that could be disregarded only by the most phlegmatic among Miss Hillyard's acquaintances.

Two boys who had climbed through a break in the hedge enclosing private woods and meadowland on the north side of Orchard Road were intrigued to see that a small, bright red car had somehow come to be parked beneath some trees. They approached it cautiously, encouraged by the remoteness of its resting place to hope for glimpsed indiscretions. But the car proved to be empty.

The older boy tried the door on the driver's side. It opened. Something white and flimsy slipped off the seat and fell to the ground among wet dead leaves. The other pounced, trying to save what had fallen from getting dirty. He brushed it clumsily, leaving brown streaks.

'Look out, clot. You'll have it absolutely filthy.'

The older boy snatched. He looked at what he held, then at the neat pile on the seat.

'Christ, they're a bird's.'

Flushing, he draped the muddied slip on the seat back. It flowed down into a heap beside the other things. He tried to make it look neat, undisturbed, by giving it a few nervous tweaks and pats, but had no success. His companion looked on impassively.

'Come on. Let's scarpa.'

The older boy stepped back, ready to shut the car door.

The other put out a restraining hand; he was staring now at the clothing with keener interest.

'Hey, do you know what? She's taken the flippin' lot off. Jersey, skirt . . . Look, that's her what-d'you-call it. Stockings, an' all.' A small hesitation. '*And* them.' He pointed, awed.

'So what?' The older boy pushed him aside and closed the door as quietly as he could. 'Come on.'

Neither, in his need to seem worldly, wanted to admit to the other the feeling of unease that the incident had roused in him. But as they walked back to the road, the younger perplexed, the older pretending nonchalance, there grew between them the unvoiced acceptance that somebody else would have to be told.

There was a telephone box near the junction of Orchard Road and Marshside Road. The older boy regarded it doubtfully, then swung the door open.

'I suppose we ought, really,' he said. 'I mean, we don't have to say who we are.'

He wiped his hands down the seams of his trousers, picked up the receiver and with great deliberation dialled nine-nine-nine.

Three minutes later, he rejoined his companion.

'Right thick one, that,' he complained. 'Kept asking my name and address.'

'You didn't tell him?'

'Course not.'

'What's he going to do about the car and that?'

'How would I know? Expect they'll come over and take a look round. We'd better not be hanging about.'

The boys hurried round the corner and slipped into the shelter of an alley a few yards along Marshside Road. For nearly half an hour they kept watch and listened for the two-note bray of a police car. Then, hungry and disillusioned, they went their separate ways home.

They were not to know that a patrol car had happened to be at the far end of Orchard Road, beyond the crematorium, at the time of their call to police headquarters in Fen Street, and that a radio message had long since sent its crew to investigate.

The driver of the car was Constable Palethorp, a reticent, phlegmatic officer whose eyes were as expressive as holes in a blanket.

He was accompanied by a lean, restless man. Constable Brevitt always rode as passenger in the patrol car. This was a precaution ordained by his superiors. Fully aware of Flaxborough's distinction in having on its Force an officer who would have managed splendidly and perhaps even single-handed the suppression of the Indian Mutiny, they had no wish to test the compatibility of his panache with the requirements of the Road Traffic Acts.

'Go on, Fred – clip the stupid bugger into the ditch!' urged Constable Brevitt. He glared at Palethorp, who had braked and was watching patiently an old man who had dismounted from his cycle opposite the crematorium gates and now waited, directly in their path, for an oncoming car to pass.

'His road as much as ours,' Palethorp murmured.

Brevitt smote his own forehead with the flat of his hand and turned up his eyes. He suddenly reached over and held down the horn button. The old man jumped so violently that the bicycle slewed from his grip and fell over. It rocked once or twice and the handlebars quivered. Palethorp was put in mind of a horned animal, fatally shot but trying to get up again.

Brevitt grinned.

Palethorp said nothing. When the other car had gone, he pulled out to give the old man plenty of room and drove on. In his mirror he saw the old man heaving the cycle upright – wearily, yet with a sort of solicitude as if it were indeed a creature and not a machine.

Brevitt leaned forward against his safety belt and scrutinized the road ahead. In time with some tune within his own head, his right fist hammered gently into his left palm.

'Hang on.' He pointed. 'There's a break there, just before the bend.'

The car stopped. In the high thorn hedge a gap had been torn near the ground.

Palethorp spared it no more than a glance, but Brevitt jumped out and squatted to peer through. Experimentally, he squeezed head and some chest into the hole.

'No point,' Palethorp called. 'It's perfectly easy to get in the proper way. Past the house.'

'House?' Brevitt looked disappointed but he got back into his seat.

'Mrs Gloss. This is all part of her place. It's open ground past those trees. And if there is a car there, either somebody sneaked it up the drive during the night or it belongs to a friend of hers. Simply enough settled by asking.'

The house was a 1928 Tudor mansion, with half-timber facings over roughened white concrete. The steel-framed casement windows had criss-crossed lead strip appliqué with here and there a bottle-glass inset. A complete set of shutters had been grafted in

1937. There was a round dovecot on a pole in the centre of the broad gravel forecourt. The drive from Orchard Road was flanked, where it opened into the forecourt, by two old-style street lamps. One carried the sign 'Drury Lane', the other, 'Ye Strande'.

The patrol car crunched to a halt beside the porch, a creosoted half-barn that gave deep shelter to the big white-painted front door. Beside the door, and matching its heavy, ornamental hinges was a wrought-iron bell pull. Palethorp took firm hold of its handle and drew it down. Inside the house there sounded the unctuous double-boyng of an electric chime.

Almost at once they heard footsteps approach across a hard surface. They were brisk and spiky. Palethorp diagnosed a plump woman, short in the leg, busy. Mrs Gloss herself. Not one of the days for hired help. She was not going to relish silly inquiries by policemen.

'Yes?' The door stood open. Mrs Gertrude Gloss, O B E, had the slightly drawn look over one eye that betokened a struggle with hangover that was not yet quite won. Otherwise, she appeared alert, well groomed and not unobliging.

'We are police officers, ma'am.' The superfluous introduction was Brevitt's. 'We've had reports concerning an abandoned vehicle.' He looked accusingly at Mrs Gloss's bosom, as if prompted by association of ideas.

'I don't think I understand, officer. But perhaps you both had better come in.'

Palethorp noted the return play of the word 'officer'. He recognized a gentle warning. Only those whose social or official status allowed them to strew other people's paths of duty with the flints of criticism employed that form of address in quite so confident yet off-hand a manner.

The entrance hall was tiled in bright terra-cotta. In one corner stood a big stone jar from which splayed tropical grasses. A Tudor arch led to a white staircase laid with new-looking, flower patterned carpet. Each of four doorways, all similarly arched, had a little coloured plaster shield at its apex. Through one half-open door Brevitt glimpsed white porcelain. Downstairs lav, he ruminated, sensing need to be respectful.

Mrs Gloss led them to the lounge. They saw a wide bow-fronted china cabinet packed densely with pieces of porcelain, glasses, miniature jugs and warming pans in varnished copper, little ivory monkeys and elephants, a pair of cigarette cases decorated with designs contrived out of butterfly wings, and a set of model cowbells in six sizes, souvenirs of Chamonix.

Against the opposite wall stood a mahogany-cased grandfather clock with a brass face and a moon phase indicator. The clock was not working. Four oil paintings, all seascapes in heavy gilt frames, had been hung in line and exactly equidistantly from one another across a third wall. The room also contained a large oval rosewood table, a combined radiogram and television set camouflaged as a Jacobean sideboard, and a coterie of armchairs, obese and befrilled.

Across the back of one of the armchairs had been tossed a short fur coat.

Mrs Gloss did not sit down. Nor did she invite the policemen to do so.

'According to this message' – Palethorp made their errand sound an altogether unreasonable affair that he personally much regretted – 'the so-called abandoned car is on your property, Mrs Gloss.'

She turned with a faint smile from Palethorp to Brevitt as if inviting him to supply the second half of the joke.

'Red sports car,' Brevitt said. 'Under some trees.'

'According to the message,' insisted Palethorp.

'Abandoned?'

'Well – parked. As I say, under some trees. And there was some clothing in it.'

'Female apparel.' Brevitt sniffed, looked away, and probed one ear-hole with a piece of match which he had taken from an inner pocket of his tunic.

'How do you know the car isn't mine, constable?'

'A *sports* car, madam?' Palethorp's tone conveyed reproof.

'No, it isn't, as a matter of fact. But I've a fair idea who the owner might be.'

'You do, madam?' Palethorp, looking suddenly pleased, glanced at Brevitt. Brevitt thriftily put away his match end and from another pocket produced a notebook.

'If we could just have his name, then, madam ...'

'*Her* name,' Mrs Gloss corrected. She frowned. 'Look, how did this nonsense start, anyway? Who sent you people here?'

Brevitt's instinct was to tell her that questions were for policemen to ask and that what he wanted from her was answers and look sharp about it or else, but he managed to keep silent and let Palethorp mumble something about a nine-nine-nine call from someone who had looked inside the car.

'A trespasser, you mean,' said Mrs Gloss.

'It would seem so,' Palethorp agreed uncomfortably.

Mrs Gloss shook her head over the sad ineptitude of authority and said well, they'd better all go together and have a look and get the matter settled.

They followed a path round the side of the house and crossed a lawn that lay within an irregular embankment set with rocks and covered by masses of tiny white and yellow and purple flowers. Beyond the bank, a smaller lawn flanked an open-fronted summer-house made of boarding covered with bark strips. Hanging within from its roof on three fine chains was a round metal bowl, decoratively pierced. Brevitt supposed it to be some kind of colander for growing bulbs. Palethorp had once inadvertently attended Benediction at St Joseph's Roman Catholic Church in Southgate while trailing an indecent exposure subject; he recognized a censer.

'It's quicker this way,' Mrs Gloss explained, as they rounded the summer house and filed through a small wicket gate into a field. 'The drive goes on past the house on the other side. They can get a tractor in when the grass needs mowing.' She pointed. 'There you are – there's the car you're making all the fuss about.'

Scarlet glinted against the darkness of closely set trees about a hundred yards away on their right. They walked towards it, Mrs Gloss watching the ground as she stepped carefully in her high-heeled shoes.

Once or twice she tripped and would have fallen but for the

ready and strong arm of Constable Brevitt. No corsets, he reflected after the most nearly democratic of these encounters had impressed him not unpleasurably with the warmth, scent and volume of her person. That evening and on several subsequent occasions before the memory faded, he was vicariously to award himself that privileged relationship with Mrs Gloss which he called 'having a tit in each ear'.

Palethorp noticed, but did not remark upon, a circular patch of calcined earth, a couple of yards in diameter, where evidently there had been a wood fire within the last day or two. The evening breeze stirred pale, flocculent ash and blackened twig fragments.

The field was of perhaps six acres. It showed no signs of recent cultivation. Palethorp guessed it would be poor growing land. There was a shallow declivity near the centre where stood a group of tall ash trees; drainage probably was not too good. And the ranks of trees that enclosed the field on three sides would deprive crops of much light and nutriment.

Palethorp peered again at the grove in the middle of the field; it was now directly on their left and about thirty yards distant.

'What's that thing in between the trees?' he asked.

'I've really no idea,' Mrs Gloss replied cheerily. 'It seems to be some kind of old monument but I don't think there's an inscription or anything.'

'Looks a bit like a vault from here,' Palethorp said. 'You know — like in churchyards.'

Brevitt, too, was staring now towards the table-like structure of greenish stone standing crookedly among the trees. He looked quickly back at Mrs Gloss when he heard her laugh. Were churchyards comical, then? Brevitt wouldn't have thought so.

'As a matter of fact,' said the amused Mrs Gloss, 'we've always called it the altar.'

Palethorp smiled politely and they walked the rest of the way to the red sports car in silence.

The two policemen padded round the car, giving it a preliminary scrutiny. They looked judiciously at each wheel in turn, examined the licence holder, eyed both number plates and gently kicked a front tyre that seemed softer than the others.

'Whose did you say it was, madam?' Brevitt had his notebook out again.

'I didn't say,' Mrs Gloss corrected, 'but I think it belongs to a lady called Miss Hillyard.' She watched Brevitt's labouring pencil for a moment and added: 'Miss Edna Hillyard.' He crossed out what he had written and began again.

Palethorp put a hand on the driver's door. 'Address?' he prompted, very quietly, then shook his head. 'No, never mind. We can soon check if it's really necessary. If she's the Miss Hillyard I'm thinking of, she works in the Corporation Offices.'

'That's right: she does.'

Brevitt wrote down some more. Then he asked: 'Did Miss Hillyard have your permission to leave her car here?'

Mrs Gloss raised her brows, pouted. 'Yes, in a general way. All my friends know they can park round here if they wish. There's not a lot of room in front of the house.'

'I suppose you had company yesterday, did you, Mrs Gloss? I was wondering about all these wheel marks, as a matter of fact.' Palethorp indicated a complex of tyre tracks across the grass. 'Ah . . .' His face brightened with sudden comprehension. 'Of course. It will have been those folk song people. Right?'

Mrs Gloss challenged neither the appellation nor the plain hint in Palethorp's tone that the sort of citizens who went hey-ding-a-ding-ing round a wet field when they could be watching television like everybody else were more to be pitied than harassed by the law. She simply confirmed that there had been a little social function the previous evening and suggested that Miss Hillyard might have had trouble in starting her motor afterwards and had been given a lift home by one of the others.

Palethorp opened the door on which he had been lightly leaning.

He looked around the inside of the car, then stretched across and gathered in his capacious hand the clothing on the passenger seat.

'The party who phoned said something about these,' he said.

Mrs Gloss looked annoyed for the first time in the interview. 'Well, I think they had a nerve. Not content with trespassing and breaking into somebody else's car . . .'

'No sign of breaking,' Palethorp interrupted.

'All right. Opening it without permission, then. Anyway, after all that, they have the impertinence to interfere with personal property and then, if you please, to bring you people over on a . . .' Mrs Gloss nearly said 'fool's errand', but diplomatically substituted 'wasted journey'.

Brevitt watched the other policeman sort through the clothing and lay it, one article at a time, on the car bonnet. It consisted of a bright orange sweater, a short skirt in dark green corded velvet, white nylon slip, tights, a pair of black lace briefs and a matching brassière.

'And what do you make of those, madam?' asked Brevitt. He sounded rather pleased himself.

'What do you mean, *make* of them? I suppose they're the girl's laundry. She'll not thank you for getting them dirty again on there.'

Obediently, Palethorp gathered up the clothes. But instead of putting them back in the car, he looked them over again with a dubious expression.

'Funny that they should be an exact set,' he said. 'If they're laundry, that is. I'd have thought there'd be more than just the one each of some of them.'

'What my colleague means,' Brevitt explained, 'is that it looks more as if the lady in question had stripped off.' As used by Brevitt, the word 'stripped' was so evocative that Palethorp had to thrust his head inside the car and pretend further search in order to conceal his embarrassment.

Mrs Gloss stared sternly at Brevitt. 'That is the most preposterous suggestion, constable. You seem to have forgotten that I am the owner of this property. People who come here do so at my invitation and for perfectly respectable purposes. What on earth do you think goes on here? Nudist conventions?'

Flustered and contrite, Brevitt mumbled scraps of a formula about 'routine inquiries'. He was relieved – and not a little surprised – when Mrs Gloss's tightly-set lips twitched and then parted in mischievous amusement.

'Pulling your leg, laddie,' she confided gently, leaning very close and giving his thigh a playful tap with the backs of her fingers. At once she stepped away again to watch Palethorp's exploration of the back seat of the car, but not before Brevitt had caught a whiff of liquor of one of the more boudoir-ish kinds. Sherry, he thought. Or maybe raisin wine.

'I think,' Palethorp said when he had emerged from the car, 'that we had better leave everything as it is, Mrs Gloss. We'll have to make a report, of course . . .' He paused. 'The lady's shoes, by the way – they don't seem to be here.'

'Why should they be? People don't take shoes to the laundry.'

'No, of course not.' He left it at that.

They walked back to the house, where the policemen declined Mrs Gloss's offer of a cup of tea 'or something'. She promised to telephone as soon as the car was collected by its owner, and stood between them at the porch to give the arm of each a parting squeeze.

'Funny,' ruminated Palethorp on their way back to the station, 'how you can be wrong about somebody. I thought at first she was going to be very upstage. "Orficer",' he mimicked, remembering. 'Yet she turned out quite nice, really.'

Brevitt loudly sucked air between his lip and a couple of teeth in an attempt to dislodge a remnant of breakfast bacon. 'I know what *she* wants . . .' He explored the teeth with the tip of his tongue while he reached for the pocket in which his match end was kept. '. . . and I don't reckon I'd mind giving it her, either.'

Palethorp took his eyes off the road long enough to give Brevitt a look of wondering disapproval.

In the lounge of Aleister Lodge, Mrs Gloss poured herself a tumbler of wine, drank a quarter of it and carried the rest to where a plum-coloured telephone stood in a window embrasure. She dialled a Flaxborough number.

'Have you,' she asked someone she addressed as Amy, 'any idea of where our prize-winner got to last night? After the presentation, I mean.'

Amy said she personally had been too busy searching for a lost recorder to notice the comings and goings of others, but why the concern?'

'She has not collected her motor-car and some policemen have called about it.'

This evinced an awed echo of the word 'policemen'. Mrs Gloss described the visit in greater detail.

'Of course I remember she was there at roll-call,' Amy said slowly after a pause, 'and I did see her taking part in the last dance before my instrument was mislaid but ... Oh, dear, I wish I could be more helpful. I suppose she could not have ...'

'Yes?' prompted Mrs Gloss.

'Well, gone home with ... You know – afterwards, I mean ...'

'Now that *is* out of the question. Completely and utterly.'

Amy had to agree. She suggested two or three alternative escorts. Mrs Gloss said she would call them. She did not sound enthusiastic.

When she had rung off, she poured more wine and propped herself against a pile of cushions in the largest armchair. Soon there entered the room a cinnamon-coloured cat so plump that it appeared to be wearing an extra fur. It crossed the carpet with a condescending waddle and heaved itself up beside Mrs Gloss.

'Hello, Hecate,' said Mrs Gloss. She rubbed the cat's chin and gazed at its all but closed eyes.

'And where the devil has Sister Edna flown off to, eh?'

For a second, Hecate opened topaz eyes wide and stopped purring. Then it settled again into somnolent contemplation of Mrs Gloss.

Chapter Three

'IF LUCILLITE IS IN YOUR HOME, I'VE BROUGHT GOOD news from Dixon-Frome!'

Detective Inspector Purbright looked at the apparition on his doorstep and tried to relate it to the more familiar aspects of life in Tetford Drive at a quarter to nine on a Friday morning.

Standing before him was a young woman dressed in a costume of what appeared to be white plastic. Basically a doublet, tightly belted and flaring below the waist, the garment was stiffened at the shoulders into what Purbright could only compare to aeroplane engine cowlings. From these a short cape hung at the girl's back. She wore white tights and white plastic boots and carried a white plastic satchel.

'You're not Supergirl?' inquired the inspector, with what he judged to be the appropriate blend of humility and hopefulness.

For reply, the girl pointed to her chest. The name LUCILLITE in pale blue lettering was surrounded by a representation of golden rays.

'Have you got the three packets like the advert said on telly?' asked the girl. Her large, very earnest eyes made the question sound extremely important.

Purbright abashedly shook his head.

'You sure? I mean, you'll not get the Gift, unless. Hadn't you better ask the wife?'

'I'm sorry. I don't think that would do any good. We don't happen to have bought any' – he glanced again at her name plate – 'Lucillite.'

'What, not the Introductory Offer?'

'I'm afraid not.'

'Don't you want the Gift?'

'Perhaps the opportunity will come again one day.' Purbright smiled and edged back in preparation for shutting the door.

'But the Lucies are only here for today. We go on to some other roads tomorrow.'

'Lucies?'

'Yes – us.' The girl gestured towards the road. Purbright stepped out from the doorway and saw with something of a shock that his caller was but one unit of a whole cadre. Girls in exactly similar garments were standing at doors, opening and shutting gates, or staring up at windows from one end of Tetford Drive to the other. The scene had something about it comparable with the discovery of the overnight infestation of one's garden by a colony of cabbage whites, creatures individually engaging but collectively intimidating.

'I tell you what,' said the girl. 'Never mind about the packets – see if you can get the answer to one of the Simple Questions.'

Purbright looked at his watch. 'I think I'd rather finish my breakfast, if it's all the same to you.'

The girl treated this observation with the indifference it deserved. She glanced at a card she had taken from her tunic pocket and recited carefully:

'What is the secret of Lucillite's power to give your wash the sort of lightness and brightness and whiteness that will set all your neighbours talking?'

Purbright adopted an expression of intense mental effort.

'Only . . .' prompted the girl, watching him.

'. . . Lucillite . . .' she added, a few moments later.

Purbright shook his head. 'I'm being really very stupid.'

'. . . has . . .'

'No, it's no use. I'm sorry.'

'. . . sa . . . saponi . . . saponif . . .' The girl mouthed the syllables with all the patience of a teacher of deaf Hottentots.

Purbright felt the burden of his obligation becoming too much to be borne much longer.

'It's no good, really it isn't,' he said firmly. 'Why don't you try the lady next door? She's more intelligent, and she gets around more than I do.'

The girl sighed. She looked up and down the road, then came close.

'Only Lucillite has saponified granules.'

Purbright snapped his fingers. 'Of *course*!' He knuckled his brow in self-reproach. 'The things one can forget!'

For the first time in the interview the girl's solemn expression thawed. She gave him a little chin-up smile that wrinkled her nose.

'You can have the Gift now.'

Opening the satchel at her side, she took out and handed to Purbright first a sample packet of Lucillite Family Wash Granules, then – reverently – a yellow plastic frame made in the form of a spoked wheel, the spaces between the spokes containing polythene windows of graded degrees of smokiness.

'The Gift?' Purbright asked softly.

She nodded. 'It's a Scintillometer. You see . . .' She took it from him. 'You turn these little windows against your shirt or whatever you want to wash until you get one that matches, then it says here' – she indicated the rim of the wheel – 'how much Lucillite you have to use to get it white.'

'And bright.'

'That's right.' She handed him back the Scintillometer and began re-fastening the strap of her satchel. 'Pity you didn't have those packets, though. You could have gone in for the Paradise Island competition.'

'Gosh,' said Purbright.

'It's a special promotion for Dixon-Frome and it's because there's been a lot of consumer-resistance in places like . . .' She broke off, looked up from her satchel-strapping. 'What's this placed called again?'

'Flaxborough.'

'Yeah, Flaxborough. But I can't give you the invite, not without the packet tops. I only wish I could.'

'Never mind,' said Purbright. 'I've always got these, haven't I?' He cheerily waved the packet of Lucillite and the Scintillometer and withdrew.

Half an hour later, in an office that would not even have made bottom reading on the Scintillometer, Inspector Purbright began to read a report in the laboured but legible handwriting of Constable Palethorp. He was less than half-way through when he heard the sound of scrap iron in epilepsy that signified that somebody was climbing the spiral staircase from the ground floor.

'I thought you might like some tea.'

'That's very thoughtful of you, Sid.'

Purbright cleared a space on the desk top to accommodate the two large mugs borne by Detective Sergeant Love. He cautiously sipped at the steaming rim of one of them without taking his eyes from Palethorp's report.

'What,' he asked, 'is all this about an abandoned car and folk singers and laundry, for God's sake?'

Love's face, pink and patient like a boy martyr's, held in addition something of the innocent pleasure of the pre-informed.

'You mean the Edna Hillyard business?'

'If it's her car that's over at Orchard Road, yes. Although why we should assume that it's been abandoned I really cannot see.'

'Funny place to leave a car,' Love said.

'It would have been at one time. What you call funny places are the only ones where you *can* leave a car nowadays.'

The inspector read to the end of the report. He shrugged. 'Well, unless this girl has been reported missing . . .'

'She hasn't,' Love assured him. 'Not as per the present. But she's not a girl. She's thirty-four.'

'How do you know?'

'Well, you know who she *is*, don't you?'

Purbright looked blank.

'Niece of old Rupert Hillyard,' Love supplied. 'She came here from Glasgow with her mother in 1954 and went to the High School for a year. She was seventeen.' The sergeant smiled sadly, as if at some fragrant memory.

Purbright good-naturedly gave him a glance of inquiry.

'I remember the age, actually,' Love said, 'because she came into the station to ask if one of us would sign her passport application. It was the year Flaxborough was knocked out of the Eastern League. She would have been, wait a minute . . . yes, twenty-four when Doctor Hillyard died in prison. Did I say twenty-four – no, twenty-five, it must have been. Good lord, nine years . . .'

'Sid. Please.' The inspector had raised his hand. 'We've established the woman's age. All we want to know now is whether or not she's come to any harm. I've yet to be convinced that whoever made that nine-nine-nine call wasn't trying to be funny.'

'Would you like somebody to ask around? She works for the Council. They might know something in her department.'

'Tomorrow, Sid. Wait until tomorrow. If she hasn't turned up by then, we'll take some action.'

Love nodded, then rubbed his chin. 'Of course they do reckon,' he said, 'that she's a bit . . .' His lips pouted, seeking *le mot injuste*.

'Oh, naturally,' said the inspector. He measured with lack-lustre eye what was left of his tea, then quickly drank it down.

The telephone rang just as Love was about to leave the room. The inspector motioned him to stay.

'All right. Bring him along.'

Purbright put back the phone. He straightened some papers, half rose to glance at the condition of the only other chair, sat back, sniffed.

'Guess who's coming to see us.'

Love co-operatively took the empty mugs off the desk and put them on top of the filing cabinet.

'The vicar,' said Purbright. He joined fingertips and smiled tightly in parody of pastoral solicitude.

For an instant, Love looked alarmed. Then he frowned and made rapid survey of the office as if expecting that something particularly unseemly had been left about.

The door opened with the suddenness of a sprung trap. 'Christ!' said Love, spinning to face it.

He found himself regarded fixedly by the small, angry eyes of a man not much more than five feet tall but of considerable shoulder breadth. The man, whose complexion was like an open stove, wore a suit of the peculiarly apposite colour of coke.

'Do you habitually blaspheme, young man, or was that a genuine case of mistaken identity?'

The Reverend Clement James Grewyear, MA, DD, Vicar of Flaxborough, continued to stare at the speechless Love until the sergeant took refuge in urgent exploration of one of the drawers of the filing cabinet. He then turned to the inspector, but did not abate the gravity of his scowl.

'Do take a seat, vicar.' Purbright had stood up behind his desk and was indicating the visitor's chair.

Mr Grewyear hitched up his coke-coloured trouser legs and lowered himself into the chair without taking his eyes off the inspector. Purbright reflected that the vicar seemed to take literally the definition of his calling as that of a fisher of men: his gaze had all the tenacity of a two-hundred-pound line.

'You must come with me immediately to the church, Purbright.'

The inspector waited for amplification, but Mr Grewyear added nothing. He clearly expected Purbright to respond forthwith. Several seconds went by.

'Something has happened at the church, has it, sir?'

'That,' snapped Mr Grewyear, 'is putting it very mildly indeed. Come along, man.' He stood up.

'I'm sorry vicar, but you really must be more explicit. Are you referring to an accident? A crime? I have to know the kind of assistance you want me to give.'

Mr Grewyear said coldly and quietly: 'You are not one of my communicants, I believe, Purbright.'

Purbright shrugged in apology for recusance.

The vicar nodded. 'No, well, you will probably be none the wiser when I tell you that somebody – or something – has been perpetrating abominations.'

'That certainly sounds serious.'

'It *is* serious. You do not suppose I should be here otherwise, do you?' There was a smokiness in the vicar's eye that warned Purbright not to dispute the point: even though he was not a church-goer, the Chief Constable was, and Mr Grewyear was obviously sufficiently stoked up to carry his complaints a good deal further than Fen Street.

'Sergeant.'

'Sir?' Love disinterred himself from the filing cabinet.

'The vicar believes that there has been a case of sacrilege at the Parish Church. Will you accompany him there and let him show you what has been going on. You'd better pick up Harper on the way. Tell him to take his bag and a camera.'

Mr Grewyear looked at Love as a wealthy hospital patient might have regarded an apprentice plumber co-opted to remove his prostate.

'The sergeant will make a note of the details,' Purbright explained, 'and if he thinks it necessary I shall come over myself a little later. But I am sure you will find him a most experienced and capable officer.'

Saying nothing more, but dark with doubt, the vicar rose and walked to the door. Love scurried to open it and followed him out.

The vicar's car was at the police station entrance. It was an American-built Ford of about the same floor area as the Lady Chapel in the parish church.

Love and Harper sat in the back and wondered how the five-foot vicar was going to pilot the machine from a driving position that obliged him actually to reach upward in order to grasp the wheel. He showed no hesitation, however, and soon the vast car was sweeping along East Street towards the Market Place.

From the rear, Mr Grewyear's upstretched arms gave him the appearance of administering extreme unction to those pedestrians who had stepped or been jostled from the narrow pavement and were now leaping out of the way of the car's elephantine fenders.

Love drew Harper's attention to the tinted windows. 'Like being under water,' he whispered.

Harper nudged him and whispered back, indicating their driver: 'No wonder the little bugger needs a periscope, then.' He laughed noiselessly.

Love, a little shocked, quickly looked the other way.

The vicar drove across the Market Place, passed the wrong side of a traffic bollard into Spoongate and parked beneath a 'Funerals Only' sign near a gateway in the church railings.

Without waiting to see the policemen evacuate the rear hall of his car, he strutted along a path and disappeared through the wicket in the south door.

Love and Harper found him standing by the font. They walked up to him. Speechlessly, he pointed.

The heavy, elaborately carved stone cover was in its usual raised position and a plain wooden lid, padlocked, lay on the font ready for removal at baptismal services. To the very centre of this lid something had been transfixed by a butcher's metal skewer.

The policemen stepped up on the plinth for a closer view.

The skewered object was a dead frog. Between its outstretched rear legs, there had been drawn a cross. A black felt-tipped pen seemed to have been used. Farther down were words, printed by the same means.

Ad te omnis caro veniet.

Harper wrinkled his nose in distaste, but Love leaned nearer and examined the frog with considerable interest. Then he peered at the inscription and turned towards the vicar.

'What's the French all about, then, padre?'

'French?'

'This bit of writing.'

Mr Grewyear, who hated being called 'padre' perhaps more than anything else in the world, wrestled for some time with his anger before he trusted himself to reply.

Very quietly, and with eyes closed, he said at last: 'Those words, sergeant, are Latin. I construe. "Unto Thee shall all flesh come".'

Love gazed at the frog with innocent amiability. 'Quite neat, really,' he said, 'when you come to think about it.'

Harper had opened his case and was busy assembling camera and tripod. He held a light-meter at arm's length and regarded it gloomily. Then he stared in turn at the roof, the great West window and the rood screen, as if debating which one of those obstacles he would ask the vicar to have removed.

'You will record the scoundrel's fingerprints, of course, officer,' said Mr Grewyear.

Harper shook his head and sucked breath through his teeth in noisy denial. 'Never in this world, padre. What, from wood like that?' He rummaged in his case, drew out a flash bulb, and began screwing it into an attachment to the camera.

When the frog had been photographed from several angles the vicar set off towards the nave altar, imperiously beckoning the policemen to follow.

With outstretched arm, he indicated the lectern.

This was fashioned in brass in the likeness of a huge and fierce-visaged eagle. At first, neither noticed anything odd about it. Then Love spotted something suspended just beneath the bird's neck.

It was a dead mouse and it had been hung from its tail with the aid of a piece of wire in such a way that the great brass bird appeared to be about to eat it.

'Well, I never,' Love said, hoping to please.

The vicar muttered something about satanic rites.

Harper took four more photographs after brushing the eagle's neck with some fine grey powder and saying 'Nix' to himself.

By now, several visitors to the church had begun to show interest in the proceedings.

An elderly couple, having discovered the sacrificial frog, were casting indignant glances in the direction of the vicar and his companions, whom they apparently assumed to be vivisectionists.

A woman holding two small girls by the hand pretended to read a ledger stone while awaiting her opportunity to see what had been done to the lectern.

The boldest approach was made by an American, who cordially invited Harper to advise what shutter speed and aperture would do justice to that wonderful old church. He was pretty old himself – a lean, brown, sinewy vine of a man, hung with cameras like a crop of leather-podded fruit.

Mr Grewyear coldly but courteously told him that he had – unintentionally, no doubt – interrupted a canonical investigation of the most serious kind. Was that so, exclaimed the onlooker, much gratified. Well, if the Reverend said so – and he withdrew to the North aisle.

The vicar proceeded to the revelation of the third and most startling piece of iniquity.

This was nothing less than a lifelike image in modelling clay of Mr Grewyear himself, dressed in miniature vestments and suspended in a string noose from the pulpit canopy.

Into the model had been pushed half a dozen long pins.

Chapter Four

THE AREA PROMOTION DIRECTOR OF DIXON-FROME (Domestic Detergents Division) stared at the Deputy Chief Brand Visualizer of Thornton-Edwards, Arnold and Konstatin, Dixon-Frome's consultancy in charge of the Lucillite account, and inquired: '*Now* what the bloody hell do we do?'

Both men were between thirty and thirty-five years old. Their suits looked soft yet impossible to crease. So did their faces. Black shoes, carefully cleaned to a degree just short of shine, encased restless yet always precisely poised feet. About the persons of these men hung, faint but unmistakable, the odour of deodorant.

The name of D-F's APD (DDD) was Gordon. TEAK's DCBV was called Richard. None of the friends and colleagues of either man ever used his second name or abbreviated his first.

'If he hasn't turned up by this afternoon, Gordon, we shall have to go ahead without him.'

'Yes, but Richard, look at it this way. Persimmon has the how-pull when it comes to maximum venue participation. Right?'

'Right.'

'So he's absolutely integral – but integral – so far as local product *acceptance* is concerned.'

'In an above-the-line situation, Gordon.'

'Above the line. Sure. I'm with you on that. But what is it we're really aiming for, Richard? D-F is short on Folk-fond – and I mean short. So ...'

'Folk-fond we can get, for God's sake, Gordon. You are talking *image* now. Folk-fond – that's an image situation. But first things first. Before product acceptance, product *presentation*, right?'

'If you want to co-ordinate visuals, Richard, by all means co-ordinate visuals, and we're with you a hundred per cent, but this *is* Friday, May the second, and Persimmon has bloody well disappeared.'

'Hang on. We'll just kick that one around a bit, shall we? One – have we really lost him, disappearance wise? Or is he just temporarily snarled up in a bottle situation?'

'No, no. Drinkwise, he's absolutely neg. Eastern Super rate him clear on that.'

'Fine. O.K. So Persimmon might not be back in time for the campaign film. We need to reckon with that – but seriously. Right?'

'But seriously, Richard. Right. Now you're in mesh.'

'Right. Now, we just kick this around a bit more, do we? Point number two. Reserve customer participation – that we have not got. No, I admit we should have thought about RCP.'

'Oh, but timewise ...'

'Timewise nothing, Gordon. Forgetting to provide RCP was plain ad-bad. I beat my breast, I really do. However – next case. Persimmon had forty, fifty washwives handpicked and primed. But we don't have his list. Therefore selected washwives are strictly non-viable material. Remedy?'

'D-F would probably sanction reasonable loading with pro-extras.'

'Flown in? Time's short, Gordon. It would cost.'

'No more than to cancel filming.'

'Another thing, Gordon. Exposure factor. Washwife pro-extras are certified resistant to detergent dermatitis. You know as well as I do that's why there aren't many of them. So their faces are familiar screenwise. You'd be absolutely right to tell me D-F don't want shadow image coming through in Lucillite promotion.'

The Deputy Chief Brand Visualizer of Thornton-Edwards, Arnold and Konstatin rose from the padded swing-and-spin think-chair in front of the great rear window of the forty-foot campaign cruiser and helped himself to another vodka and celery juice at the hospitality locker. He enlivened the drink with a short burst of soda from a receptacle labelled: ZING-POD by *Dixon-Frome* (*Northern Nutritionals Division*) and resumed his seat.

The Area Promotion Director of Dixon-Frome (Domestic Detergents Division) made two slow revolutions in his own think-chair while he tapped one knee with a pair of spectacles that had enormously thick, square, black frames. The first time round, he said: 'I don't want to angle this question to get an over-responseful reaction, Richard ...' and the second time round, he said: '... so I'll put it this way, right?

'Right. Now, Richard, you are the Product. Put yourself right there. The Product. I say this to you. Fifty consuming washwives recruited at the local supermarket want to use you, but they can't because the supermarket manager is their identity key and no one knows where he is. O.K. Hold on to that. Now, then – fifty pro-extras could be slotted in, but film of them would look like a re-issue and very non-fresh, so they do not get slotted in. Hold on to that, too. Right. So who do you want to use you? A Product in a

Dilemma is how I see this, Richard. Just by asking these questions, just by personalising the Product, something starts to jel. No, wait a minute. Don't say anything yet. There's a sort of sex thing here. I'm almost certain there is. Now, what? Rejection fantasy? No, no – too linear. I know – call it Use-Wish. Use-Wish, Richard – how does that roll you as a bit of motivational structurizing?'

'Use-Wish . . .'

'Remember you're Lucillite. Identify. That's all I want you to do. Identify. Now – get rolled up. Like a spring. Fine. Tight with Use-Wish. I really think we've got something here, Richard. O.K. Now let it come.'

'Sex-thing, it is, by God . . .'

'Great. Great.'

'No, you're dead right, Gordon. I'm really with you on this. Christ, but Use-Wish – it's brilliant. But brilliant. A sort of Product-soul – that's how you read?'

'That's how I read. Right. So *be* Lucillite. Come on, give OUT, Lucillite.'

'I'm granules. I'm a lonely lover made of granules . . .'

'Great. Come on, come on, come on . . .'

'I'm in a box. Imprisoned in a box.'

'Yes.'

'But there are women all round me. And they say, what is this? What does this do?'

'Women?'

'Washwives.'

'Great.'

'And I tell them: I don't *do* anything. I want to be used – used up – turned into foam and sluiced away.'

'Guilt eradication.'

'And I shout out: Darlings, feel my granules. They are for you . . .'

'Spermatozoa image! Marvellous.'

'Open my box . . .'

'Pandora complex!'

'Fly fixation, actually.'

'Oh, this is four-star, Richard. Bloody four-star. Christ, wait until I tell them at D-F.'

'Wait a minute, though. I'm still Lucillite. Still the Product. And I know what I want these women to do. I want to be delved into. Grabbed. Emasculated. De-granuled. The final orgasm of being de-organed!'

The climactic six words were delivered by a man suddenly wide-eyed and holding aloft a fan of tensed fingers.

D-F's Area Promotion Director released pent-up breath. 'My God,' he said softly. 'Mantis motivation!'

The other watched him, alert but silent.

'You see what this means, Richard!'

TEAK's DCBV nodded. He blew gently upon the nail of his left thumb.

'An ad-clens revolution. A turn round of the whole concept. Everything up to now has been slanted on women wanting to please men. But *do* they?'

'Exactly. *Do* they? We've been hammering away for years on this whiteness thing. And why? Because Motivational Research said whiteness represented lost virginity.'

'Every washday the woman got her hymen back so she could offer it again to her mate. Sure, sure. You remember the Vurj campaign, Richard? Always a shot of washwife handing the Vurj pack to man in white hubbyshirt.'

'God! How off-beam can one get? Listen, this is how I see it, Gordon. Copulation equals children equals drudgegrudge. Right?'

'Right.'

'What colour drudgegrudge? White. Because of millions spent on washimage, right? Now, then. White equals the Product. Lucillite equals white equals copulation, equals drudgegrudge.'

'A multidirectional equation ...'

'Sure. Now you see where everybody's been going wrong, Gordon. They've tried to make the Product a love-object.'

'Instead of ...'

'Exactly. A hate-focus. Or castration substitute, if you like.'

'The implications are pretty terrific, Richard.'

'Policywise, my God, yes! Dynamite.'

'Maybe we should have had Antony in on this.'

'He's getting cameras set up. In any case, we'll have to stick to format until D-F and TEAK can conferencize.'

'I suppose so.'

'Pity.'

'Yes, indeed.'

'Gordon ...'

'Yes?'

'You realize we haven't any consumer-participation laid on yet?'

'God, I'd forgotten. No use waiting for Persimmon. Look, what about getting Hughie to organize this. He's done CP organizing before.'

The adman went into the interior of the campaign cruiser. He called back: 'Which mobile is Hughie on?'

'Number two.'

'Roger.'

The prodman heard a murmur of conversation in the talkout stall.

When he returned, the adman said that Hughie would brief his Lucy-team and issue them with extra giftbait.

The first women recruited by the Lucies arrived shortly after twelve o'clock. They were from the Council estate off Burton Lane. A party of three from Windsor Close had linked with the Simpson Road and Abdication Avenue contingents. They were closely followed by a straggling dozen from Edward Crescent. Some had brought sandwiches and flasks of tea. Almost all wore their best clothes and more than their usual amount of make-up. Several of the younger ones had packed swimsuits in their shopping bags, but none admitted having done so.

The campaign cruiser was easily enough identified. It carried the word LUCILLITE in letters two feet high along each side. There rose from the roof on supporting brackets the representation of an attractive female clutching a packet of Lucillite and gazing up, like a saint contemplating her own halo, at a thinksbaloon inscribed 'For Stains that Defy – Saponify!'

The cruiser was parked on a half-acre of uncultivated land that lay between the river and the northern end of Jubilee Park Crescent. The area was low lying and its liability to be flooded each spring gave it a grey and streaky appearance; what grass grew there was short, sparse and wirelike.

On this impoverished terrain had been set a broad, white-painted platform surmounted by an arch of trellis over which two drumfuls of 'Bowermaster' plastic vine had been unwound. At each side of the platform was an imitation medieval fair booth. That on the left bore a notice in Gothic type: *Ye Townspeople's fouled cloutes taken here*. The notice on the right-hand booth read: *Collect ye fayre and sweete cloutes here*.

An outsize washing-machine occupied the centre of the platform.

By one o'clock, more than thirty women had collected around the great caravan. Two Lucies emerged from their rest-room amidships and began to check names and describe in simple terms what was going to happen. More detailed directions, they said, would be given by the gentlemen from The Company and The Film People.

The crowd grew to fifty or more. Instinctive segregation was beginning to be noticeable. The more animated elements, those from the Burton Lane estate, kept close to the cruiser, ready to profit from neighbourhood solidarity should anything be offered from its doors on a first-come-first-served principle.

Less voluble, but no less vigilant ladies, whose homes lay in the avenues and closes south of Pawson's Lane, moved slowly in small groups around the platform. This not only enabled them to avoid a social admixture which, they were considerate enough to realize, would have embarrassed their less fortunately placed fellow townswomen, but it was calculated to give them a head start if the platform and not the caravan should prove to be the focus of the afternoon's activities.

A third group, the smallest, loitered on the river bank in graceful contemplation of the upper air. Every now and then they peeked at tiny gold watches, glistening amidst the fur of coat-sleeves like the eyes of little animals. These women were residents of Stanstead Gardens and its tributaries, Brompton, Mather and Darlington Gardens, and they were on hand partly out of curiosity and partly on account of the rumour that a ten-guinea fee was to be paid everyone selected for actual screen appearance.

Precisely at one-thirty, the Assistant Environmental Research and Liaison Executive in charge of the number two mobile and called Hugh by his peers, leaped briskly up the three steps to the platform and held up his arms.

'Ladies . . .'

The factions began to draw together to form a single audience. Even the Gardens-dwellers ventured within listening distance. They turned to one another, trying out smiles.

'Ladies,' cried the A E R A L E, 'as you know, this is a big day for' – he frowned for a second, snapped his fingers – 'for Flaxborough. With your kind assistance and' – he glanced at the sky – 'that of the beautiful weather you seem to enjoy in this part of the country' – good-humoured groans – 'we intend to put this town on a million television screens. Right, everyone? Right. Now you know what that means, don't you? It means that some of you lovely ladies – no, don't laugh, I can safely say that seldom have I seen so high a proportion of attractive women in all the crowds that have come to testify to the power of our Product – it means, I say, that some of you luscious ladies will have the chance you have been waiting for – and which, believe me, you so richly deserve – the chance of being a real film star! What do you think of that, eh? Fabulous? Fabulous, right. So we'll get right along with all the wonderful things that are in store for Flaxborough while this fabulous weather holds and while all you lovely ladies are still smiling. Smile, smile, smile, that's the style, right? First of all, there's a fabulous young man I want you all to meet. He's our Location Visual Kinetics Executive – and anyone who can say that gets a free packet of Lucillite here and now, I promise you, ladies – can *you* say that, madam? – no, never mind, we'll just call him Antony, shall we? Antony, come up here and meet all these lovely ladies . . .'

And soon they were all friends: the ladies both of humble station and high degree; Hugh, with his chubby chops, a nose like an aubergine, and eyes restless as riot police, darting always here and there in the crowd to see that the quips and sallies were being properly acknowledged; black-bearded Antony, who wore heavy gold ear-rings and manipulated his camera like a harpooner; and the four Lucies on herd control and powder-room whisper duty.

Neither the Area Promotion Director of Dixon-Frome nor their consultancy's Deputy Chief Brand Visualizer had yet put in an appearance. They were taking a working lunch at the Roebuck in order to discuss in depth the new concept of Mantis Motivation in the domestic detergent field.

No such advanced theory lay behind the programme of filming and interviews from which a two-minute commercial would eventually be sculpted by the Tele-kinetics Division of TEAK. The idea to be promoted was simply that Lucillite was of such remarkable cleansing potential that it would enable clothes to be washed even in the polluted water of a modern river.

The treatment of the finished film was to be in a style combining historico-fantastical and chemo-whimsical elements.

Some shots had been taken the previous day. Polystyrene rocks had been set in the mud at the water's edge, and Lucies in seventeenth-century gowns filmed while they dunked seventeenth-century shifts in the river, slapped them on to the polystyrene rocks and belaboured them with plastic paddles. This performance would be condensed into the few seconds' screen time sufficient for viewers to be told that in Good King Charles's days rivers ran pure – pure enough for washing the family's clothes. There would follow the interpolation of some stocky library shots of industrial effluent to point the question, 'But would you put your husband's shirt into *this*?'

Hugh, held all the time at close range by Antony's lenses, moved among the women like a faith-healer with a full head of steam. He halted before a benign-looking woman on whose coat was pinned the tiny 'L' monogram that showed she had been interviewed by a Lucy, found reasonably articulate and co-operative, and coached in the art of giving prescribed answers with apparent conviction.

'Would *you* like to try doing your weekly wash in that river, madam, as they did in Good King Charles's golden days?'

'Ha, ha,' said the woman with great care and solemnity. 'You must be joking of course.'

Hugh shook his head, put one arm round the woman's shoulders and smiled into the middle distance. 'My dear, you won't think I'm joking when I tell you what I'm going to do. You've brought your weekly wash along here today?'

'Yes I have. I don't know what my hubby will say I'm sure.' The woman stared steadfastly at the microphone and waited.

'Fabulous. Well, I'll tell you what I'm going to do. I'm going to tell one of those young ladies to take your things and – no, wait for it – and WASH them in that dirty old river water. Now what do you say to that? He gave her shoulders a squeeze and grinned round at the assembly.

'Well all I can say is good luck to Lucillite and its sapo-ni-fied gra-nules but I must say you are taking something on this time.'

Hugh released the woman from his evangelical embrace and without sparing her another glance he began to wind up a few yards of slack in the microphone cable.

'Lovely,' said Antony. 'Marvellous.' He made cabbalistic motions with a light-meter. 'I want the river shots now. That lovely boatman. Before the light goes.'

'We'll have some more of these little personal chats later, shall we, ladies?' Hugh was addressing the women in general. 'That will be fabulous, and I'm looking forward to it, I truly am. But for the moment I want you all to gather over there by the river and stand – yes, that's right, just stand there – and look out over the water at the boat. Like you were waiting for Bonnie Prince Charlie. You all know who Bonnie Prince Charlie was? Of course you do. That's marvellous. Just stay like that a minute. Fabulous . . .'

Into Antony's ear he inquired: 'Where's that prick who's supposed to be taking the bloody boat out?'

The boatman was eventually discovered asleep in his craft, moored a hundred yards up river. He was a Flaxborough man ('a genuine local', in Antony's enthusiastic phrase) and the admen had recruited him the previous evening on the strength of his assurance, given with a wealth of circumstantial detail in the bar parlour of the Three Crowns, that he was a ferryman of long experience and wide renown. His name was Heath.

'Aye, aye, cap'n!' he responded with great presence of mind, on being jolted from sleep by an angry shout from Hugh. He scrambled to the stern of the rowboat, unknowingly loaned by a drinking acquaintance, and cut the rope that secured it to a baulk of timber. The boat began to drift offshore, slowly revolving.

Heath searched for whatever means of locomotion the boat possessed. There were no oars. He managed to pull out a seatboard. Using this as a paddle, he got the craft near enough to the bank to make himself heard by his patrons.

'Ahoy, there . . . I'll belay her down wind a point and get her to where you said. You go and hoist your film gear and she'll be there before you can spit.'

Heath had been punctilious in one respect: he had donned the costume devised by the T E A K Tele-kinetics Division for his role – indeed it had so taken his fancy that he had been wearing it continuously since the previous evening. It consisted of a scarlet and gold waterman's doublet, Nelsonian breeches and a highwayman's hat left over from a stillborn campaign on behalf of Dick Turpin Y-fronts (The B-I-G Holdup).

The plan was for this picturesque figure to row out to midstream, mime a baling action to make it seem he was filling the antique brass-bound plastic tub in the prow, and return to the shore. A series of brief clips would convey an impression of the operation and of its sequels: the transfer of the supposed river water into the washing machine ashore and the supposed addition of the miraculously saponifying Product, in order that a collection of the town's most gruesomely stained articles of apparel might supposedly be cleansed to the astonishment, edification and high delight of the beholders.

Heath's intended course was marked by three poles that had been driven at low tide into the river bed at twenty-yard intervals. These rose some ten feet above the present water level and served the primary purpose of supporting a banner that read: BRIGHT, BRIGHT–NEW LUCILLITE.

Having with difficulty brought his boat to the bank close by the first pole, and exchanged his extemporized paddle for the oars that Hugh had commandeered from a beached dinghy near by, Heath spat on his hands and struck a nautical attitude.

'Everything shipshape, cap'n?' he inquired of Antony, already clamped to his viewfinder.

'Lovely. Lovely. Carry on. Marvellous. Now the rowing. Lovely. Pull. Try and keep together. You're Captain Bligh. Yes, lovely. You're Bligh, duckie. Intrepid. Obsessed. Yes, yes – marvellous. Knot your neck muscles. Now a teeny bit of agony. You're being lashed. Ooo ... lash, lash, lash. Lovely ...'

When he had been for some time out of range of these murmured exhortations, Heath judged the moment appropriate to stop rowing and to go through the baling routine. The third pole, he noticed, was only a yard or two away. He picked up the reproduction eighteenth century grog pannikin that had been supplied with his costume and dipped it in the river, then emptied its contents into the tub. He repeated the operation half a dozen times.

A shout came from the shore. Heath looked back to see Hugh waving and pointing meaningfully at the boat. Antony had stopped filming and seemed to be making gestures indicative of impending self-destruction. Heath, much puzzled, cupped his hand to one ear.

'Get the bloody thing off!' came over the water from Hugh. 'It's right in the bloody picture!'

Heath frowned, shrugged and inquiringly doffed his three-cornered hat.

'No!' bellowed Hugh. 'Not that.'

Heath put his hat on again.

'In the water,' Hugh shouted. 'There. Just by the stern.'

Heath peered over the prow.

'Stern! Stern!'

'The back!' screamed Antony. Heath gave a great quarter-deck salute of comprehension and clambered aft.

What he saw was enough to disconcert more seasoned mariners than Heath. Waterborne just below the gunwale and staring up at him with bulbous, bloodshot eyes was the head of some monstrous animal. Strips of hide floating from the severed neck had caught on the farthest banner-supporting pole.

Heath stared for nearly half a minute at the creature's chaps, blackened as if by mummification, at its bull-like nostrils and partly submerged horns.

Then, quite suddenly, it dawned on him that the thing was too buoyant to be real. He poked it with an oar. It bobbed, sending an impression of wood, of hollowness, up the oar. He leaned out and tugged the leather strapping free from the pole. Heaving the head into the boat took scarcely any effort at all.

'Beg to report sea monster in the scuppers, cap'n!'

The homeward-bound Heath, delighted with the discovery so late in life that he could row, grinned over his shoulder at the assembly on the bank.

A few of the women smiled back. The others, who had heard some of the things which Hugh and Antony had been saying to each other about Heath's odyssey, remained grave-faced.

As soon as the boat touched ground, Hugh yanked out the head and swung it on to the turf behind him. In a terribly audible whisper he ordered Heath to turn the boat round and go through his whole routine again but not like a piss-boiling twat this time or God help him he'd stitch his ears to his arsehole and *please* but *please* to remember this whole thing was more serious than the Holy Ghost so no more bloody jokes ...

Heath embarked on his second voyage to the accompaniment of another stream of those delirious little cries of encouragement which seemed to issue from Antony quite automatically whenever he aimed a camera at anybody.

Hugh, his solicitous affability restored to full pressure, mar-shalled the washwives into new positions for interviews and amazement shots.

The Area Promotion Director of Dixon-Frome and the Deputy Chief Brand Visualizer of Thornton-Edwards, Arnold and Kon-statin arrived back from their working lunch in the A P D's Sholto-Clore Mark I I I Retaliator. They watched the filming for a few minutes from the observation window of the campaign cruiser, then closed their eyes in order to internalize a few of the day's ideas.

Only two people seemed disposed to take notice of the great mask that lay on the grass, the spring sunshine drawing from it faint wraiths of steam.

One was Mrs Flora Pentatuke, who had been watching from the opposite bank during Heath's first excursion.

The other also was a woman. Her name was Miss Amy Parkin and although she was of exceptionally short stature, she somehow had contrived that afternoon to get her face on to more than half the footage of Antony's film.

Chapter Five

SATURDAY MORNING IN FLAXBOROUGH IS NORMALLY AN undemanding, leisurely interlude between five days of labour and the athletic, alcoholic or concupiscent demands of the week-end. There is an open street market at one end of the town and at the other an auction of such various objects as henhouses, bags of onions, fishing rods, rolls of wire, saplings, tortoises and second-hand hearing aids. The shops in between are packed with citizens exchanging news and opinions and occasionally buying something. Inns do a moderate trade, but the availability of their liquor is of secondary importance to the comfort and seclusion of their bar parlours. The drivers of the cars wedged irrevocably in narrow streets do not engage in the empurpling bouts of mutual recrimination that are the sole enlivening indulgence open to the city motorist; they sensibly go in search of talk and refreshment until such time as the situation be resolved by the Flaxborough equivalent of natural selection. Even policemen, from Chief Constable Harcourt Chubb to the rawest cadet in Fen Street, subscribe – in normal times – to the preservation of Saturday morning as a strictly social amenity which could be blighted by the slightest excess of zeal on their part. 'Let it mulch until Monday', is one of the favourite advisory metaphors of Mr Chubb, a keen gardener in his considerable spare time.

But the day that followed the opening of the Lucillite promotion campaign was not normal – or certainly not to a degree that would have permitted Inspector Purbright and his colleagues to remain inoperative.

For one thing, Edna Hillyard had not yet made a reappearance at her lodgings or her place of work or, as far as the police were aware, anywhere else in the town.

For another, the wife of Mr Bertram Persimmon, of 3 The Riding, Flaxborough, had reported her husband missing since Wednesday.

A third thoroughly disconcerting circumstance was the arrival at the police station of five journalists from London papers anxious to know about a Black Magic Cult which had turned Flaxborough into a Town of Fear.

Purbright sent word to the duty sergeant that if the five gentlemen would be good enough to await him in the station recreation room they would be rewarded with a press conference.

Sergeant Love expressed apprehension but Purbright brushed aside his doubts with the observation that the newspaperman of the present day was no longer all hip flask and trespass but a civilized practitioner who would respect confidences and reciprocate helpfulness. Thus whistling in the dark, so to speak, he led Love downstairs to the recreation room.

Purbright took stock of the waiting five and was a little surprised to find that they did, indeed, look different in type and temperament from national pressmen as he supposed Love would recall them. The dirty raincoats with epaulettes and leather buttons had gone; as had the scuffed brown brogue shoes, the underarm clutches of early editions, the blue ribbon of smoke ascending from the mouth-cornered cigarette past the permanently closed eye that gave the face its abiding expression of quizzical world-weariness. These men looked less abusive and less abused. Purbright guessed that they ate more expense-account lunches than their predecessors and fewer railway pies. For a moment, he wondered if the old habits of thought had been jettisoned with the shabby coats and the chain-smoking.

'Inspector, what are the police doing about all these black masses that are going on down here?'

Purbright sighed. *Plus ça change* ... 'Ah,' he said brightly, 'I'm glad you asked me that ...'

To the home of Mrs Gloss on Orchard Road went Detective Constable Pook, primed by Purbright to ask further questions about Edna Hillyard and to bring her car back to police headquarters.

Mrs Gloss did not look particularly pleased to see him but she invited him into the lounge. 'Another cup, Edie,' Mrs Gloss called through the kitchen door as they passed.

A very short, plainly dressed woman was sitting beside the table on which coffee and a plate of biscuits were already set out. Pook recognized her as a teacher from the Dorley Road junior school.

'Morning, Miss Parkin,' he said.

Amy Parkin's convergent eyes were trained at points in space a little beyond and to each side of his head. She wished him good morning.

'Mr Pook is a policeman,' explained Mrs Gloss, 'and he has come to take Edna's car away.'

She held out her hand for the cup and saucer which a sallow, straight-haired young girl wearing an apron had brought in.

'Help yourself to a biscuit, officer.'

He did so.

'I understand,' Pook said, regarding the KreemiKrunch Kookie that would release the real taste of the country at the first bite, 'that Miss Hillyard was last seen on Wednesday night.'

'Well, that was when I personally last saw her. I cannot speak for other people, naturally.'

'You saw her then as well, did you, Miss Parkin?'

'I?' Miss Parkin sounded surprised. Then she noticed the folded copy of the *Flaxborough Citizen* which Pook had taken from his pocket and was smoothing, napkin-like, across his knee. 'Oh, yes. Certainly I saw her. At our little function. But only very briefly.'

Pook nibbled the KreemiKrunch Kookie and allowed his taste buds to be beguiled by a country-style combination of dehydrated milk solids, soya rusk, sodium monostearate and saccharin.

'I see she won some sort of a prize,' he said.

'A title only,' Mrs Gloss said quickly. 'Nothing tangible.'

'Not a cup, then? It says here "Maypole trophy".'

'You shouldn't take things in newspapers too literally,' Miss Parkin said.

'That's true,' added Mrs Gloss. '"Trophy" in this case isn't used in a material sense, you know. It's a sort of honour, that's all.

'The members know what it means, and that's what matters, isn't it?'

Pook nodded at Miss Parkin's sapience and looked again at the *Citizen* report while he drank some coffee and demolished the rest of the KreemiKrunch.

'What's a faggot-master?' he inquired.

Mrs Gloss frowned. 'If you *must* know, we generally have a little bonfire to brighten up our outdoor meetings, and Mr Cowdrey looks after it. He has had experience with the Scouts.'

'I know,' Pook said, without looking up from the paper. He somehow made the acknowledgement sound like a notice of impending prosecution. The two women glanced at each other.

'What time was it when you last noticed Miss Hillyard?' Pook asked Mrs Gloss.

'I really couldn't tell you. It was towards the end of the meeting. Elevenish, perhaps.'

Pook looked at Miss Parkin.

She waved a hand vaguely. 'About then, yes.'

'Dancing, was she?' asked Pook, having referred again to the newspaper report.

'I believe she was.'

Miss Parkin nodded agreement.

'It says here,' the policeman went on, 'that there were refreshments. What sort of refreshments, Mrs Gloss?'

Mrs Gloss's expression hardened. 'Is that relevant, officer?'

'It could be, madam.'

'How?'

'Well, it's not for me to speculate, but the lady did leave her car here. Perhaps she had reason to think that it was the wisest thing to do.'

Mrs Gloss was silent for a moment. She shrugged. 'You could be right. But it is not for me to speculate, either. I only know that the bar . . .'

'The "quaffing bench"?'

'If you prefer to call it that.'

'It's what the paper calls it.'

'I see. The point is, though, if I may return to it, that any notion of unregulated drinking on anybody's part can be dismissed from your mind at once. The refreshment was the one customarily served at our meetings – a very wholesome drink made to an old country punch recipe.'

'Chiefly home-made wine,' averred Miss Parkin.

'Ah,' Pook said. (Purbright once had observed that one of what he called Pook's 'rancid monosyllables' was as intimidating as a search warrant.)

'About Miss Hillyard,' Pook said. 'Has either of you ladies any idea at all where she might have gone after you last had sight of her?'

Miss Parkin replied first. 'One would have expected her to return to her apartment.'

'Apartment?'

'She has rooms in Cheviot Road,' said Mrs Gloss.

'That's rather a long way from here, isn't it? If she walked, I mean. And late at night.'

'There were others here with cars. She probably got a lift home.'

'In that case, there might be somebody who could tell us what happened to her on the way. Because she certainly didn't arrive at her lodgings.'

Pook brought out this piece of reasoning with the air of having forced some wily miscreant into a corner.

Mrs Gloss made no comment. She poured more coffee for Miss Parkin, refilled her own cup, and moved the remaining biscuits to the side of the table farthest from Detective-Constable Pook.

Miss Parkin took small but audible sips from her cup and gazed unsympathetically past the head of coffeeless Pook. Although the room was warm, she was dressed in the same thick, stiff cape which she had been wearing the previous Wednesday night. Her hat, in matching material, was round and hard-crowned and of broad brim, like a lifeboatman's. When she put down her cup and wiped her lips with a handkerchief produced from beneath the cape, there was a faint scrubbing noise.

'Just one more question, I think, Mrs Gloss.' Pook consulted some notes he had made in the margin of his copy of the *Citizen*. 'Could you tell me if Mr Persimmon, the supermarket manager, is a member of your society?'

'Persimmon?'

'That's right. Mr Bertram Persimmon. Lives off Partney Drive.'

Mrs Gloss shook her head dubiously. 'I very much doubt it. Do *you* know, Amy?'

'We do not have a Mr Persimmon. That is for sure.'

'There you are, then, officer. Your final question is answered.' Mrs Gloss made as if to rise.

'Was Miss Hillyard an acquaintance of Mr Persimmon, do you happen to know?'

'I haven't the faintest idea. And now, if you wouldn't mind . . .'

'Can *you* answer that, Miss Parkin?'

'No.'

Pook stood up.

'I understand my colleague left the key of Miss Hillyard's car in your safe keeping, madam.'

Mrs Gloss stepped to the Jacobean television sideboard and pulled open a drawer.

'Do be careful how you drive it round the side of the house, won't you, officer. We don't want to lose any of the bedding plants.'

For a moment she kept the keys in her hand, ignoring his outstretched palm.

'You do have a driving licence, I take it?'

When the policeman had gone, both women waited in silence until they heard the distant grind of a starter succeeded by the bursting into spasmodic life of the sports car's engine.

'I don't think I liked him very much. Did you, Amy?'

Miss Parkin grunted and thoughtfully tugged at a whiskered

mole under her right ear.

'I wonder,' she said very quietly, 'where he lives.'

The five pressmen, Purbright soon found, had been commendably busy since their arrival in Flaxborough the previous evening.

They had sought out the Vicar, pierced his hostile reticence, and flattered him into providing a colourful account of the discoveries in the Parish Church.

They had found several shopkeepers willing to testify to disturbing but unaccountable interference with trade by what they called 'rum goings on'.

A Miss Lucilla Teatime, secretary and treasurer of the Edith Cavell Psychical Research Foundation, had been prevailed upon to describe the level of poltergeist activity in the area as 'well above that which we investigators of paranormal phenomena would expect to find in the circumstances'.

And the unknown lady whose telephone call to a London newsagency had aroused Fleet Street's interest in the first place had since asserted – again anonymously, but this time in a letter addressed to 'The Gentlemen of the Press' and left on the reception counter at the Roebuck Hotel – that she had personally attended more Black Masses in Flaxborough than she cared to remember.

'Even making allowance for exaggeration,' said the representative of the *Sunday Dispatch*, a young man with the beginnings of a Fu Manchu moustache, 'I would have thought there was enough in this story to have worried the police. *Are* the police worried, inspector?'

Purbright smiled apologetically.

'If I say yes, it will mean that the constabulary doesn't feel confident to deal with the powers of evil. If I say no, I'm inviting the criticism that we don't believe in them. I would prefer to be allowed the middle course of benevolent agnosticism: tell me where a black mass is going on – or likely to take place – and I'll see if there's anything we can or ought to do about it.'

'What you've said,' quickly observed a girl with a pretty but worried face and a shaggy motoring coat, 'strikes me as sort of . . .

oh, I don't know, sort of uninvolved. I mean, like you had a lot of permissiveness around out here in the country – you know, the Provinces – and sort of wanted to turn a blind eye. I mean, I'm not criticizing you, or anything, but . . .' All the time she was talking, the girl kept capping and uncapping a fountain pen and fixedly staring at it.

'Would you say you had a permissive society here, inspector?'

This question was issued on behalf of the readers of the *Empire News*, whose representative, a plump youth in Victorian style trousers, flowered shirt and velvet jacket, was clearly devout in desiring the answer to be yes.

The girl with the pen, a *Sunday Pictorial* feature writer, looked up and gave her colleague a grateful smile.

'I'm not sure that I know what you mean by permissive,' Purbright said. 'The police certainly don't go around harassing people in deference to the morally pretentious. We don't believe that citizens can be sorted back into the right beds by rule of truncheon. We do, on the other hand, try to dissuade them from raping one another – galloping their maggots in public – that sort of thing. Or is it something else you have in mind? Something more sophisticated, perhaps?'

A constable, dispatched earlier to fetch coffee from the canteen, appeared with a tray. Cups were distributed. One of the two journalists who declined, the *Daily Herald* man, put another question.

'Is it true that people are afraid to go out after dark because of black magic rites?'

'Not as far as I'm aware.'

'But we have been told' – the *Herald* man glanced round at the others – 'by four or five people in the town that they've either been bewitched themselves at some time or they know of others who have.'

There were murmurs of agreement, although a lanky grizzle-haired man from the *News Chronicle*, older than the rest, interposed the remark that free drinks would buy testimony to anything.

Purbright, who saw that direct confirmation of the truth of this opinion would not be popular, observed instead that strangers might be forgiven if they mistook for veracity that eagerness to please which was so notable a canon of Flaxborough hospitality.

'I'm very sorry,' he went on, 'if it seems to you that *I* could be a little more eager to please in this matter, but I'm sure that such experienced journalists as yourselves would prefer me to be absolutely prosaic and factual. Policemen who make conjectures, however attractive they may be from a news editor's standpoint, are really of no more use to you than those who sit on facts.'

The reporter from the *Dispatch* had begun to put a question about pin-stuck images when there came through the door a man of about sixty wearing a light grey overcoat and carrying a walking stick and yellow washleather gloves. His bearing was careful, his expression one of courteous inquisitiveness. Purbright greeted and introduced him as Mr Harcourt Chubb, the chief constable of Flaxborough.

'This lady and these gentlemen,' the inspector explained, 'are journalists' – Mr Chubb raised one eyebrow – 'and they are here to ask questions about witchcraft.' Mr Chubb's second eyebrow went up and he gazed disbelievingly at the girl from the *Sunday Pictorial*.

Purbright turned to the pressmen. 'Is there anything you'd care to put to the chief constable while he's here?'

Mr Chubb instantly pursed his lips and shook his head. 'My dear Mr Purbright, I wouldn't dream of interfering with your prerogatives.' He took a step towards the door. 'Just you carry . . .' Sudden comprehension of the enormity of what the inspector had said pulled him short. 'Questions about *what*?'

'Witchcraft, sir. Black magic. Necromancy.'

'Good gracious me. Where?'

'Here, sir. In Flaxborough.'

There was silence. Then the chief constable said 'I see.' He gave the pressmen a bleak, puzzled little smile of farewell and departed.

The man from the *News Chronicle* said it appeared that anxiety about the alleged instances of satanism had not spread to the upper ranks of the police force.

'It hasn't, actually,' said Purbright.

'Not even when they know that a girl has disappeared and may have been used as a human sacrifice?'

Four journalists snapped attention to the fifth. He was the floridly attired *Empire News* reporter and he was blushing partly with triumph, partly with annoyance at the impetuous discard of his own advantage.

Purbright knew that nothing excites deeper suspicion and resentment in a newspaperman than the countering of an awkward question with the retort: Who told you that? He considered, then replied carefully:

'It is true that a young woman of thirty-four has been missing – in the sense of being absent from both her work and her lodgings – for the past two days. We have no reason to suppose that she has come to any harm, although, naturally enough, we shall feel easier when she reappears.

'The suggestion by your colleague that this woman has been the victim of, what, a ritual murder – is that your meaning, sir?' – the *Empire News* man nodded – 'Yes, well, that suggestion is unsupported by any evidence known to me.'

There was a rattle of conversation, from which, after a few moments, intelligible questions separated.

'What's the girl's name, inspector?'

'Edna Hillyard.'

'Married?'

'We don't think so.'

'Address?'

'Cheviot Road. Number eighteen. Incidentally, if you do wish to question her landlady, who is inoffensive and knows singularly little, I rely on you not to embarrass her.'

In reply to another question, Purbright added that the landlady was called Mrs Lanchester.

'Has the girl no family?'

'Not in this area. She moved here with her mother some years ago, but the mother is now dead. There are relations in Scotland, I believe, and we are trying to get in touch with them.'

The *Sunday Pictorial* girl spoke. 'Look, if you don't think anything's happened to this Hillyard person – I mean, you don't *sound* terribly concerned – not that one expects policemen to wax hys*ter*ical or anything . . . but after all she *is missing*, and one can't help wondering why the sang-froid, as it were. You do see what I mean?'

'Oh, certainly. And there is a reason, as you've obviously guessed already. Miss Hillyard is an independent sort of young woman. She gets around. Her reputation is one of unpredictability.'

'You mean she's disappeared before?' asked the *Dispatch*.

'I mean she gets around, as I said. Disappear is a rather Gothic way of putting it.'

'A good-time girl?' brightly suggested the *Herald*.

Purbright gave a worldly shrug.

'And you don't think she takes part in this Voodoo Cult you've got here?'

'Miss Hillyard,' Purbright said patiently, 'is employed in the department of the Medical Officer of Health. She is also, I understand, a member of the Presbyterian Church. Of those facts, gentlemen, you are at liberty to make what you will.'

After the press conference, Purbright made his way to the chief constable's office, where Mr Chubb was in recuperative retreat in the interval between exercising six of his Yorkshire terriers and attending a Rotary lunch.

'What's all this nonsense about witches, for heaven's sake? I thought you were pulling those fellows' legs just now, but they all looked very serious.'

Purbright explained. Mr Chubb looked more dubious than ever.

'You mean they've been going round the town listening to a lot of silly gossip. That's what it boils down to.'

'To be fair, sir, it isn't a subject they're likely to learn anything about without listening to gossip. We don't normally issue official bulletins or Wanted-for-Witchcraft posters.'

'Yes, but *you* don't believe this ridiculous story about Miss Whatsername, do you?'

'Miss Hillyard. No, sir. Nor do they. But it's not a question of belief. Newspapers are a branch of the entertainment industry, not a research foundation.'

'You say you are not worried about this woman, Mr Purbright.'

'Not unduly. As I told the press just now, she has something of a reputation for unconventional behaviour. But there's another thing – and this I didn't tell the press. We learned this morning that a man called Persimmon has also been missing since Wednesday. The possibility of their having gone off together is well worth considering.'

'Not *Bert* Persimmon, surely?'

'Bertram. Yes, sir. Middle-aged. Store manager.'

'But he's . . .' Mr Chubb was about to say 'vice-chairman of the Conservative Club' when he remembered his inspector's perverse inclination to disregard the relevance of social lustre to a presumption of innocence. 'But he's married,' he said instead.

'He is indeed,' the inspector confirmed. Almost zestfully, he added: 'Isn't he vice-chairman of that club of yours, sir?'

'Possibly. I don't know all the officials' names.' Mr Chubb was examining his shirt cuff. 'By the way . . .' He looked up.

'Yes, sir?'

'About this unpleasantness at St Lawrence's. You'll do what you can to get to the bottom of it, won't you? Old Greywear isn't the easiest chap in the world to deal with, but he means well. It's not nice to have a lot of dead animals left around in one's church.'

'I think it was the effigy that annoyed him most. It was an exceedingly good likeness. I've asked Policewoman Bellweather to make a few very discreet inquiries among the Arts and Crafts people. There may be a lead there.'

'You say there were pins stuck into the thing?'

'Yes, sir.'

The chief constable shook his head. 'Childish tricks some of these people get up to. One wonders sometimes how their minds work.'

The inspector decided that it would only add to Mr Chubb's perplexity if he were to detail the disposition of the pins. He took his leave and prepared to drive out to The Riding and the home of Mr Bertram Persimmon.

He was going out of the building into the central yard where the cars were kept when the duty sergeant intercepted him.

'That thing, sir...'

The inspector halted and listened courteously.

'Roberts collected it after that woman rang up yesterday and I didn't know whether you'd want it put among the lost property or what. Not', the sergeant added with ponderous drollery, 'that I can imagine anybody wanting to get it back again.'

'Perhaps I'd better have a look.'

The sergeant crossed the office and opened one of the doors of the row of cupboards that extended along the opposite wall. There rolled forth, as if from the blade of a concealed guillotine, the great horned head that boatman Heath had retrieved from the river.

Purbright gave an involuntary start, then moved nearer.

The sergeant shifted the head with his boot so that it confronted his superior officer in full face if not with due respect.

'That's not lost property,' Purbright declared almost at once.

'How do you mean, sir?'

'It was pinched.'

Kneeling, the inspector turned the head about and explored its texture.

'Two or three years ago. From the museum.'

'Oh.' The sergeant looked abashed. The burglarious entering of the Heritage Room of the Municipal Museum in Fish Street by some over-eager legatee had caused much local indignation at the time. It was most remiss of any police officer to have failed to recognize the stolen article.

'Never mind,' Purbright told him. 'You can't be expected to remember every fertility rite outfit that gets lifted from a museum.'

'Is that what it is, sir?'

'So they tell me.'

Purbright turned the head over and peered inside it, then righted it again.

'Good lord, the things people choose to turn into table lamps.'

The sergeant saw that Purbright was looking at an electric bulb holder, set between the two horns. The metal stem of a bulb, still screwed into its socket, held fragments of glass, ruby-coloured.

'I think,' the inspector said, 'that we should have this locked up carefully until someone from the museum can come over and see what damage has been done. Can I leave you to arrange that?'

The sergeant grasped the chance of self-redemption. 'Oh, yes, sir. Certainly you can.' He sprang for the telephone.

'Incidentally . . .'

'Sir?'

'Who was the woman who telephoned about that thing?'

'We don't know that, sir. She wouldn't give her name.'

Purbright frowned. 'Odd. Why shouldn't she, I wonder? There's an awful lot of anonymity about just now – had you noticed?'

'I think it's because of not wanting to get into the papers, sir,' suggested the now desperately helpful sergeant.

'That,' said Purbright, making for the door, 'I can well understand.'

Chapter Six

'OH, GOD, YES,' SAID MRS PERSIMMON WHEN PURBRIGHT spoke her name interrogatively at the front door. 'Oh, God, yes,' she said again when he announced his own. Then, 'Oh God, come in,' she said, and raised her eyes so that he could see their whites as he stepped past her into a hall perfumed with the lavender of Croon, the only furniture cream containing ionized beeswax. Purbright feared that the interview was going to be a harrowing experience.

On her silent invitation, he entered a room whose big bay window commanded a view of the front lawn and the tall hedge that hid it from the road. Mrs Persimmon closed the door by leaning her back against it. She remained in that position for several seconds, breathing deeply. She put one hand on her breast.

'Oh, God, you've found him.'

'No. No, we haven't actually. But you really mustn't distress yourself, Mrs Persimmon. There's no certainty that your husband has come to any harm.'

Purbright's words appeared to have gone unheard. She continued to stare into space. The hand edged slowly off her breast and under her arm. She abstractedly scratched herself.

'Of course, you don't know what I've been through.'

She launched her body away from the door and walked across the room. Pausing by a semi-circular table set against the wall, she adjusted the position of two china figures that stood upon it. 'Oh, God!' She impetuously passed a hand over her hair without disarranging it.

'Perhaps it would be better if you sat down, Mrs Persimmon.'

Purbright indicated a square-cut sofa covered in orange plastic. She hesitated, then lowered herself into diagonal occupation of the sofa, one thin white arm along its back (like toothpaste, Purbright reflected).

The inspector found a chair for himself and sat opposite her. He felt in his pockets and produced a ball-point pen and an old sales receipt, blank on one side.

'I understand you last saw your husband on Wednesday.'

She put a hand over her eyes. Purbright took the gesture to be affirmative.

'At what time, would you say? Approximately.'

The shield of fingers remained over the pale, back-tilted face. 'When he left for business. About ten o'clock.'

'But the store opens at eight-thirty, surely?'

'My husband is not a counter hand, Mr, er...'

The correction, Purbright fancied, had been delivered with a trace more acerbity than he would have expected from a putative widow.

'Did he not return home that day for a meal?'

'No.'

'He usually has lunch in town, does he?'

'Always. He eats at the Roebuck. They reserve a special table for him.'

'In the evening, though – weren't you surprised when he didn't come home on Wednesday evening?'

'Oh, no. It was his "samaritan" night.'

'I'm sorry – his . . .?' Purbright turned his head slightly, as if to present his keener ear.

'His "samaritan" night. Mr Persimmon does social work. I thought you would have known that, Mr, er . . .'

'Purbright.'

'Mr Purbright. Yes, he received his O B E for that. He's on lots of committees.' Mrs Persimmon had removed the hand from her face. She was looking a little stronger now.

'I'm not sure that I quite understand what you mean by "samaritan" night, Mrs Persimmon. There is an organization called The Samaritans. Do I take it that your husband is a member?'

'Oh, no, not that organization but it's just what I've always called, that's all – his "samaritan" night. It's to help people. I expect one of the other gentlemen can tell you more about it if you really want to know.'

Purbright nodded with every appearance of having understood. 'Of course. The other gentlemen.' He held his pen poised.

'Well, there's Harry,' said Mrs Persimmon. 'You know – Sir Henry Bird.'

'Ah, yes.'

'He's a particular friend of my husband, and I should say they've done this social whatever-it-is, this "samaritan" business, as I call it, oh, for a couple of years at least, ever since . . . oh, God' – she hoisted herself forward and opened her eyes – 'but you won't go and ask him a lot of questions, will you? You'll not do that? I don't think my husband would like Harry to be bothered unnecessarily.'

'We try not to bother anybody unnecessarily, Mrs Persimmon.'

There was a pause. Mrs Persimmon straightened her posture and sat facing forward.

'Perhaps,' she said quietly, 'I've been rather hasty in sending for the police.'

Purbright watched her face. 'Why do you say that?'

'I don't know. It seems silly, though. To panic. I mean, I would have heard if anything had happened to him. Don't you think so?'

'Almost certainly you would have done, yes.' The inspector was wondering why dramatic expletives and gestures had given way first to social defensiveness, then to this unhappy deflation.

'Well, then,' she said at last, 'we'd better just forget about it for the time being, shall we?'

She stood. Purbright motioned her to sit down again. He sighed gently.

'Look, Mrs Persimmon. Today is Saturday. You have told me that you last saw your husband on Wednesday. His absence during that night did not surprise you because you knew he was doing some kind of social welfare work. Very well. But he did not come home on Thursday night either. Nor last night. So you telephoned us this morning and reported him missing.'

'Yes, I'm sorry, I...'

'No, don't apologize, Mrs Persimmon. I don't at all consider your phone call to have been hasty, as you put it. What I *do* find difficult to understand is why you waited so long before making it.'

She considered.

'We don't live in each other's pockets, you know,' she said coldly. 'Me and my husband, I mean.'

'I don't suppose you do.'

'Well, then – what are you making all the fuss about?'

'I came because you asked for help.'

'All right. Well, now you can go because I don't want any after all.'

The childishly crude retort Purbright recognized as a symptom of deep unease. He could not quite decide whether Mrs Persimmon was aware of the possibility of her husband's having decamped with another woman. Was it scandal she feared? She clearly was the kind of person who rated neighbourhood opinion very highly. And yet he doubted if this was the only or even the main reason for her distress.

'Mrs Persimmon, you must forgive my asking this, but are you perhaps just a little afraid of your husband?'

A reflex frown of annoyance faded quickly. The tall, thin, angular, expensively-dressed woman seemed suddenly to suffer a kind of interior unstarching. Very softly, she said: 'He's not always the easiest man in the world to get along with.'

'Is this the first time he's stayed away from home for more than the one night?'

'No, it's happened two or three times before. But always over a week-end. He didn't lose any time at the shop.'

'And did he tell you where he'd been?'

'No.'

'Didn't you ask him?'

'Not directly. He doesn't like being what he calls quizzed.'

'But did you find out? From somebody else, perhaps?'

She shook her head. 'I think it was in Brocklestone he stayed during one of the week-ends. A friend of mine mentioned afterwards that she'd seen him there. But *he* never said, and I didn't ask.'

Purbright considered whether he should take further advantage of Mrs Persimmon's meekness of mood by sounding out what knowledge or suspicions she might have concerning Edna Hillyard. He decided against. He asked instead if she could give the name of anyone else associated with her husband's 'samaritan' activities – just in case, he said, it proved necessary to widen inquiries into his whereabouts and movements on the night of his disappearance.

Mr Persimmon, she replied, had spoken from time to time of three colleagues in that particular branch of his social work. They were Sir Henry Bird, mentioned already, and also Dr Cropper, the Borough Medical Officer, and the Vicar, Mr Grewyear.

The inspector said he was sure that three such distinguished gentlemen would be not only reliable but discreet informants should the need for their co-operation arise. For the time being, though, he counselled patience and faith in the likelihood of Mr Persimmon's having taken himself off somewhere simply to think out the perplexities of life. It did happen with people of his age, and, as Mrs Persimmon had herself acknowledged, her husband seemingly was not a man to share his problems.

Not the problem of Miss Hillyard, anyway, Purbright added in a personal aside to himself as he smiled encouragingly at Mrs

Persimmon and rose to take his leave. At the door, he put his final question.

'Is your husband interested in folk singing or anything in that line?'

Mrs Persimmon's immediate 'Not that I know of – why?' was distinctly derogatory in tone.

'Oh, no reason,' said Purbright. 'I just wondered.'

Sergeant Love was combining with business the pleasure that any healthy, youngish, innocently good-looking policeman is almost bound to feel in the company of totties, Flaxborough's generic term for all presentable and responsive females. Totties were predominant among the employees in the Town Hall and in no department could there be a more pleasing selection, Love decided, than in the offices of Dr Halcyon Cropper, Medical Officer of Health.

The doctor was absent at a conference in Ipswich, but the chief clerk – whose function seemed to be mainly that of a sort of girl-herd – told the sergeant that he was welcome to interview whom he pleased. Love looked round the room with as nearly blank an expression as he could manage in face of such largesse and said he would 'try that one'.

The clerk beckoned his choice, a girl called Sylvia Lintz, who had straight, short, straw-coloured hair, long but plump legs, and what Love's mother would have called a fine, strong chest.

'The sergeant,' the clerk said to her, 'wishes to ask some questions. About Miss Hillyard.'

Sylvia glanced quickly at Love, alarmed.

'Oh, no, nothing, er – well, not as far as we know,' the clerk soothed without conviction. His eye covertly ranged the other girls in the room. What's he worried about, Love wondered.

'Perhaps,' the clerk said to Sylvia, 'you'd better take him into the stock room.' He rubbed his chin dubiously. 'Unless you can think of anywhere better.'

The stock room was about eight feet square, windowless and lined on three sides with shelves loaded with packets of forms, stationery, and other kinds of office equipment. It contained a small table and chair. Love fetched another chair. He left the door wide open. They sat, Love stiffly, the girl demurely, the table between them.

'You do know Miss Hillyard's missing, don't you?' said Love.

'Well, I know she hasn't been to work. Not since Wednesday.'

'Has there been any talk about her being away?'

'Not really. Not at first, anyway. She often has a day off.'

'More often than other people?'

'I don't know that I'd say that.'

'Has she ever told you why she had these days off?'

'I haven't asked.' The reply was made with slight hesitation.

Love tried to look extra kind. The effort somehow resembled a wind-repressing discipline.

'What you say won't get her into trouble, you know,' he said. 'We just want to be given some idea of where she might have got to.'

The girl was silent a moment. She traced a spiral pattern with a finger tip on the table top. 'I think Edna's a bit ... well, you know...'

'Promiscuous?' dared the sergeant, feeling the unfamiliar word bring something of the satisfaction of boldly squeezing Miss Lintz's thigh.

She considered the question without sign of embarrassment then said simply, 'Of course, she's a lot older than most of us.'

'Yes, I can see that.'

The girl smiled. Ooo, but you're scrumptious, the sergeant silently told her. Aloud, he asked if Miss Hillyard had ever confided to her the names of such admirers as had seduced her from service in the public health sector.

'Not to me, she didn't. She was thicker with Mavis and Vi than anybody else. *They* might tell you. Shall I see if Mr House can spare them?'

'Mr House?'

'He's the gentleman you've seen already. The head clerk.'

'If you wouldn't mind.'

'No trouble,' said Miss Lintz sweetly. She got up.

Love rose as well, partly out of politeness but mainly because he felt that otherwise the girl might be left with the regrettable impression that decrepitude rather than authority dictated his remaining seated.

There were times when the sergeant wondered whether his long and loyal courtship of the person still optimistically described by his mother as 'your young lady' had not been attenuated by mutual passivity; a probationary period of fourteen years did seem adequate to forestall any charge of foolhardiness.

As he watched the departure of Miss Lintz's splendidly untrammelled legs and lively bottom, oscillating within its brief tourniquet of skirt, he recalled with a sense almost of awe that this nineteen-year-old daughter of the one-time editor of the *Flaxborough Citizen* was a child of six when he, Love, had worked on his first murder case, the slaying of old Marcus Gwill in Heston Lane. He would buy his Agnes a dinky nylon nightie that very afternoon. If he could get away, of course. And if the store wasn't too crowded, as it well might be on a Saturday . . .

Mavis O'Conlon and Violet Beach arrived together.

Violet was tall, with thin arms and shoulders but paradoxically heavy legs. She looked as if she would be difficult to knock over. Her cool, pale-lashed eyes were steady but mistrustful. She had a habit of caressing her left shoulder with her right hand, the forearm resting protectively across her small bosom. Love thought her pretty in a rather delicate way which he attributed vaguely to her having been sired by the manager of the Field Street branch of the Provinces and Maritime Bank, a notably pussy-footed gentleman.

Miss O'Conlon presented a contrast as startling in its way as the disparity between the profession of her companion's father and that of Mr O'Conlon, bookmaker. Mavis had a mouth wide enough to be kissed with moderate satisfaction by two men at a time, and, if Love was any judge, which at that moment he thought he was, hers was the disposition to let them. Generosity was implicit in brown, questing but not calculating eyes, a slightly side-tilted head and a throat, plump and uncreased by habitual affectation of modesty, that channelled regard at once to its confluence with breasts of astonishing amplitude. There, after some seconds, the sergeant discerned a little gold cross, suspended upon a fine chain.

'Got it for my first communion,' confided Miss O'Conlon in a deliciously husky voice, tinged with brogue.

Love gave a start and turned a brighter than usual pink. He went in search of an extra chair.

'Did the other young lady,' he asked when the two new arrivals were settled, 'tell you what I wanted you for?'

They looked at each other doubtfully, then back at the sergeant.

'Well, it's about Edna, isn't it?' said Mavis O'Conlon.

'Miss Hillyard,' her companion amplified.

'That's right.' Love tried to keep his gaze away from the environment of Mavis's crucifix (her 'Christ of the Andes', as Dr Cropper once had dubbed it). 'You're both friends of hers, I understand.'

'Sort of.' Violet did not sound eager to commit herself.

'Oh, but sure we're friends,' said Mavis quickly and with emphasis, taking no notice of Violet's nervous side glance.

Love went straight to the point. 'Does either of you know where she is? Today, I mean. Right now at this moment.'

'No idea,' said Violet. Mavis, suddenly solemn, shook her head.

'This really could be important. I don't want you to cover up for her because of her job. You're not doing that, are you?'

This time it was Violet who shook her head. Mavis said Jesus no, she'd not dream of doing any such thing but what did the pollis think had happened to the poor woman for God's sake?

Love hastily assured her that there was no reason so far to suspect that Miss Hillyard had come to harm. The fact remained that no one seemed to know where she was, so it was only right and sensible to make a few inquiries.

Yes, the girls agreed. So it was.

'That little car of hers, now. Does she normally use it a good deal?'

Every day, they said. Edna was very fond of driving around in her car.

'So you wouldn't expect her to go off anywhere without it?'

They certainly wouldn't. Not unless something had gone wrong with the works, of course.

'Laundry,' said Love. 'Does either of you know what she does about laundry? Dresses, undies – that sort of thing.'

Mavis gave a good-natured shrug in acknowledgment of the sergeant's innocence. 'Washes them, darlin' – what else?' She was, Love noticed again as she made herself more comfortable in the chair, a well-nourished girl and she undulated very pleasingly within her own undies and that sort of thing.

'Washes them herself, you mean? At home?'

'That's right,' said Violet. 'She always does her ironing on Tuesday night. That I do know.'

'So you wouldn't expect her to take a pile of clothes to a laundry in the town.'

'I've certainly never known her to do that. Have you, Mavis?'

'Not on *our* sort of money,' said Mavis.

Violet glanced at her with prim reproof. 'It's not a question of *affording*. One likes the fabric to be treated properly.'

'Has Miss Hillyard a lot of friends?'

Violet turned in consultation to Mavis. 'Would you say that she's a lot of friends? In numbers, perhaps. But not that many really staunch friends. Would you say she has many staunch friends?'

'She gets sniffed around after plenty.' Miss O'Conlon sounded amiably matter-of-fact.

'That's not a nice thing to say,' exclaimed Miss Beach. 'Not a bit nice.'

'It's true. And it's truth the pollis'll be wanting, surely?'

Love confirmed this supposition. 'You mean she has men friends – several men friends?'

'Jesus, she's every right to have made a bit of a collection at her age. I mean, you get the liking. Y'know? You'd not be blaming her?'

'Not in the least,' declared Toleration Love. He pondered a moment. 'It would help, though, if you could tell me if she has any particular preferences at the moment.'

'Particular's not the word I'd have used meself, but maybe it's special you mean. In the sense of extra keen, like. Hungry. Y'know? Now wait a bit. Do *you* know, Vi?'

73

Miss Beach, whose face clearly indicated that she found all such speculation offensive, gave a tight little headshake.

'Hey, that fellow from the garage – whatsisname – Blossom. Has she finished with that one?'

Miss Beach remained silent.

Miss O'Conlon snapped her fingers – an accomplishment that Love found endearingly raffish in so feminine a witness.

'Len Palgrove ... Now she was having it with that one. That I do know. *Defi*nitely.'

'Don't be horrible, Mavis. I don't know how you could say that about Mr Palgrove so soon after his bereavement.'

'Bereaved, was it?' Miss O'Conlon's eyes enlarged mightily for the benefit of the sergeant. 'Listen, he wasn't so eaten up with grief that he couldn't lay twenty quid in cross doubles with my old man on the morning of the funeral. Da nearly refused it out of respect for the dead but he knew the bets wouldn't have a snowflake in hell chance. Anyway ...'

'The point is,' Love broke in, 'that we'd like to know where Miss Hillyard is likely to be *now*. It's at least two years since Mrs Palgrove was ... since she died. Are you saying for certain that the friendship between Mr Palgrove and Miss Hillyard is something that's going on at the moment?'

'You know very well it isn't,' Miss Beach said reprovingly to Miss O'Conlon, who pursed her lips, reflected a little while, and then admitted that perhaps her information was out of date, but not by many weeks.

Further questions were put by Love, simply because the longer the interview went on, the longer he would be able to gaze with official justification at two good-looking girls. Their answers gave no lead at all to the person in whose company Edna Hillyard had been content – or obliged – to abandon her job, her lodgings and her car.

Neither girl could say that she had actually seen Edna with a man during her spare time since before Christmas. She had made oblique references to a 'friend', certainly, but he had not been produced and she had not mentioned anyone specifically by name.

Love thanked his informants and followed them back into the

main office in order to tell the head clerk that he would not require the co-operation of any more members of staff that morning.

Mr House cast an eye quickly over Miss Beach and Miss O'Conlon, as if to satisfy himself that no parts of them had been damaged or abstracted as souvenirs, and said that it was just as well because the department closed at noon on Saturdays and it was then 11.53.

Purbright seemed to find Love's account of his interviews less disappointing than the sergeant thought it sounded.

'At least we know two things now that we didn't know before. One is that although Edna Hillyard is over thirty and unmarried she's considered by people who know her fairly intimately to be far from frigid. The other is that she's taken some trouble – uncharacteristically – to keep her current affair secret.'

That, Love said, had been his impression.

'And why should she do that?'

'Reputation, I suppose.'

'Yes, but whose? What you were told by Miss O'Conlon doesn't suggest much reticence on Edna's part in the past.'

'She'd have had her work cut out to be reticent about Pally Palgrove. They reckon he leaves footprints on his girl friends.'

'And Alf Blossom?'

'He runs the South Circuit Garage.'

'Yes, I know that,' said Purbright, a little tetchily. 'I mean he's no great conquest, is he? Not socially. I'm leading up to something. You'll see in a minute.'

Love resolved to make no more irrelevant observations. 'Studwise,' he said with dignity, 'Alf Blossom isn't even in the book.'

The inspector nodded. 'So we can assume that Edna's present consort is someone she values more than she would value Palgrove, say, or Blossom, or any of those she told her office friends about. The probability is that he is married – which would explain their care not to be seen together – also respectable, and reasonably well-heeled. I'd put his age at a bit above fifty.'

'Job?'

'Profession,' Purbright corrected. He pretended to consider. 'Store manager, I should say. A fairly big store.'

Love, suspecting a leg pull, looked cheerily sceptical. 'You wouldn't know his address, I suppose?'

'My guess would be somewhere in Debtors' Retreat or up by Jubilee Park. How likely does The Riding strike you?'

Love frowned and remained silent. Then, suddenly, 'Oh, Christ! Of course...'

'Mr Persimmon, of the Bridge Street supermarket.'

'You really think they've skipped off together?'

'Their simultaneous disappearance does rather suggest it.'

'It could be coincidence.' Love's slowness to catch the inspector's drift of thought had left him feeling less than generous.

'In London or New York, perhaps,' said Purbright. 'But there's not much random duplication in a town of fifteen thousand inhabitants.'

'What about her car, though?' Love protested.

'Well, they don't need two. It isn't usual to elope in a convoy.'

'Then there's her job. His, too, for that matter.'

'I gather his head office is giving the books a good looking over.'

Again the sergeant was visited with a sense of having missed a significant possibility. 'Oh,' he said, gloomily.

Purbright relented. 'Of course, there's no evidence at the moment of anything crooked having gone on. We'll have to wait for the audit.'

'Perhaps,' said Love, 'it was just a case of irresistible passion.'

'You could be right, Sid. How nice it would be if you were.'

Chapter Seven

ON THE EVENING OF SATURDAY, 3 MAY, THERE WAS HELD an emergency meeting of the Flaxborough Branch of the Sabbath Conservation Society at the elegant home in Mather Gardens of Mrs H. L. Framlington, JP. There was a good attendance, despite the brevity of notice that circumstances had dictated, and the tastefully decorated drawing-room contained not one empty chair.

Mrs Framlington presided. She sat behind a dark mahogany

table on whose polished surface lay a thick, black-bound book, a black candle in a squat holder of polished brass designed like a bishop's mitre, a small enamelled incense bowl on a trivet, and a tumbler of water.

By her side was the secretary, Mrs Pentatuke. Her alert, slightly bronzed face wore a grim half-smile as she peered through her harlequin-framed glasses round the room and ticked names on a list she had taken from between the leaves of the book. Pausing in this task, she leaned forward to light an ochre-coloured cigarette at the candle flame. The smoke she blew forth aggressively over the hat feathers of the nearest members smelled of sulphur.

Mrs Pentatuke was fully dressed. She wore an outfit in bottle-green woollen fabric. On the floor by her sturdy, nylon encased calves lay a large handbag, a stumpy, furled umbrella and a pair of gloves of the same shade of violet as her shoes.

When she had finished putting ticks on her list, Mrs Pentatuke nudged Mrs Framlington, who had been contemplating dreamily the cornices of her elegant drawing-room, and indicated with a nod the incense bowl.

Mrs Framlington smiled vaguely, patted her grey, wispy, untidy hair, and accepted the box of matches that Mrs Pentatuke handed to her. She managed with the third match to ignite the tip of the small heap of material in the bowl. There rose a grey fume, thin at first but then broadening and becoming laden with sooty motes. There was a smell of singed poultry. Mrs Framlington glanced apprehensively at her ivory-faced wallpaper.

'Amen, evil from us deliver but temptation into not ...' Mrs Pentatuke's ringing tones brought to a sudden end the murmur of witchly small-talk. The Coven was in session.

Mrs Framlington half rose from her chair and bobbed a welcome to the assembly. Then she sat again, leaning slightly forward and resting a hand against the right side of her neck in readiness for its being cupped as a hearing aid.

'Ladies ... ah, sisters, sisters and warlocks.... It's most gratifying to see such a good turn-out this evening. This, of course, is not the regular meeting, as you all know. Our next little get-together was not due until the end of this month, but we did feel – that is, the ladies, the sisters, rather – the sisters and Warlock Gooding of the Sabbath sub-committee, did feel that in the circumstances . . .'

'Point of order, madam chairman!'

The interruption came from the bald-headed man who had taken part in the Walpurgis-night Revel in rolled-down stockings and motoring pennons. His costume now was considerably more formal but there was still noticeable in his eye a certain wildness that contrasted with a countenance which one might have thought expressly designed to hover over hymn-books.

'Yes, Warlock Parkin?' Mrs Framlington's hand rose behind her ear.

'Shouldn't Maiden Pentatuke have read the minutes first?'

Maiden Pentatuke did not wait for Mrs Framlington to consult her.

'Certainly not,' she called. 'This is an emergency meeting and there hasn't been time for minutes to be copied into the book. They'll be read next time.'

'Emergency meeting,' Mrs Framlington echoed, nodding her head very decisively at Mr Paracelsus Parkin. 'No time to be copied.' She was a little afraid of Mr Parkin, brother of evil-eyed Amy. He was a former Baptist lay preacher who had been drummed out of the Church on account of his too liberal interpretation of the word 'lay'. He was reputedly addicted to muscle culture and stamp collecting, and more than one member of the Coven suspected that his adherence to wizardry was less for love of the black art for its own sake than in the selfish hope that he might become sufficiently skilled in its practice to wreak personal vengeance upon his late accusers, in particular the Rev. William Harness and Miss Bertha Pollock of the Flaxborough Borough Welfare Department.

'I was saying,' resumed Mrs Framlington, 'that the Sabbath Sub-committee thinks that certain events of the last few days could be of great importance to . . . to our little gathering, and that they ought to be discussed.'

She looked inquiringly at Mrs Pentatuke, who thereupon barked 'Without delay'.

'Without delay,' said Mrs Framlington. She assumed a straighter posture and took a few sips of water.

'Unfortunately, as some of you may be aware, I was prevented by sickness from attending the Sabbath in person at Roodmas, so I hope that you, Madam Maiden' – she turned to Mrs Pentatuke – 'will correct me if I betray ignorance on any particular point.'

Mrs Pentatuke drummed her long fingers on the black minutes book and stared stonily out of the window.

'Of course,' Mrs Framlington went on with a fond, reflective smile, 'I was really amongst you all in a sense that night.' She looked up. 'Through my Familiar, you know. Did any of you see my little Billy Boy – no, Belial – my little Belial flying about? I did let him out of his cage, you know, and he flew around for quite a while looking for the keyhole in the bedroom door, bless him, and when I woke in the morning there he was, back on his perch again, and I knew – I *knew* – well, because I'd dreamed, you see, and anyway he was chattering away thirteen to the dozen – "Looo-cifer, Looo-cifer, Bicky for Billy, Looo-cifer..."'

'Point of order, Sister chairman!'

A plump hand was held aloft by a man with a neatly trimmed beard. His conventional shopkeeper's suit of dark serge hid and constrained the pale belly that had bounced and flopped above a velvet loincloth three nights before.

He was Henry Pearce: draper, toxophilite and husband of Mrs Tossie Pearce, whose choice of widow's weeds as her orgy costume had been prompted solely by sensual eccentricity and in no degree by wishful thinking. Indeed, Henry himself had provided the outfit from his discovery in a corner of the stock-room of a cache of apparel hidden away by some long dead, thrifty predecessor in the corsetry trade.

Mrs Framlington did not at once see the raised hand. She peered nervously round the room. Mrs Pentatuke leaned across and tapped her shoulder, then pointed out the interrupter.

'Just half a minute, Sister chairman,' said Warlock Pearce, in the tone of a long-suffering shop steward. 'With all due respect, I think I can say that we did not come here today to hear about the doings of your little Belial.'

He paused and smiled thinly at a mutter of approval that came from some half-dozen members of the Coven.

'I think I can fairly say that. I mean to say, the Familiars do get a fair crack of the whip. There's the annual tricks competition for one thing. But I don't think I need go on about that. Time and place for everything. What we *do* want to know, and what my good friend Warlock George Gooding and the sub-committee want to know, is this...'

Mrs Framlington, goaded by digs from Mrs Pentatuke into asserting her authority, quaveringly demanded: 'Isn't that rather a lengthy point of order, Warlock Pearce?'

'Never you mind about length, Sister chairman,' retorted Mr Pearce. 'I've got the floor and I'm going to put my question. It's about the police...'

'Black blisters and the scalding weeps be on 'em!' shouted a stout, red-faced woman from her seat at the back of the room. She was Mrs Margaret Gooding, the Sabbath participant who had worn woollen drawers and claimed to be a drinker of baboon blood.

'... the police, I said,' repeated Warlock Pearce, 'and if Sister Gooding wants to move a curse as an amendment, that's up to her, but what I'm asking is in regard to a point of order, Sister chairman, which is, and I put it to you fair and square – Who called them in when Sister Hillyard took off, as is her right as a witch, I don't think anyone will quarrel with that.'

Mrs Framlington looked perplexed. Not sharing with Mr Pearce the privilege of membership of Pennick Rural District Council, she was unaccustomed to the somewhat dislocated language in which the affairs of that and similar authorities habitually are conducted. She turned to make mute appeal of Mrs Pentatuke.

'All Warlock Pearce means,' ruled Mrs Pentatuke brusquely, 'is that you should get straight to the point about police inquiries into whatever's happened to Edna Hillyard. He suggests, if I understand him aright, that there was a tip-off of some kind.'

'Who says that *anything* has happened to Sister Edna?' called out Warlock Parkin.

One or two others made noises of support.

'The police want to take their long noses out of what doesn't concern them or they might find the same thing happening to those said noses as I had the pleasure of seeing happen last Lammas to the nose of a certain party in the Post Office who steamed open a certain letter.'

The reference seemed a familiar one – at least to Mrs Pentatuke, who raised her eyes and sighed 'Lucifer all-bloody-mighty! Not again!'

Mrs Framlington tapped the table with a pencil.

'If we can just have a little order, I will ask our Sister who has actually been *visited* by the police to tell you what she thinks it is all about.'

Mrs Gloss stood up and gave a brief account of her questioning by Detective-Constables Palethorp, Brevitt and Pook. She said it was her opinion that the interrogation had been of an unnecessarily importunate kind. Why, one might ask, had no fewer than three policemen been sent to her house? None had offered any good reason to suppose that Sister Edna had come to harm. She believed her so-called disappearance was being used as an excuse for police persecution. Small wonder that ratepayers resented having to find huge sums of money for the maintenance of law and order. Was this what they were to understand by law and order? She for one could think of other names for it.

Immediate warm applause was punctuated by cries of 'Witch-hunt!'

Mrs Gloss, who appeared no less surprised by her own oratory than gratified by her audience's reception of it, sat down in a glow and pretended to have lost her gloves among the cushions of her armchair.

'That,' said Henry Pearce as soon as he could make himself heard, 'is all very well, but the question with me, Sister chairman, and with respect, is this. There wouldn't be hordes of these policemen pushing into all our homes now if somebody hadn't carried information. I think that the . . .'

Among several conflicting shouts of protest was one from Miss Amy Parkin.

'They found her car, didn't they? And her clothes. It was only to be expected that they'd go round asking questions. I very much resent the insinuation of ... of subversion that's been made by Probationary Warlock Pearce.'

There were calls of 'Hear, hear!' and 'Withdraw!'

The object of the derogatory reference to rank, purple with fury, began to recite a curse, but his wife pulled him to his seat.

Mrs Framlington, finding appeals by pencil-tapping ineffective, opened a small metal box that stood beside the incense bowl and tried to tip a little of the greenish powder it contained upon the almost dead embers. In her agitation she cascaded a good ounce of powder into the bowl.

The resultant upsurge of thick, greasy smoke would have done credit to a burning tyre dump.

'Suppurating Satan!' muttered tall, scraggy Warlock Gooding as he shambled past the chairman's table to fling open the french windows. None was so ungrateful as to rebuke him for blasphemy.

The debate was adjourned so that members might take advantage of Mrs Framlington's invitation to stroll in the garden for a few minutes 'in order', as she phrased it, 'to renew our store of Life Force from the great Pan'.

It was remarks of this kind which had done much to render invidious Mrs Framlington's position as Coven chairman. The less tolerant members called her an old folksie, a white witch, and other uncomplimentary names. She was not what Thornton-Edwards, Arnold and Konstatin would have termed 'orgy-orientated' and although she never voiced criticism of those channels in which self-expression tended to flow at the quarterly Sabbath, her early retirement from the ceremony or, on occasion, failure to attend at all, left no one in doubt of her lukewarm attitude.

The truth was that Bertha Framlington had drifted into witchcraft for no better reason than that it lay in much the same latitude as other and earlier interests of hers. This lofty, raw-boned, untidy-looking woman, with her round, steel-rimmed glasses; thick stockings, always rumpled; woollen garments that gave the impression of having been tossed upon her as upon a chair-back, by their true owners; her expression of troubled but kindly anticipation as she listened to others, which she did with mouth a little open, for she was inclined to deafness; this woman who walked with long, uncertain strides as if bolts had worked loose in her leg joints, was the widow of the one-time proprietor of a small wines and spirits business which now had been merged into the Bride Street supermarket. She was a vegetarian whenever she remembered to be. She had once stood for the Borough Council as an anti-fluoride candidate and polled fifty-eight votes. A dedicated reversionist, she considered Arthur to have been the last British monarch worthy of the crown. She would have re-instituted the maypole and the setting out of bowls of cream for goblins – despite lack of response to a saucer of Carnation Milk she three times thrice had left on the elegant porch of 3 Mather Gardens. Witchcraft, to Mrs Framlington, was a Robin Goodfellow affair, a branch of home arts and crafts. She found it more sociable than Primitive Methodism, her late husband's hobby; less bloodthirsty than whist drives; and not so damp as Spiritualism, which she had tried also, but briefly.

On its re-assembly, the Coven was served with refreshments. There were cups of tea brewed with what Sister Pearce, who had brought it, asserted to be font water. The tea certainly tasted odd ('like mildewed vestments', Warlock Parkin appreciatively pronounced it, to the benefit of his reputation as a cognoscente) and Mrs Framlington swallowed only enough to carry down one of the biscuits contributed by Sister Gooding. These were grey and gritty with pink flecks and were handed round by their creator with the gloomy but insistent generosity of a distributor of the means of fulfilling a suicide pact. Sister Gooding had never divulged the recipe for her confection, which Mrs Gloss flippantly called her Crypt Crumble, and the curious had to make what they could of her husband's enigmatic 'She's got a cousin who works at the hospital, you know.'

The discussion was resumed. Sister Henrietta Hall, the wife of the manager of a car-hire firm in St Anne's Place, said that her husband had spoken of newspapermen arriving in the town from London. They had been asking questions about the Craft, and there was talk of photographs.

'Photographs? What photographs?' Warlock Parkin had swung round in some alarm.

'In the church, he says.'

'Photographs of what?' asked Amy Parkin.

'Things,' darkly replied Sister Hall, at the end of her seam of information.

'That's quite true, actually,' confirmed Sister Gloss. 'One of my cleaning women has a son in the police, and she came in this morning with a tale about the vicar having been found hanged in his own pulpit...'

'No!' exclaimed Warlock Parkin, eyes a-glitter.

'... not that he had, of course. It was an effigy of old Grewyear and he called the police in to see it. That and a couple of other little arrangements, as a matter of fact.'

Mrs Framlington peeked anxiously at Maiden Pentatuke. 'That was never authorized, was it? Doing Mr Grewyear!'

The black minutes book was consulted. 'Not in this month's programme, certainly,' said Mrs Pentatuke. 'Could Sister Gertrude be more specific about the other things the police are supposed to have been shown?'

'"A mouse that was hanged and a toad impaled."'

Significant glances were exchanged around the room. Mrs Gloss had spoken quietly but with a rhythmic intonation that she had not used in speaking of the effigy.

Silence was broken by Tossie Pearce.

'"With this spell be your coffin nailed",' she recited reflectively.

Some of the others nodded. The mouse and toad combination seemed to be an old favourite.

Mrs Framlington, though, looked anxious. 'Those little creatures hadn't suffered, had they?' she inquired of Sister Gloss.

'Well, how would I know? *I* didn't put them there.'

'Has anyone seen the vicar today?' Mrs Framlington asked, with rather less concern.

'He looked all right at four o'clock, wolfing cakes in Brown and Derehams.' This information came from Sister Parkin.

'Ah,' observed the more sanguine Mrs Pearce, 'but we mustn't forget that cramps don't usually come on until the third day and it's not before the seventh that they vomit nails.' She turned to Mrs Gloss. 'Did you say one toad or two?'

'According to my cleaning wo...'

The slamming of the minutes book on the table signalled Mrs Pentatuke's wrathful rise to her feet.

She glanced down contemptuously at Mrs Framlington, then addressed the meeting.

'This is all absolutely out of order. I do not think that anybody fully realizes the seriousness of what has been going on. The secrets of our society are threatened. One of our sisterhood has been taken and none knows where. Meddlers and inquisitors will use her vanishing as an excuse to harass us and seek the source of our power and chain our spirits. Thus I tell. Thus I warn. We are all in great peril. There is but one course to take, and that without delay.'

Slowly and with every muscle and tendon from wrists to shoulders tensed, Mrs Pentatuke raised her arms until both long, outstretched forefingers pointed horizontally ahead.

'We must raise the Grand Master!'

For nearly a minute, they all stared in shocked silence at the statuesque figure.

Then an almost incoherent whisper came from Mrs Framlington. 'Yes, but...'

She cleared her throat very delicately, and tried again.

'But we don't ... we don't know who he is.'

Silence descended again.

So, gradually, did Mrs Pentatuke's arms.

'He is the Grand Master,' she stated hollowly, as if from sleep. 'If we call, He will come.'

'Do you really think we ought to?' asked Mrs Hall, looking round at her neighbours.

None offered an opinion.

Then a smooth-faced, chinless man with thin hair and protuberant eyes, who had said nothing up to then, shuffled to the edge of his chair and spoke. He was Jack Bottomley, landlord of the

Freemasons' Arms, and leading singer in perpetuity of the Flax-borough Amateur Operatic Society.

'This lady who's missing,' rasped Mr Bottomley, in a voice whose original fruitiness had long since been dehydrated by perennial performance of *The Desert Song.* 'I wonder if I could make a suggestion.'

'By all means,' said Mrs Framlington, eager for an excuse to put off the mess and trouble of a conjuration.

'Well, it might not work, of course, but I was reading just the other day in "B and C" that if you can get hold of some hair of anybody you want to find and burn it in front of a mirror, that person will appear. I thought I'd better, you know, sort of mention it.'

Mr Bottomley cast down his glance. Off-stage and away from his pub counter, he was a shy and nervous man; necromancy was for him a refuge from fears of inadequacy – or so Mrs Gloss had said more than once.

'What edition?' Mrs Pentatuke snappily inquired. She had left the table and was standing before a tall, glass-fronted bookcase.

'Well, er, that one, actually.'

'Seventeen forty-three.' Mrs Pentatuke spoke with a brusque-ness that reproached Mr Bottomley's lack of precision. She opened the case and pulled out a book whose leather binding looked dry and powdery, as if it had been stored in cocoa. It was one of the most frequently consulted volumes in the Coven lib-rary, and known simply as "B and C" in abbreviation of its full title: *With Broom and Cauldron, Being The True Confessions of Goody Nixon.*

Mrs Pentatuke licked a finger and sought first a place in the index and then a specified page. They watched the alert, oscillating eye behind the spectacle lens quickly devour print. She slammed the book shut.

'Exactly as I thought. It's one of the virgin things. Out.'

She squeezed Goody Nixon back between *A Chronicle of De-monology in the Eastern Counties, 1587–1694,* by Albert and Theresa Horne and Patrick's *Dictionary of Herbs and Tinctures.*

'How do you mean?' asked Amy Parkin. She sounded not very

friendly.

'I mean,' said Mrs Pentatuke, walking back to her seat, 'that it only works with virgins. Anyway, we'd have to find the woman first to cut some of her bloody hair off, wouldn't we?'

With the ill-advised persistence of a self-doubter, Mr Bottomley coughed and said: 'But I don't quite see how our lady secretary can be so sure that this won't work, madam chairman. I mean, Miss Hillyard isn't married, is she?'

Before Mrs Pentatuke could raise steam for a fitting retort, Mrs Framlington said kindly: 'No, of course not, Mr Bottomley; but that is rather a good point about our not having any of her hair for the experiment. Don't you think?'

Mr Bottomley shrugged and lapsed into despondency.

An impatient tapping was heard. It was being made by Mrs Pentatuke's shoe against the leg of the table.

'We're wasting time, you know,' she said, without looking at anyone in particular. 'The sooner we have the protection of the Master's power, the sooner we can be sure that our terrestial existence will not be harassed by policemen and newspaper spies. I have warned once, I have warned twice. Split the mandrake with grattle and grice!'

'Stew their balls in badger bile,' yelled Mrs Gooding, with alliterative fervour.

Mrs Pentatuke turned up her eyes.

'O Master, come soon among us!'

Mrs Gooding nodded violently.

'He is like a ramrod of fire! Go-orrrh!'

She let out her breath with a noise like a winded horse and gave an ecstatic shuffle with her posteriors. Mr Gooding bestowed on her a sidelong glance of mild proprietary curiosity.

Amy Parkin and Mrs Pearce were having an argument about pentagrams, which the latter insisted on calling pentagons.

Mrs Gloss had discovered a hand casually laid upon her shoulder from behind. It was that of Paracelsus Parkin and, as Mr Parkin leaned forward to pay closer attention to something the chairman was murmuring, the hand slid through the neck of her dress. Mrs Gloss kept very still and dignified.

So, too, did Mrs Hall, who now regretted having spoken about the happenings in the church – partly because her sparsity of information had made her look ineffectual in relation to Mrs Gloss, proud claimant to not merely one cleaning woman but a plurality; and partly because she feared that the conjuring of the Master, so forcefully advocated by Sister Pentatuke, would almost certainly entail a general casting off of garments, which she, Mrs Hall, did not much fancy in broad daylight.

'Sisters and warlocks,' cried Mrs Framlington, aware at last that no one had been taking any notice of her for the past five minutes, 'I really must ask you to preserve a little order in this discussion...'

Mr Parkin's hand contracted playfully within Mrs Gloss's brassière. 'Honk, honk!' he whispered into her ear.

'... which, after all, is concerned with a most serious matter. It would be most unfortunate if our little group were to find itself involved in a police investigation – particularly at a time when, as you have heard, some representatives of the national Press are in the town. We do not want any misunderstandings, do we? They could, if publicized, do some of us great harm.'

Mrs Gloss, OBE, Chairman of the Standing Conference of Conservative Ladies, looked grave. So did Mrs Pearce, Honorary Secretary of the Flaxborough Society of Mead Makers; Mrs Hall, vice-president of the Ladies' Branch of the British Legion; and Mr Gooding, who for years had been trying to get into the Masons by sending gifts of his fretwork to members of the Royal Family.

'What I do think is regrettable,' continued Mrs Framlington, 'is this quite unauthorized piece of spell-casting in the parish church. Sister Pentatuke is right to warn us of the possible consequences of, er, tactlessness in the exercise of our arts...'

'That,' Mrs Pentatuke broke in, 'is not what I said. I warned and warned thrice of harm intended by spies and strangers. I have never sought to stay the hand of sister or brother in mal or moil, in dark or light.'

'I beg your pardon, Maiden Pentatuke.'

'Granted, Sister chairman.'

There was a long pause. Mrs Framlington looked expectantly at several members in turn. Mrs Gooding spoke.

'Couldn't Warlock Bottomley get all these newspaper people or whatever they are into his pub? It would be easy enough then for him to . . .' She began to laugh wheezily – 'to put a few drops of . . . of . . .'

This was as much of the suggestion that Mrs Gooding was able to offer before the palsy of her amusement rendered her altogether inarticulate.

'No, he jolly well couldn't,' declared the horrified licensee of the Freemasons' Arms.

'Let us be practical,' Mrs Framlington urged. She noticed that Henry Pearce had stood up and was looking at a piece of paper on which he had been writing a few notes. 'Yes, Warlock Pearce?'

'To test the feelings of the meeting,' Pearce said slowly, 'I am going to propose the following motion from the floor in regard to matters arising from what was said by madam secretary. That this assembly hereby authorizes the officers of the organization, known for security reasons as the Flaxborough Branch of the Sabbath Day Conservation Society, to conjure or otherwise obtain the presence – no, the attendance – the attendance for advice purposes of the Being we call for security reasons the President of the said Branch. And that we agree' – Mr Pearce glanced about him, then looked down at the paper again – 'to co-operate in any ceremony or other activity deemed necessary by the said officers in order to raise the said President.'

Mr Pearce folded the paper twice, put it into his pocket and sat down.

'I second that proposition,' called Mr Parkin, withdrawing and raising his right, warmer, hand.

'Me, too!' Mrs Gooding was fumbling with a button at the side of her skirt.

Mrs Framlington searched with hopeful eye for evidence of contrary counsel. She looked for a moment at the unenthusiastic face of Mrs Hall but it remained averted. No one else seemed to wish to say anything.

'Carried unanimously,' announced Mrs Pentatuke, before Mrs Framlington could call for a vote. 'I think,' she added, rising energetically to her feet, 'that the curtains had better be drawn just in case anyone wanders by.'

Mr Parkin hastened to respond.

From within the tent of her tortuously uprising inside-out skirt Mrs Gooding was making little growling noises of pleasurable anticipation.

Her husband moved to the other side of the room and began slowly to unknot his tie in front of a gilt-framed wall mirror in which he could watch the reflected disrobing of Mrs Gloss. It looked, he thought, very artistic in the greenish gloaming produced by the closing of the curtains.

'Potions, everybody!'

This rallying cry came from Mrs Tossie Pearce on her return from a brief excursion to the kitchen. She shut the door behind her with her foot. On the tray she carried were five big black bottles.

'Do you mind using your cups?' she inquired cheerily.

To Mrs Pentatuke, ecstatically unbuttoning her dress, the question seemed to be a reminder. She came out of her trance.

'Gosh, I must just ring home,' she said to Mrs Framlington, and hurried to the door. 'I left Lionel some liver in the oven. Mind if I use the phone?'

She disappeared before the owner of the house and telephone could reply. Mrs Framlington reflected that Mrs Pentatuke's forcefulness of character could be a little trying on occasion.

She looked about her. Everyone seemed preoccupied and rather excited. Tossie Pearce's home-made wine – this particular *crû*, she believed, was Sage and Blood Orange – had no rival in the county as an aphrodisiac. Would they take offence if she were to put newspapers over the furniture? Perhaps. Feeling apprehensive but quite impotent, she edged unobtrusively to the door, slipped through, and closed it behind her. She had decided to spend an hour weeding the herb garden.

On her way to the kitchen and the back door, she heard the voice of Mrs Pentatuke telephoning in the hall. She did not consciously listen to what Mrs Pentatuke was saying. Later, though, it was to occur to her that there had been something odd about the call – about the tone of voice which Mrs Pentatuke had used.

Why, Mrs Framlington was to ask herself, should a homely conversation about braised liver have sounded so threatening?

Chapter Eight

THE FOLLOWING MORNING, MRS FRAMLINGTON DROVE her sedate, seven-year-old motor-car into the Market Place and parked it with three wheels in the roadway and the fourth half-way across the pavement. This untidiness did not matter much, for it was Sunday and the streets were deserted except for an occasional blear-eyed wanderer in quest of cigarettes or milk or the *News of the World*. Mrs Framlington wanted none of these things. Nor did she join the thin straggle of citizens making their way to the south door of St Lawrence's in response to the great waves of bell-music that had been assaulting the town since before eight o'clock. She took the perimeter path round the Church Close and halted before the door of a tall, narrow, Georgian house that looked as if it would have one or, at the most, two rooms on each of its three floors.

Mrs Framlington remarked expansively to the woman who opened the door – a woman slightly younger, perhaps, than herself but of gracious manner and a pleasing mildness of countenance – that she had never heard the parish bells in better voice.

'What a lovely peal and how splendidly it seems to sing out right over one's head,' she exclaimed, clasping her hands and gazing up at the vast honey-coloured cliff of the tower.

The other woman smiled and shook her head. She took Mrs Framlington's arm and drew her inside the house, then closed the door.

'Now, dear,' she said sweetly, 'what was it you said? I could not hear a word for those bloody bells.'

'I said,' replied Mrs Framlington after the smallest of pauses, 'that I would give anything for a nice cup of coffee.'

'You shall have one. Immediately.' And Miss Lucilla Edith Cavell Teatime waved her guest to ascend the twist of narrow, white-painted stairs.

Miss Teatime's sitting-room on the first floor had a much more spacious air than might have been deduced from looking at the outside of the house. It was light, with big areas of polished wooden floor, a few heavy rugs and a minimum of slender-legged furniture that seemed to stand about in attitudes of well-bred deference. The two armchairs, that now were facing the window and its view of the church and the laburnum trees by the west porch, were small but dumpily hospitable in their petticoats of flowered chintz. Mrs Framlington sat in one of them and began sorting out in her mind the reasons for her visit while Miss Teatime busied herself with the preparation of coffee in the tiny adjoining kitchen.

Just as the laden tray was arriving through the doorway, the pealing of the bells abruptly ceased.

'Thank God for that,' said Miss Teatime. She glanced at her guest. 'If you'll pardon the allusion.'

She put the tray down on a low table and settled herself into the other armchair.

There was a whisky bottle beside the coffee jug. Miss Teatime indicated it as she took up Mrs Framlington's cup.

'Hemlock?' she inquired waggishly.

Mrs Framlington shook her head. Her earlier ebullience seemed to have evaporated.

Miss Teatime poured straight coffee for her, then dispensed her own fifty-fifty formula.

It was several minutes before Mrs Framlington gave a little shudder, blinked away her dreamy expression and put down her cup.

'There are times,' she said carefully, 'when I find myself just the teeniest bit out of sympathy with ... you know.'

'Really?' Miss Teatime's tone implied nothing but a desire to help.

'Well, some of them do go *on* rather. I am a keen Pagan person myself, but I feel that one cannot be always flying in the face of so-called civilization. There must be give and take in all things, don't you think?'

'You are so right,' assented Miss Teatime solemnly. 'Although it does seem at times that the take tends to predominate somewhat grossly.'

'The trouble with our little group,' went on Mrs Framlington, 'is what begins to look like a division of attitudes. I had hoped that a common consciousness of the Universal Spirit – the Earth Force, as I like to call it – would unite us in purpose. But I'm afraid it hasn't. There is no use in denying that there are *factions*. And some of us fear that serious trouble will result.'

Miss Teatime thoughtfully uncapped the whisky bottle.

'I did warn you, my dear, did I not, that unwelcome attention would be attracted to your organization if some of the members persisted in their more malodorous practices.'

'Yes, but how can I stop them? They are very much under the influence of Mrs Pentatuke. As you know, she is a strong Brockenist. I remember on one occasion I had to advise some friends of mine privately against accepting her offer of help as a baby-sitter. It was most embarrassing, but one has to draw the line somewhere.'

'An intimidating woman.'

'Oh, yes. And terribly *carnal*. I think she must have something wrong with her glands.'

Miss Teatime poured more coffee.

'Am I to understand, then, that your being Coven chairman gives you no real authority over these more wayward spirits?'

'Oh, I do not delude myself in that respect, Lucy. I know why I have been favoured with the chairmanship. I happen to have a large, pleasant and secluded house where our meetings can conveniently be held. That I don't mind so long as there are no *rites*. Mrs Gloss is welcome to accommodate *them*. She has more domestic help to clear up the mess.'

'Forgive me, but I cannot quite free myself from the impression that witchcraft is not strictly your *thing*, as I believe they say nowadays. Cannot you send Mrs Pentatuke and her cronies packing if you see danger in continued association?'

Mrs Framlington stared into her cup.

'When one is a Justice of the Peace, a marriage guidance

counsellor and a member of the boards of governors of two schools,' she said quietly, 'one has to be careful with whom one associates – but a good deal more careful from whom one then *dis*sociates.'

There was a pause.

'Yes, I do see what you mean.' With a pair of embroidery scissors, Miss Teatime probed the end of a cheroot before lighting it. 'Yours is not the happiest of positions.'

'Oh, but you must not misunderstand me,' said Mrs Framlington more brightly. 'I would not for the world be anything other than a witch. "A witch am I in blood and bone, a steadfast daughter of the moon."'

'I take it, though,' remarked Miss Teatime, drily, 'that your enthusiasm would not extend to riding into the magistrates' court on your broomstick.'

'Well, precisely. Even witches must be discreet. I wish Pentatuke and Parkin and old Mrs Gooding could see that.'

'And Miss Edna Hillyard?' Miss Teatime regarded her guest as blandly as if she had just asked her the time.

'You know about that?'

'I certainly have heard that the girl is considered by the police to be a missing person. I know, of course, as well as you do, that she is a member of the Flaxborough Folklore Society, in the midst of one of whose little revels she is supposed to have disappeared.'

'That is quite true,' acknowledged Mrs Framlington. She sounded tired.

'Is there anything you think I can do?'

'I really don't know. In any case, I don't see why you should be plagued with our worries.'

'My dear Hetty, that is nonsense. I owe you and your band of helpers a great deal. We work professionally to considerable mutual advantage, as you know well.'

'The Coven doesn't know, though,' said Mrs Framlington, uncomfortably.

'It is better,' replied Miss Teatime, 'that we should remain unaware of our own virtues; otherwise, we might be tempted to set a price upon them.'

'What do you suppose you can do? It is the possible publicity that I dread, of course. That we all dread. All but' – Mrs Framlington smiled mirthlessly – 'the baby blood brigade.'

Miss Teatime watched an expelled stream of cheroot smoke decelerate and form a sun-creamed vortex above a bowl of wallflowers in the window recess.

'Has it occurred to you,' she asked, 'that publicity is exactly what some person or other seems determined to attract? I am thinking, in particular, of the not very savoury exhibition in the church over there.'

'Poor little things,' said Mrs Framlington absently. She gave a start. 'But how did you know about that? I only heard myself yesterday.'

'Have you not read a newspaper this morning?'

'The *Sunday Times*. But not all of it, of course.'

Miss Teatime put down her cup and rose to cross the room.

'An elevated taste in reading matter can be a disadvantage sometimes.'

She handed Mrs Framlington a copy of the *Sunday Pictorial* that had been folded back to display the headlines: 'PETS EXECUTED IN CHURCH OF BLACK MASS TOWN: ''END NUDE RITES'' DEMAND MUMS.'

'Good God!' exclaimed Mrs Framlington. She fumbled for glasses to read the smaller print.

A quarter of a mile away in the police headquarters in Fen Street, Inspector Purbright was sampling and comparing a number of newspaper stories, of which the account in the *Pictorial* was one. They were highly diversified in terms of reported fact, but a reader as attentive as the inspector could scarcely avoid the conclusion that all had originated in the one town of Flaxborough and purported to describe similar events.

Common to every report was the use of the words witchcraft, black magic, mass, sacrifice and cult. In three cases, nude and orgy had been incorporated as well. Satanism was offered by the *Dispatch*, while the *Express* daringly added necromancy ('say it neck-romancee').

Purbright decided that the piece in the *Empire News* promised to be, if not the most enlightening, at any rate the most imaginative and morally pop-eyed of that morning's contributions to what he once had heard aphoristically defined as the Anals of Journalism.

Flaxborough, Saturday.

These were the questions on everyone's lips today in this sleepy little market town...

Does the Devil ride out to claim dupes and victims amongst their neighbours?

Who, or what, offers sacrifices of animals in their ancient parish church at dead of night and in hideous parody of Christian ritual?

Are the flitting figures that have been glimpsed in near-by woodland those of members of a witch cult taking part in the bestialities of their 'Sabbath'?

And what has happened to pretty, fun-loving typist, Edna Hillyard, who has not been seen since she said goodnight to friends at a folk-dance festival on Wednesday?

Seeking answers to these question, I have discovered that facts even more disturbing – facts that might be connected with a Voo-doo type kidnapping – have been reported to the police.

The informants have not dared give their names.

For fear stalks this quiet country town, where apple-cheeked farmers – usually ready with a friendly word or a rural quip – now turn away at the sight of a stranger and touch the silver coins in their pockets to ward off evil.

One man not afraid to talk, however, is bluff river-boatman 'Yormer' Heath. Mr Heath it was whose gruesome discovery of a devil mask in the river set off police inquiries into the disappearance of attractive, vivacious folk-dancer Edna.

'Yormer' told me: 'We have been stalked by fear for some time in this quiet old town. I cannot rightly put a name to what troubles us, but it is evil, evil – like that unspeakable object which I hauled out of the water.'

I asked 'Yormer' Heath if he had heard any reports of the notorious Black Mass being celebrated in Flaxborough.

'Definitely,' he replied.

Did he personally know of any witches in the locality?

Certainly, he did, and so did many of his friends.

Yes, there had been sacrificial rites in the parish church and other places, and he would definitely describe those responsible as fiends in human form.

And the missing girl?

'Everybody in this town loved Edna Hillyard,' declared 'Yormer' Heath as he went into the dusk after answering my questions in the quaint old Three Crowns inn, 'and we shall not rest until we find her.'

Purbright, pleasantly intrigued thus far, was sorry to find that the story deteriorated in the next few paragraphs to a repetitious chronicle of assertions by 'a local shopkeeper', 'a clergyman', 'housewives shopping in the old Market Place' and other traditional fictions of the thwarted or bar-bound journalist. But then his interest quickened anew.

In charge of the hunt for Edna Hillyard is Detective-Superintendent R. Parbright, golden-haired seven-footer known by the criminal fraternity of this remote area of rural England as 'Apollo'.

Superintendent Parbright talked to me in the Operations Room of Flaxborough Police H.Q. He said he was unaware of the townspeople's reluctance to go out after dark because of black magic rites.

'I'm an agnostic,' the superintendent declared. He added that he did not know what was meant by the word 'permissive' and said he would like to take the opportunity to deny allegations that his men went round the town breaking up adulterous associations with their truncheons.

I asked him what progress had been made in the search for Edna Hillyard.

'We are still looking for the evidence that this thirty-four-year-old good-time girl has been used as a human sacrifice,' replied Superintendent Parbright.

As he spoke, I heard somewhere in the distance the screech of an owl.

In this town of fear, even the night-birds are edgy.

The chief constable made a diversion on his way home from church in order to call at the police station. He found Purbright sitting with Sergeant Love in the general office on the ground floor. They were drinking coffee. A small avalanche of newspapers covered a desk.

Mr Chubb slowly drew off his gloves. His expression was that of a surgeon at the end of an unsuccessful operation on a particularly rich patient.

'You know, Mr Purbright, I seriously doubted at the time your wisdom in entertaining those newspaper people.'

The gloves were deposited in Mr Chubb's bowler hat, which, with his walking stick, he placed carefully on the top of a filing cabinet. He motioned Purbright and Love to resume their seats.

'I didn't entertain them half as lavishly as they have entertained me, sir.' Purbright nodded towards the pile of newspapers. He wondered how far down the social scale was the journal that Mr Chubb would confess to having read.

'Do not let us play with words,' admonished the chief constable. 'What I mean is that all this inflammatory nonsense would never have got into print if you had refused to be interviewed. Whatever possessed you to bring up the subject of human sacrifices? My paper actually quoted you as saying something about my men going round the town with truncheons and stopping adultery. Really, Mr Purbright!'

The inspector looked shocked. 'But surely, sir. *The Observer* hasn't...'

Mr Chubb hastily made correction.

'No, I'm wrong. It was a paper the vicar showed me. But that doesn't make the matter less serious.'

Purbright debated the likelihood of the chief constable's appreciating an explanation of the tactics of the newspaper interview but decided against.

'I'm sorry about this, of course, sir, but I think you'll find that where information is refused altogether the press can be very vindictive – as one might argue it has a right to be.'

For a moment, Mr Chubb turned upon the inspector that gaze of sad and perplexed reproof with which he habitually reacted to outlandish opinion. Then he examined the buttons on the cuff of his coat.

'Mrs Chubb tells me,' he said, almost casually, 'that she was taking some of the boys for a walk yesterday' (the 'boys' were a swarm of Scotch terriers bred and fostered by the Chubbs) – 'when one of them was attacked by a beast belonging to a woman named Gooding . . .' He raised his eyes. 'Do you know of a Mrs Gooding?'

Purbright shook his head and glanced questioningly at Love, who said at once: 'Could be Mrs Margaret Gooding, sir. Beatrice Avenue. Husband, George. We've had complaints about him shooting arrows in the garden. I believe he writes to the Queen a lot.'

The inspector looked proudly at Mr Chubb, as if to solicit reward there and then for omniscient Love, but the chief constable merely nodded.

'That's her. The dog is black and very vicious. Mrs Chubb naturally remonstrated with the woman. Now here's the significant thing – at least, it could be significant. This Gooding person was rather offensive and she ended up by saying (now just let me get this right) yes, by saying: "You'll be getting a call from my Meffie later and he'll wind your bowels round and round the bed post." '

'Good lord,' said Purbright. He tried to look more surprised then he felt at this fairly ordinary example of dog owners' rhetoric. 'Who's Meffie, though – the husband? I thought he was called George.'

'She was referring,' the chief constable said very deliberately, 'to her dog.'

'Her *dog*?'

'Certainly. Mrs Chubb had no doubt whatever about that. The woman indicated the beast while she was talking. My Meffie, she called it. Several times.'

The inspector, at a loss to see the relevance of this incident to the earlier subject of Mr Chubb's complaint, waited for a hint.

'No smoke without fire, Mr Purbright.'

'I suppose not, sir.'

There was another silence.

'No, I didn't understand either,' conceded the chief constable at last. 'It was Mrs Chubb who opened my eyes, so to speak. The dog, you see – Meffie. Well, Meffie's not a dog's name. I mean, no one would call a decent self-respecting animal Meffie, would he?'

'Certainly not,' agreed Purbright, anxious not to protract what seemed to him an idiotic excursion into Petology.

'But Mrs Chubb realized straightaway that the name was short for something else. *Now* are you with me?'

The chief constable's face was as nearly expressive of excitement as either of his officers had ever seen it. Love said 'Ah!' loudly, out of sheer nervousness.

'The sergeant's got it,' said Chubb, almost jocularly, to Purbright. 'What about you?'

'I'm afraid I'm rather dense this morning, sir.'

'I'm afraid you are, Mr Purbright. Perhaps the shock of ' – he glanced at the pile of newspapers – 'so much notoriety has not yet worn off. When it does, you might reflect that Meffie is an abbreviated form of Mephistopheles.'

There was a pause.

'You think, then, do you, sir, that Mrs Gooding may be associated with the kind of activities described – or hinted at, rather – in these newspaper stories?'

'I leave you to draw what inference you care to.'

Purbright consulted his own Familiar. 'Has Mrs Gooding ever been in trouble of any kind, sergeant?'

Love answered without hesitation.

'Only for not having a dog licence. I think that was two years ago. And we were called once to a bit of disturbance with neighbours. They reckoned she'd got into their garden during the night and sprinkled everything with battery acid, but there was never anything proved.'

'Beatrice Avenue,' observed Mr Chubb, 'went down badly after that dreadful business a few years ago at number fourteen. There were some very nice people living there at one time.'

Purbright reflected, not for the first time, that the chief constable was inclined to regard vice and violence as systemic infections, mysterious as dry rot, that might be checked but never completely eradicated from the neighbourhood corpus in which they once had manifested themselves. Their spores, it seemed, were secreted in local property values which thereafter steadily and irrevocably shrank, the process being known by Mr Chubb as 'going down'.

'Would you like me to have Mrs Gooding questioned?' Purbright asked. 'What she said to Mrs Chubb might well be construed as a threat. And then there is the possibility of her dog coming within the definition of a dangerous animal, not under proper control.'

The chief constable vetoed this suggestion at once. Mrs Chubb did not bear a grudge and would not, in any case, care to be involved.

Purbright began to tidy up the newspapers.

'I expect you will have noticed that there is no mention of Mr Persimmon's disappearance in any of these stories, sir.'

Mr Chubb's tone was still chilly.

'Let us be thankful for small mercies.'

'His wife, I think, is less worried than she would like us to believe. His spending a night away from home and without warning is no novelty, apparently. She may or may not suspect that he has gone off with another woman – my impression after talking to her is that her husband's fidelity is not the most important thing in life for Mrs Persimmon.'

'She is very interested in flower arrangement,' volunteered Mr Chubb. 'The Club committee room is beautifully done out sometimes. Tell me, though, Mr Purbright – why are you so sure that Bert Persimmon is carrying on with this Hillyard girl? There's been no whisper at the Club.'

'Coincidence, mainly, sir. I agree there has been an absence of gossip, but that in itself would tend to confirm that Miss Hillyard's lover is a person of some local consequence. Both would be careful to keep the affair quiet.'

'You're guessing, you know.'

'Yes, sir. I am.'

'But the girl's clothes that were found in her car – how do you explain those?'

'She had been attending this folk dancing thing and I should think the arrangement was for him to pick her up there when it finished, or when she could slip away. She was probably hot and sweaty, so she changed into a fresh outfit there by the car. She wouldn't want to go back to her lodgings so late in the evening, and possibly draw her landlady's attention to the man she was going off with.

'There was absolutely no sign,' the inspector added, 'of a disturbance in or near the girl's car. The clothing was not damaged in any way and it had been left in a neatly folded pile, except for a slip that looked as if it had been dropped on the ground and picked up again.'

Mr Chubb pouted thoughtfully. 'All terribly speculative,' he complained. 'It seems to me that there is nothing whatever to connect these two people.'

'Other than their simultaneous disappearance, sir.'

'Well, yes; that's a pretty negative argument, after all.'

Purbright hesitated. The chief constable's disputatious mood was out of character. Either he was spinning out the interview in order to absent himself from some kind of domestic unpleasantness, or he was genuinely apprehensive lest the Edna Hillyard affair provide the press with even more dastardly material.

'There is,' the inspector said, 'one link that I haven't mentioned yet. It may come under your heading of speculation, but I'll tell you what it is, if you like.'

'Please do.'

'According to Mrs Persimmon – and I have not yet confirmed what she said – her husband works in some welfare capacity in partnership with three other well-known people. One, as we might expect, is the vicar. Sir Harry Bird is another. And the third is the Medical Officer, Dr Cropper, in whose office Miss Hillyard is employed.'

Mr Chubb wrinkled his nose. 'A bit thin, Mr Purbright, isn't it?'

An incoming call set off the buzzer of the unattended switchboard. Constable Braine clattered into the office and stared vaguely about him. Purbright waited until Braine had picked up the receiver before he spoke again.

'Tenuous perhaps at first sight, yes, sir. But an introduction might easily have resulted. I don't know yet the nature of what Persimmon's wife called his "samaritan" activities, but they could be something to do with moral guidance.'

'You mean that is what the girl was in need of?'

'I mean nothing of the kind, sir. But women of generous and uninhibited temperament do have the misfortune to attract the attention of well-meaning people. That could...'

'Excuse me a moment, sir.'

Constable Braine had appeared at Purbright's elbow.

A dignified nod from Mr Chubb conferred permission to speak. Braine straightened his shoulders.

'That was Henry Cutlock on the phone, sir. The fisherman. He was ringing from the staging at Five Mile Bar to say they'd picked up a body, sir. He thinks they'll be berthing in just over an hour.'

Purbright looked up at the clock.

'Tell the ambulance station to have someone at the harbour by a quarter to one. You'd better warn them that the body's been in the sea. Then get on to the hospital. Where's Bill Malley?'

The Coroner's Officer was likely, according to Braine, to be either at choir practice or playing darts in the Railway Hotel.

'Leave a message with his wife, then, will you? And I'd be obliged if you'd raise Harper in case we need pictures.'

Mr Chubb witnessed all this ordering of affairs with grave approval. It was not until Constable Braine had completed the commissions so far entrusted to him, however, that Purbright put the question which the chief constable had been waiting to hear answered.

'Did Henry say whether it was a man or a woman?'

'Man, sir.'

'Any hope of its being identifiable, did he think?'

'Oh, but he knows who it is, sir. It's the manager of that supermarket at the corner of Bride Street. Mr Persimmon.'

Chapter Nine

THE MORTUARY AT FLAXBOROUGH GENERAL HOSPITAL was set distinctly apart from the main group of buildings, as though the relationship was an embarrassment. It probably was, for whereas the hospital presented in 1912 brick baroque the florid and self-confident face of a doer of Good Works, the mean-visaged concrete and asbestos mortuary lurked like some necessary but resented menial, bearing mute witness to the philanthropist's fallibility.

It was not the failure of hospital treatment, charitable or otherwise, that accounted for the latest occupancy of the mortuary, however. Bertram Persimmon had died either by drowning or – and the police surgeon inclined to this opinion after a preliminary examination of the body – from a deep wound in his neck.

'How long would you say he'd been in the water?'

Purbright was looking down at the white, boneless-seeming body of what the pathologist's report was to describe as a 'well-nourished male, aged 45–50, with some excess of adipose tissue but otherwise generally healthy apart from a degree of arterial deterioration consistent with age and sedentary occupation...' To the flaccid flesh of arms and legs, black hairs, still wet, clung like draggles of weed. The thick patch in the middle of the chest was less dark. Around the head, damp strands of grey were tangled. They, more than anything else about the corpse, suggested defeat and helplessness. Purbright discovered that he had the foolish desire to comb them into order.

'Difficult to tell. Two days. Three days. Ay-ay-ay-ay...'

This last sound was a favourite comment of Doctor Fergusson; it was a kind of brisk keening for human frailty.

Purbright watched the sun-burned poll of the little Scotsman as he short-sightedly peered and probed, turning over folds of skin, exploring bone structure and tracing with delicate fingers the lip of the great wound in the side of the neck.

Fergusson shook his head and tut-tutted.

'And what, my lad, were you doing to get this great hole dug in you?'

He straightened and said, this time to Purbright: 'It's one hell of a jab, is that.'

'Could it have happened while he was in the river? A chop from a propeller – something of that sort?'

'Not in a hundred years, laddie. Dearie me, no.' Fergusson bent again. 'I'm not making any bets but I'll be surprised if we don't find that this was what put paid to him.'

'Have you any idea how a wound like that might have been caused?'

'I have not.'

'A knife?'

'No, no – not a knife. I'd say not a blade of any kind.'

'A spike, then?'

Fergusson did not refute this suggestion quite so promptly, but on reflection he thought a spike, in the sense of a spiked railing, say, was not the most likely weapon.

'What about a sharpened stake?'

'Ah . . .' The doctor raised a finger to the side of his nose and considered. He took a close look at the wound.

'Could be. Aye. Something at least two inches in diameter at the thick end. A stake – you might be right.'

He looked suddenly over his shoulder at the inspector. 'Why? Have you found one?'

'Heavens, no.'

The doctor sighed and busied himself with his bag. The catch snapped shut. He walked to a sink and began washing his hands.

'As a matter of fact,' he called, 'I once saw a wound very similar to that one. The fellow hadn't been in a river, though. They'd pulled him out of a stockyard.'

He turned off the tap and glanced around. 'Hell, isn't there even a towel in this place?'

Purbright pointed to a paper towel-dispenser farther along the white-tiled wall. 'Stockyard?' he repeated.

'Aye, he'd been gored,' said Fergusson. 'By an Aberdeen Angus.'

The inspector stared ruminatively at the corpse. He bent down and examined an area of the throat a few inches to the left of the main wound. The flesh was bruised and close scrutiny revealed a number of small, irregular gashes.

'What do you make of that, doctor?'

Fergusson thrust his head into partnership with Purbright's. He pouted, unimpressed.

'Superficial cuts and abrasions. Bodies do get knocked about on their travels, you know.' He straightened, reached for his bag.

'No, wait a minute.'

The inspector took a pencil from his pocket and indicated with its point what appeared to be a bright red incision at the edge of the damaged area.

'I took that to be blood, but of course, it can't be – not after a longish immersion in water. Try tweezers.'

'Hey, this isn't the PM yet, laddie. You'll get me shot.' But Fergusson, intrigued himself, produced a small pair of forceps and investigated.

The scarlet line proved to be the edge of a hard object embedded in the flesh. The forceps gripped and began to withdraw it.

Fergusson dropped the find into a small porcelain dish. It was a curved fragment, about half an inch long, of very thin ruby-coloured glass.

The bells of St Lawrence's had just begun to make their second major assault of the day upon the ears and vestigial consciences of Flaxborough when six policemen, accompanied by a policewoman, sat down to consider plans for the investigation of the death of Bertram Persimmon. It was six o'clock.

A big rectangular table had been pulled into the middle of the CID room. At its head sat the chief constable, wearing half-moon spectacles that gave him an air of school-masterly sapience. Purbright was at the opposite end of the table. The two longer sides were occupied by Detective-Sergeant Love, Detective-

Constables Harper and Pook, and Sergeant William Malley, the Coroner's Officer.

The policewoman was Sadie Bellweather, and she sat a little apart from the others, with a shorthand notebook on her knee.

On the farther side of the room a tea chest had been upended to serve as a display plinth. It bore the bull's-head mask which Purbright had retrieved for the occasion from a locked compartment in the lost property cupboard.

The chief constable spoke first.

'There are just a couple of points I think we should be clear about before we go any further, gentlemen. Firstly, there is no doubt, I take it, that the body is that of Mr Persimmon?'

'That's so, sir,' confirmed Malley, a very large man indeed, whose matching store of amiability had not been noticeably diminished even by the disruption of his Sunday evening. 'Mrs Persimmon has been down to the hospital already and identified him.'

'And the inquest?'

'Formal opening and adjournment in the morning, sir.'

Mr Chubb looked straight down the table to Purbright.

'You've seen the body, of course – as I have – and your opinion is that Persimmon could not possibly have received that injury by accident. Am I right?'

'Let me put it this way, sir. I find it quite impossible to visualize an accident that would have had precisely the results that we've seen here. The wound is consistent with the man having been gored. But it would be asking a lot from coincidence to suppose that he had happened to be on the brink of the river at the time. There are other factors which I shall mention shortly, and they do fit in with a picture of deliberate violence on somebody's part.'

'In short,' said Mr Chubb, 'we are faced with a case of murder.'

'Murder or manslaughter, sir. The distinction need not trouble us at this stage, as you rightly point out.'

The chief constable was still pondering this mysterious compliment when Purbright got up and walked over to the tea chest.

All looked towards the bull's head, Mr Chubb with cold

appraisal, Malley stolidly, Love and Harper craning like tourists anxious to get their money's worth, Pook indifferently, and Policewoman Bellweather with that rigidity of mien with which she had trained herself to confront all things unusual or distasteful, from a motor accident to a rashly proffered penis.

Purbright stationed himself by the mask like a lecturer.

'If you don't mind, I'd like to tell you what I can about this thing without your coming any nearer. Forensic are sending someone over, and there will be hard words if we are caught handing it around.

'The curator of the Fish Street Museum, from which you'll remember it was stolen a couple of years ago, says that it was used – or rather that others, of which this is an eighteenth- or nineteenth-century copy, were used – in religious celebrations of a kind that the press likes to call fertility rites. You could say it had associations with paganism – magic – witchcraft, if you prefer – but my main concern at the moment is with its physical properties.

'You can take it from me that this is an extremely durable article. Webster, the curator, thinks it is oak under all the varnish. The horns are actual bull's horns, but they have been set in the wood at an upward rather than a forward angle. The carpentry is excellent: neither horn has worked loose even after God knows how many years. Both horns are sharp.

'This harness' – Purbright pointed to the broad leather straps – 'would cross round the chest and keep the thing on pretty firmly.

'The mask would float with the help of a little trapped air. Which is why it is here now and not at the bottom of the river where I suspect someone either excessively optimistic or simply in a hurry thought it would end up.'

Sergeant Malley took from his mouth the empty pipe he had been sucking and signalled with it his desire to ask a question.

'You feel confident, do you, inspector, that Persimmon was killed with that thing?'

'Absolutely.'

Malley nodded and blew, like a gentle whale, while he formulated his next question.

'Do you have that opinion because both the body and the mask were found in the river within a fairly short time of each other?'

'No, not just because of that. Doctor Fergusson will be assisting at the PM a little later this evening, but I might as well mention one of the more interesting discoveries that he's made already.'

'Now, here' – the inspector pointed delicately with a pencil – 'there has been fixed fairly recently to the top of the mask, exactly halfway between the horns, a small electric bulb holder. The bulb is smashed, but its base is still screwed into the holder and there is enough glass left to be compared with fragments of the same bulb that might turn up elsewhere.'

'As they have, presumably,' said Mr Chubb.

'In the neck of the corpse, actually. And the glass is rather distinctive. One would call it ruby, I think. The bulb is of the kind that is hung on Christmas trees. Forensic will be able to say for certain if the glass matches, but I have no reason to doubt that it does – nor that we have here the weapon that killed Persimmon.'

'I quite agree with you,' said the chief constable.

The inspector gave a small bow.

'What I cannot understand,' went on Mr Chubb, 'is why the fellow, whoever he is, went to all that trouble. It's a terrible enough thing to kill somebody, God knows, but to dress up as a cow with all that electric paraphernalia in order to do it . . . We're obviously dealing here with a diseased mind, gentlemen.'

The others observed silence of a duration suitable to the profundity of the chief constable's conclusion. Love was the first to let curiosity off the leash again.

'Where's the battery?' he inquired, pertly.

'Inside,' said Purbright. He pointed again with his pencil. 'Under some padding. The wiring is quite neat. It comes out at the side – just here – and connects with this rheostat switch.'

'Rheostat?'

To the aid of perplexed Malley came Harper. 'It's a dimmer. You know. Like a car's dashboard light.'

'Ah,' Malley's own elderly vehicle all but lacked a dashboard, let alone a rheostat, but he thought he understood.

Constable Pook, who was frowning a good deal, asked what the inspector supposed the idea of the switch and so on had been.

Purbright shrugged. 'Your guess would be as good as mine. According to Webster, this kind of mask sometimes had a candle set between the horns. It was lighted during the ceremony to add to the general impressiveness of the occasion.'

'But whoever wore that thing,' Love said, 'wouldn't get much dancing done. Not with a lighted candle on his bonce. It would blow out.'

'As I understand it, he wasn't expected to dance, sergeant. All he had to do was to sit and be worshipped.'

Harper spoke. 'I think I get the idea of the rheostat, sir. If there's been any worshipping or that sort of thing going on, that is. The fellow inside that mask would want the thing to be artistic, wouldn't he? A gradual fading in and out. I mean, it would look stupid if it just went on and off like a traffic light.'

Mr Chubb, looking a little exasperated by the disquisition on electric circuits, suggested that it was time to consider other lines of investigation and how best they might be followed.

Purbright returned to his place at the table. He straightened two sheets of notes that lay before him.

'Because Persimmon appears to have been killed in so bizarre a fashion,' the inspector began after a pause, 'the temptation is to concentrate on that aspect of the crime. To try and trace, for instance, the person who originally stole or later came into possession of that mask. Inquiries will need to be made, certainly, but we shall be lucky if they are productive; it's amazing how invisible things become once they have been pinched from a museum or an art gallery.

'We also shall need to treat seriously, though not with credulity, the stories of witchcraft that have been going the rounds in the last few days. It would be foolish to ignore the ritual associations of the mask. Again, though, I'm sure the chief constable will wish me to stress the importance of sifting concrete and relevant evidence from all the portentous rumour which so readily froths up during investigations of this kind.

'More in the nature of conventional inquiries will be the effort needed to find out what sort of person the dead man was and how he spent his time – particularly, of course, during Wednesday, when he was last seen alive. Persimmon was well known and there should be no lack of information concerning his open activities...'

'Open?' Mr Chubb had raised one eyebrow.

'Yes, sir. There could have been others, of which direct evidence is unlikely to be forthcoming.'

The chief constable glanced apprehensively in the direction of Policewoman Bellweather.

'Be that as it may,' he murmured.

'Which brings me,' resumed the inspector, relentlessly, 'to the matter of Edna Hillyard's disappearance. When it was first known that Persimmon, too, had vanished, Mr Chubb rightly described as guesswork my connecting the two events. It was, at that time, conjecture – though not, I think, wild conjecture. Less than half an hour ago, however, I received a telephone call from the manager of the Neptune Hotel at Brocklestone. He confirmed, with dates, what he had told me when I rang him earlier in the afternoon. Persimmon and Miss Hillyard stayed together at the hotel on three occasions during March and twice in April.'

'The manager told you that?'

Mr Chubb's involuntary emphasis on 'Manager' suggested that even in murder investigations there existed areas of confidential dealing that were not lightly to be exploited.

'Yes, sir. Barraclough. He's reasonably co-operative provided he can be convinced that we are not spying on his guests simply for the sake of being officious.'

'I was not thinking in terms of Mr Barraclough's willingness or unwillingness to impart information,' said the chief constable. 'What I find surprising is his ability to furnish you with the correct names. I had always understood that people who stay at hotels for immoral purposes are inclined to use pseudonyms.'

'Is that so, sir? Ah, well, Mr Barraclough has a very wide local acquaintance and a good memory. I suspect he would not need to rely too heavily upon his hotel register for identification.'

Sergeant Malley testified that the manager of the Neptune had not only a memory like a filing system but a particular talent for recognizing averted faces and even, some said, fugitive backsides.

'Does the inspector mean that Miss Hillyard could be at Brocklestone now?' asked Pook.

'She could be anywhere,' Purbright replied. 'But Brocklestone is one of the less likely places. She certainly is not at the Neptune, and has not been there since last month. No, in view of what has happened to her lover, the possibility that most worries me is that she finished up in the same place as he did.'

Mr Chubb stared, frowning, at the inspector. Purbright realized that the man was genuinely grieved by the suggestion. What he had not expected, though, was Mr Chubb's patent surprise. Purbright felt sorry for him.

'After all, sir, no one has had word of this woman for four days. Persimmon's death must change radically whatever theories we might have formed previously. I admit my own view was decidedly over-complacent.'

Sergeant Love spoke. 'We don't know for certain that she was still his girl friend. She'd knocked around a good deal before and the people who talked to me about her didn't strike me as thinking that she was likely to settle for anybody in particular.' Love leaned round Harper to address the chief constable directly. 'She's not what you might call a home-loving girl, sir.'

Mr Chubb pouted dubiously. 'That may be so, sergeant, but I'm afraid the only hypothesis we can afford to accept is that both these unfortunate people were involved in the same event. We must hope it did not have the same outcome for both of them.'

'One of my proposals,' Purbright said, 'is that apart from trying to find out what happened on Wednesday night, and where, we should assume that Miss Hillyard is still alive and make a special effort to trace her. With your agreement, sir, I should not rule out door-to-door inquiries. The county people might help with men.'

Mr Chubb made a note on the pad before him. 'I'll have a word with Hessledine,' he said.

Harper asked Love something under his breath, then spoke aloud. 'Does anybody know if Mr Persimmon had a car?'

Yes, Malley said, a big Ford, he thought a Zodiac, was almost certain a Zodiac.

'Do we know where it is now?'

Purbright acknowledged the point to be a good one. He added – but inwardly – that there was no excuse for his having failed to think of it himself, then sent Love into the next office with instructions to telephone Mrs Persimmon and ask if her husband had been using the car on the day of his disappearance.

'Surely,' said Mr Chubb to the inspector when Love had departed, 'she would have mentioned the car to you when you called on her yesterday if her husband had taken it with him?'

'She was somewhat distraught, sir.'

'Yes, I can understand that. Even so, cars are pretty expensive items, you know.'

'His probably had been provided by the firm.'

'You think so?'

'It's customary.'

'Ah.'

Love returned with the information that Persimmon's car, the registration number of which he had obtained from the widow, had not been seen by her since the previous Wednesday morning. Nor had she thought about it. Was it, perhaps, in the parking bay behind the supermarket? She had no other suggestions to offer.

Chapter Ten

WITH THE AIR OF A GENEROUS SPORTSMAN LENDING HIS second best golf clubs to a friend who has never played before, the County Chief Constable acceded to Mr Chubb's request for help in the hunt for Edna Hillyard.

Six uniformed men and two detective-constables were relieved of their duties in Chalmsbury, Brocklestone and some of the smaller county divisions and told to report at Flaxborough, where, if the search should prove protracted, they would be found lodgings.

Purbright awaited the result of his call to Ayrshire, where lived Edna's only traceable relatives. If door-to-door inquiries were to be made, recognizable duplicates of a photograph of the woman would have to be run off. Neither her landlady nor any of her friends interviewed so far possessed a picture.

The day before the county men were due to be briefed, a carefully wrapped, framed portrait arrived at Fen Street. It was of a five-year-old child with whimsically gappy teeth and dressed in a gauze fairy costume and ballet shoes.

The inspector showed it to Love.

'Her auntie in Scotland produced it. It's all they've been able to turn up. You've seen the girl. Is this going to be any good?'

'No,' said the sergeant.

'No hint of features? Nothing that might just connect in people's minds?'

Love shook his head firmly.

Purbright put the photograph aside. 'Could we get a drawing made, do you think? We've got to have something for people to be shown.'

'Have you tried the *Citizen* office?'

It was, the inspector reflected, just as well that Love had a kind of built-in guilelessness that prevented his exploiting or even gloating over the gaffes and shortcomings of his superior officers. So gross a lapse as failure to go straight to the local newspaper file as the most likely source of a picture hardly bore thinking about.

'My dear Sid, you mean you haven't been round there yet?'

'I can't remember that you asked me to.'

Purbright regarded with fond admonishment the pink face of Love, helpful, unsurprised.

'Never mind,' he said at last. 'You've had a lot to think about. It's often the most obvious things that get overlooked.'

The sergeant nodded, forgiving himself.

Ten minutes later, he was searching through the efficiently maintained photographic index of the *Flaxborough Citizen* in Market Street.

As Purbright, upon reflection, had surmised, Miss Hillyard was by temperament the sort of woman who might be expected to have had a history of entering beauty competitions. The most recent, apparently, had been only five years ago when she was twenty-nine. Love withdrew and gazed with admiration upon the print entitled 'Miss Arcadia Ballroom, 1966'. It showed a large but well-proportioned brunette, whose sexual attractions – without question considerable even in straight presentation, so to speak – had been lent breath-catching emphasis by a choice of costume that not only was flagrantly translucent but seemed to have been shrunk on like the wrapping of a vacuum-packed ham.

'She looks fairly capable of looking after herself,' Purbright said, trying to feel confident.

He handed the print back to Love. 'Get Harper to run off two or three dozen copies.'

With twelve of the duplicated photographs in his pocket, the inspector called at the Roebuck Hotel and asked if he might see one of the gentlemen associated with the detergent advertising campaign currently mounted in the town.

He was ushered into a small, brown room, papered in simulation of panelling and hung with as many sporting prints as could be accommodated in single file around the walls. The room smelled of gin, with an underlying tang of horseradish sauce.

Three men and two women sat round a mahogany dining-table on which lay a jostle of pamphlets, correspondence and what Purbright took to be accounts or statistical extracts. Several bottles and two siphons were grouped in the centre of the table. On a sideboard were more bottles and a portable film projector.

The girl who had acted as the inspector's guide retreated and shut the door behind her without attempting introductions.

Purbright found himself being eyed sourly by the room's five occupants.

'I am an inspector of police and my name is Purbright.'

At first no one moved. The inspector had a momentary impression that the three expensively dressed, gloomy-looking men and their languid companions supposed his appearance to be connected with some puritanical local application of the liquor laws. Then he realized that their depression was rooted in some earlier and more serious cause.

'Which of you gentlemen is the Lucillite representative?'

The man called Gordon gave a start and leaped nimbly to his

feet.

'Terribly sorry, inspector. We were rather preoccupied conference-wise. I'm Dixon-Frome, DD Division. This is Richard, our consultancy colleague' – a nod and a purr from the adman – 'and Hughie, of course, who is our Assistant Environmental Research and Liaison Executive.'

'And anyone who can say that gets a free packet of Lucillite right here and now!'

The man with the aubergine nose was suddenly erect and grinning. He pumped Purbright's hand, then stood back and upped and downed him in an appraising gaze of enormous geniality.

'Fabulous! Absolutely fabulous!'

To Purbright's astonishment, he found an arm round his shoulder and Hugh's grin bobbing about a couple of inches from his face.

'Let us,' said Gordon, elbowing Hugh aside like an over-exuberant dog, 'not forget the most important members of the team. Sheila darling...'

He reached toward but did not touch the hand of a girl whose most immediately noticeable features were lemon-blonde hair, tight wash-leather shorts and a butt-end of cigar on which her mouth worked as tirelessly as a boxing promoter's.

'Sheila's our Personnel and Welfare Executive,' Gordon said.

'Detergents Division, Domestic,' squeezed wetly past Sheila's cigar butt.

Purbright thought he detected a note of irony and held her glance a little longer, but the girl's eyes remained solemn.

He looked away to a plump, sallow-complexioned young woman who had been examining a sheaf of photographic stills and making rings upon them with a white crayon.

'Hendy,' Gordon announced, extending his hand towards her. 'Assistant Co-ordinator, Visual Kinetics.'

Hendy examined two more stills, marked them, then looked up at the inspector. She gave him a smile like the movement of a camera shutter and resumed her task.

'Fabulous,' murmured Hugh, for no reason that Purbright could determine.

'I'm sorry to interrupt you in conference,' the inspector began, 'but I do think that there are one or two ways in which you can be especially helpful to us.'

'To the police, you mean?'

'I don't wish to put it quite as narrowly as that, sir. To the police, yes; but in the main to the community. There has been a murder in the town and a woman has disappeared. We are very anxious to trace her quickly. If she is not already dead, that is.'

Hugh's face registered disbelief, then horrified surprise, and set after a few more modifications into the lineaments of grave determination to see justice done.

'But that's terrible, inspector. Really terrible.' He turned to Richard. 'Isn't that terrible, Richard?' And to Gordon. 'Gordon – did you hear what the inspector said? Isn't that terrible? Hendy darling...'

Purbright waited for the equitable distribution of Hugh's dismay to be completed.

'You'd heard nothing of this business, then, sir?' he asked Gordon.

'Not a word. But we aren't exposed, really, to the neighbourhood thing. Not in any viable sense, are we, Richard?'

'I wouldn't say we were, Gordon, no. I mean, we haven't personalized communications outside the wash-psychology thing. There just isn't...'

'Who's dead?'

Sheila was looking up at the inspector. The cigar butt, perilously short now, seemed about to be ingested within her puckered lips.

'He's a shopkeeper,' Purbright said. 'Or rather, a store manager.' He saw interest flare suddenly in his audience.

'Not a supermarket manager?' prompted Gordon, hesitantly.

'That's right, sir. A man called Bertram Persimmon.'

'Christ!' Richard said.

Purbright looked from one to another. 'Did any of you know this man, then?'

'Well, I don't know that we'd actually *met* him, had we, Richard? Not in a social situation.'

'He was a great person,' Hugh interposed fervently.

'I have an idea,' Richard said to Gordon, 'that we did see him once – person-to-personwise, I mean. Wasn't he at the pre-promotion thing at the Dorchester? Right?'

'Right. Well, probably, anyway.'

'Right.' Richard turned to Purbright. 'Persimmon rated with Dixon-Frome. I know you'd like to know that. You mustn't think of Flickborough as right off the map. I'm with Thornton-Edwards – on the Lucillite account, right? – and I don't think I'm breaking our client's confidence when I tell you this is a potential zoom-zone. I can tell the inspector that, can't I, Gordon?'

'Sure. Anything.'

Hugh, in reverie, shook his head. 'A very, very sincere person. No, I mean *really* sincere.'

Purbright had been wondering for some time about the talk's curious quality of disjointedness. He indicated Hugh with a nod and asked Gordon very softly: '*He* knew Persimmon, then, did he?'

Gordon looked surprised.

'No, no – none of us knew him. Why should we? He was supposed to have got things laid on, that's all. And he let us down. Of course, what you say does explain why. But we've been bleed-ing blood over the past couple of days, we really have.'

'Would you like to tell me more about this letting down, as you term it. Persimmon was supposed to have made certain arrange-ments, was he?'

'You could say that. Sure. Richard here will tell you his consul-tancy had Persimmon lined up for product co-operation. Right, Richard?'

'Right.'

'You mean he was going to sell your washing powder in his shop?'

There was a brief silence. Richard and Gordon looked at each other.

'Oh, dear,' said Gordon, quietly.

Richard stroked his smooth chin, spicily fragrant with 'Gun-room' after-shave.

'Mr Persimmon,' Richard explained to the inspector, 'is – or was – the manager of a supermarket which is the local unit of the merchandizing division of Northern Nutritionals, a subsidiary of Dixon-Frome, which as you know is controlled by the Wyoming Cement Corporation.'

'The boot and shoe complex?' offered Purbright, unable to help himself.

Richard's expression of patient patronage parted to allow a glint of surprise and admiration.

'Exactly,' he said. 'So you will see that Persimmon was but a cog, a very small cog, in our product promotion machinery. But one specific task he did undertake – he was to issue private invitations to forty or fifty local washwives to take part in some film work for television commercials.'

'I'm sorry – local what?'

'Washwives,' Gordon said. 'Women whose life-style depends for an enhancement element upon the know-how of the detergent industry. We don't apologize for a word like that, inspector. It's a tell-word, and tell-words are what we like to use. Right, Richard?'

'Right.'

'Do I understand,' asked Purbright, 'that the forty or fifty invitations were not in fact issued by Persimmon?'

'They were not,' said Gordon. 'We had to use our own home-call operatives to recruit the ladies at the last minute. The day was not entirely successful.'

'Have you any idea at all of what prevented Mr Persimmon from doing as you had expected?'

'We were told by his staff on Friday morning that nothing had been seen of him for two days. Two whole days, for God's sake. Richard here practically orgasmed and I can't blame him. The location and everything had been set up. Even a marvellous boat-man character. Then, pfft – no washwives. Nary a bloody one.'

A disgracefully wayward but attractive notion had blown through the casement of Purbright's imagination.

'This man's disappearance,' he said slowly. 'Could it have been of critical importance to the campaign you'd all come here to launch?'

The Deputy Chief Brand Visualizer of Thornton-Edwards,

Arnold and Konstatin nodded with grave emphasis. It seemed to Purbright that the adman saw nothing outrageous in the situation at which he had hinted; perhaps his world really was one that admitted the nobbling of supermarket managers in the cause of The Product.

'Oh, but surely,' began Purbright, drawing back from the brink.

Hendy was on her feet. She stepped in front of the inspector and thrust at Gordon the photographs she had been marking.

Gordon sorted through them quickly and handed two or three to Purbright. On each he saw, ringed in white, the malevolently cross-eyed visage of Miss Amy Parkin.

Hugh's arm was clamped round Purbright's shoulder before he could step clear.

'Can *you* understand, inspector, what makes people do those terrible things? I think they must be sick, don't you? Don't you think people who do these things must be sick?'

'All that film,' lamented Richard. 'Every last shot.'

'Spoiled?' ventured Purbright.

'My God! Image-wise, anything like that slays, but slays. Listen, all these are bad-ad – jokes, sarcasm, knocking animals, politics, death. Right? But worst, worst, worst is deformity. Limps, squints, leg-irons. They're bad-ad *in profundis*.'

'This was fixed,' asserted Gordon, tapping the pile of prints.

Purbright turned. 'By?'

'No names.'

'G and P, darling, for a ducat.'

Sheila had stretched herself almost horizontally in her chair and was holding to her eye, telescope fashion, an empty gin bottle.

'No names,' repeated Gordon.

Sheila grinned, as at the discovery of an amusing new planet.

'All right, then. E and S. Bet you.'

'No names,' Richard said testily.

Yawning, Sheila scratched long, honey-coloured thighs with her free hand. Hendy gave her a glance of disapproval, then crossed to the door.

'I'm going down to the bar for some cigarettes.'

'Just a moment...'

Purbright was drawing from his pocket the envelope of copies of the photograph of Edna Hillyard.

He handed one to each of them and put the rest on the table.

'This young woman is in her mid-thirties now, but probably not much different in looks from when this picture was taken. She was friendly with the man we have been talking about. First of all, I want to know if any of you recognize this girl or remember having seen her at any time.'

All gazed dutifully at the picture, then signified that Miss Hill-yard was absolutely unknown to them. Only Hugh offered a comment.

'Oh, but fabulous. Absolutely fabulous!'

Extravagant concern flooded his face. 'And do you mean to say, inspector, that this poor girl has been done to death?'

'That I do not say. But, as I mentioned before, she is missing. In view of what has happened to Persimmon, we have very good cause to be anxious. The help I am asking from you people is this. You are running a promotion campaign involving door-to-door calls. Your canv...' – Purbright caught the look of pain in the Dixon-Frome man's eye – 'Your home-call operatives will be covering ground that might well yield useful information. Could they not slip in a question on the side, so to speak? You know – Have you seen this girl lately? – that sort of thing. It might be most valuable.'

Gordon pondered.

'The HCOs aren't really depth-orientated, are they Richard? I mean, in what sort of depth do you want this, inspector? We've no M-R people on this one, actually. Not at the moment.'

'M-R?'

'Motivational Research.'

'I don't really think that would be necessary. Just the straight question and the picture. We should do all the following up, naturally.'

After a little more thought, Gordon nodded.

'Sure. Sure. Will do. Sheila – extra special briefing for the Lucies in the morning, love. Right? O.K. Richard?'

'O.K. Gordon. Just one point, Sheila.'

'Point awaited, darl.'

The gin bottle, gripped now in the crutch of the Personnel and Welfare Executive, was being rocked from side to side by means of a sort of sedentary belly-dancer's technique.

'Those girls are not of the brightest. They are practically on top quiz-load already. Give them the one extra question only. Absolutely simple. "Have you seen?" And the picture. Roger?'

'Roger and out.'

For a few moments more, Sheila watched with a self-centred smile the oscillations of her bottle. Then she reached a fresh cigar from a box on the floor beside her and bit nearly an inch off its end.

Purbright returned to the subject of Persimmon, but with no real hope of progress. The manager's part in the Lucillite campaign had been settled beforehand by correspondence and a couple of subsidiary telephone calls from the London office. None of the team now in Flaxborough had met him personally or even spoken to him by phone. Apart from the hinted but quite unsubstantiated involvement of some other powerful protagonist in the detergent war, no one had been able to suggest a reason for the man's violent end.

'We get ourselves op-based on Thursday night. Persimmon is to rendezvous with us the following morning. He doesn't. We contact the store and his home. Negatively. Finalization of the campaign visuals is deadlined for May 7. Right. So we out-phase P and proceed. What else can we do, inspector? No one is so vital he cannot be redundantized.'

Having listened attentively to this summary by Gordon, Hugh directed upon the inspector a smile infinitely regretful and shrugged.

Purbright indicated the film stills. 'Are you going to have to do all that again?'

'Tomorrow,' said Richard. He looked as nearly worried as Purbright had yet seen him.

'Come hell and high water,' added Hugh, jocularly. He darted approval-seeking glances at everyone else in the room. Hendy curled her lip at him.

Twenty minutes after Purbright's departure, another visitor tapped at the door of the Dixon-Frome op-base and opened it immediately.

'Anybody home?'

Gordon, sifting disconsolately through the pages of a sales analysis, looked up to see the benign but alert features of a woman perhaps twenty years his senior. She was dressed in the kind of clothes – of excellent cut and quality but with a challenging touch of frumpishness – that proclaim the well-born who has managed to hang on to her money.

Gordon rose. He was alone in the room except for Sheila, who was asleep in her chair and faintly snoring. Hendy and Richard had gone down to the bar. Hugh, a compulsive body-cleanser, was locked in a bathroom somewhere for the third time that day.

The woman advanced into the room and subjected Gordon to close and friendly scrutiny.

'You are Dixon-Frome, of course,' she said, having nodded approvingly at the lemon hue of his drip-dry Execution shirt.

Gordon half-opened his mouth, remained motionless for a second, then snapped his fingers. 'You're TEAK...' He waited, smiling uncertainly.

'Teak?'

'Thornton-Edwards. One of their M-R execs. Right?'

She pursed her lips teasingly, then looked round for somewhere to put down her old-fashioned but very costly-looking blue seal-skin handbag. Gordon took the bag and placed it on the table. She selected a chair for herself and sat down. Her legs were surprisingly shapely.

'No,' she said at last, 'I am not from Thornton-Edwards, although I do know of them, of course. I was on the board of an agency for a number of years. Nowadays my interests lie in a direction different from advertising.'

'Oh, yes?'

'My name is Lucilla Teatime – incidentally, I should much prefer you to use it without the feudal handle, which may look well enough on company notepaper but does tend to be painfully embarrassing in conversation – and I am Operational Director of

ECPRF.'

There was a tiny pause.

'Small world,' said Gordon.

'Indeed it is,' agreed Miss Teatime. She gazed past his shoulder as if the Antipodes had just swum into view above the sideboard. Then she said, slowly and deliberately: 'Your promotion film has run into serious difficulties.'

Gordon started. 'How do you know about that?'

'Should we say, perhaps, that our lines crossed? What a pity that Dixon-Frome did not consult us in advance. The site you chose for filming is quite notorious in PR circles, you know.'

'Our consultancy was quite happy with it, PR-wise.'

Miss Teatime gave a tinkling, tea-with-the-vicar laugh.

'Public Relations ... oh dear, a small misunderstanding I fear. I was speaking of something rather less mundane. PR stands also for Psychical Research.'

'I see.' Gordon fingered his tie dubiously.

'Ah, you are embarrassed, are you not. Your idea association mechanism is in good order. It has given you the print-out. Psychic – spiritualism – table-turning and cheesecloth – mad old ladies in dark Peckham parlours ...'

He sent a hesitant little smile to meet hers. 'Well, actually ...'

'Perfectly natural,' declared Miss Teatime. 'You can have no idea of how that image still interferes with the work of purely scientific agencies. What I dare say you would term respect potential is something we have worked hard to achieve in the Edith Cavell Psychical Research Foundation.'

'Edith Cavell?'

Miss Teatime blushed. 'My middle names, actually. Rather shame-making but the Trust insisted. They meant it kindly, I suppose, but people do not realize how unworthy of them is this persistent deference to money and aristocratic connection. However, and be that as it may, you will be wanting to know, will you not, in what practical manner the Foundation proposes to assist you and your excellent consultancy.'

'I'm not sure that I see how you ...'

'Would you mind?' A little cheroot had appeared between two

of Miss Teatime's elegantly poised fingers. Gordon looked about him. He spotted a box of matches that rose and fell on the stomach of the sleeping Sheila.

Miss Teatime accepted a light with careful concentration, as if she valued it highly, then indicated the prints on the table.

'Those are some of the stills, are they?'

Gordon obediently handed them to her.

Miss Teatime donned a pair of gold-rimmed spectacles and scrutinized the first print. It showed a group of washwives, with Hugh in their midst. Each of the women was displaying a garment incredibly besmirched with foodstuffs or effluent of some kind. The scene was saved from looking like an incipient lynching by Hugh's expression of calm, almost saintly, reassurance.

Over every inch of the print ranged Miss Teatime's keen eye. Gordon heard her sudden intake of breath when she came to the section ringed in Hendy's white crayon.

'Amazing!'

He looked over her shoulder, but she was already busy upon the second photograph.

'Absolutely fascinating!'

'You see why all this work has negative use-value,' Gordon said. 'The spoilage rate is terrific.'

She seemed not to hear.

Another print was of the washwives gazing at the river in which boatman Heath was pretending to fill his medieval bucket. The floating bull's-head mask was clearly visible.

'Minoan ectoplasm!' breathed Miss Teatime.

A shot of the line-up of washwives at the display of their clothing after it supposedly had been immersed in Lucillite suds bore three of Hendy's censorship rings.

One framed a woman gazing furiously at a pair of drawers marred by an enormous black hand-print. Within another, low on the left of the picture, two dogs were unconcernedly copulating. The third contained the inevitable camera-ogling visage of the dwarfish woman with the thirty-degree squint.

Miss Teatime sat back, removed her glasses and tapped them pensively against her knee. 'I would never have believed it,' she said, half to herself.

'Well,' said Gordon, 'you've heard about industrial sabotage. Right?' He pointed at the prints, opened his mouth, shut it again, and began walking rapidly up and down. He stopped and pointed once more at the prints. 'Right?'

'The lady with the very odd eyes,' Miss Teatime began.

'Agent,' snapped Gordon. 'From P and Q probably. Or C and H. KGB even.'

Miss Teatime looked shocked. 'The Russians?'

'Kleen-Gear Biological. Do I have to spell it out for you?'

Gordon was noticeably less crease-proof than he had seemed earlier. Miss Teatime patted his sleeve.

'I think you ought to sit down,' she said gently. 'Come along. I have something to tell you which may come as a slight shock.'

He frowned, but followed her advice. There was something decidedly persuasive about this punctiliously mannered woman.

'That's better,' she said. 'Now, then; I do understand your reaction to these unfortunate setbacks, but I must tell you that you are quite wrong in your interpretation of them. You see, I happen to know the identity of the lady whose physical affliction has spoiled so much of your film. She is not an agent. And I am sure that her turning up here was an event quite uninfluenced by your business rivals.'

'Name. The name's all I want. Injunction. Right?'

'The name,' said Miss Teatime, 'is Mad Meg of Pennick. And there would be no point in applying for an injunction.'

Gordon stared at her. 'You mean she's a mental patient, or something?'

'She is dead. She committed suicide four years ago.'

'Good God!'

'Curiously enough,' added Miss Teatime, equably, 'there was nothing wrong with poor Meg's sight during life. That very unnerving squint which you may observe in these pictures was caused – according to medical evidence at the inquest – by the method she chose to kill herself.'

Miss Teatime leaned forward and spoke softly, after a glance at the still sleeping Sheila.

'Hanging.'

Her voice fell still further.

'In a chicken coop.'

Gordon began a fresh examination of the film stills, this time with horrified fascination.

Miss Teatime's manner became suddenly brisker.

'You must not worry too much about your filming tomorrow,' she said. 'This town has always been the focus for a good deal of paranormal phenomena. We know now how to cope with it.'

'You mean you can render this sort of thing non-repetitive?'

'I mean that I shall be happy to place our not inconsiderable field knowledge of the subject at the disposal of you and your colleagues. I propose to begin work on the site immediately. Tele-Radiation clearance should be complete by morning.'

'I'm not certain, Miss Teatime, that I can commit Dixon-Frome any further budgetwise.'

The finely delineated eyebrows arched a fraction.

'The Foundation, needless to say, does not solicit fees.'

'Oh, well, that's fine. We'll just play this one by ear, shall we?'

Miss Teatime rose and prepared to take her leave.

'Vibrations, as Sir Oliver Lodge used so often to remark to my father, are our only help and guide.'

She held out her hand.

'Of course, Sir Oliver did not live to see the benefits conferred upon scientific research by donations from industry.'

Chapter Eleven

INSPECTOR PURBRIGHT INTERVIEWED MEMBERS OF THE staff of the Bride Street supermarket in the white-painted closet, furnished with chair, table and camp bed, that served to accommodate in their separate seasons travelling salesmen, ladies taken queer, and shoplifters. On the wall was a first-aid cabinet. He had peeped inside it and discovered a part roll of adhesive tape and the heel of a woman's shoe.

The under-manager, whom the inspector decided to question first in deference to his seniority, turned out to be a pale but wiry youth of nineteen or twenty. He looked a pretty good box heaver. Henry Baxter was his name.

'When was it,' Purbright asked him, 'that Mr Persimmon was last in the store? Take your time and try to be accurate.'

'Half-past eight on Wednesday,' Henry replied without hesitation.

'What, in the evening, you mean?'

'That's right.'

'But isn't it half-day closing on a Wednesday?'

'Most places it is. Not here, though. We get our time off staggered. If,' Henry added, 'there's any going.'

'I see. So you were here with Mr Persimmon on Wednesday, were you? Until eight-thirty.'

'That's right. Well, we had all the Lucillite packets to overstick, didn't we?'

'Overstick?'

'With those little labels. "New – Improved".'

'Ah, you'd had new stock come in.'

'No. But the price had gone up again, hadn't it?'

Purbright backed out of this conversational cul-de-sac and asked: 'Did you notice anything about Mr Persimmon's manner that evening? Anything unusual – strained, excited?'

'Not really. He was a bit mad at having to stay late, especially at such short notice, but it wasn't the first time it had happened and in this trade you get used to being buggered about a bit by head office.'

'When you say short notice, do you mean he was only asked that day to stay behind?'

'Yeah. They rang up about three. Of course, there's a special push on this week and next. They've got girls in space suits and God knows what all. Proper circus.'

'Did you leave together at half-past eight?'

'More or less. Except that I walked and he got in his car.'

'Did you suppose he would drive straight home?'

'No.'

'You didn't – why?'

'Well, there was that phone call he made, wasn't there?'

Henry Baxter's mode of answering questions was curiously suggestive of a supposition on his part that the inspector had been a hidden observer of all his past life.

'Phone call?' repeated Purbright, patiently.

'When he knew about having to do the oversticks. He rang up this party and said he'd come straight over when he could.'

'Might it not have been his wife he was talking to?'

'Oh no, he never rang her. Not the boss. Not his wife, he wouldn't.'

'Who was it, then? Do you know?'

'Me? No, I never heard him. It was Julie who was getting stuff out of the stockroom to refill one of the special offer bins. The phone's in there.'

'You say Mr Persimmon was not in the habit of telephoning his wife. Do I take it that they weren't on very good terms?'

The under-manager shrugged. 'Well, just sort of average. I don't suppose he thought much of her, but they'd been married ages, hadn't they?'

'You'd call the relationship unenthusiastic rather than hostile, then.'

'Yeah, I suppose you could say that.'

'Was anyone – anyone at all – inclined to be hostile to Mr Persimmon?'

Mr Baxter considered carefully this wider question.

'What, customers, you mean?'

'Not necessarily.'

There was a pause. Then the under-manager shook his head.

'I can't think of anybody in particular,' he said, 'but I don't reckon he was liked much. Not by men. You know.'

'I'm not sure that I do know, Mr Baxter. Effeminate, was he?'

'Far from it. I'd say he was a randy old sod, if he hadn't been my boss.'

'I think we can take it that his death absolves you from professional loyalty, Mr Baxter.'

'Right. Then that's what he was.'

Julie Bollinger, bin-filler and shelf-recharger, entered Purbright's presence with a draggle-tailed awe that argued years of parental warning of the policeman who would fetch her away if she didn't eat her dinner. She was sixteen years old, sallow and straight-haired, and looked as if the threats had failed in their purpose.

Purbright got up and gave her his chair. She perched on the edge of it and covered bony knees with large red hands.

The inspector squatted on the farther end of the camp bed and waited until she glanced his way, when he gazed admiringly at a huge buckle of chrome and coloured glass on her belt.

She saw him looking and was pleased and just a little reassured.

'Julie, you know that Mr Persimmon is dead and that we think somebody killed him. Obviously all this has nothing to do with you, and I'm not going to bother you with a whole lot of silly questions. But there's one thing you might have remembered from last Wednesday which could be important. Now listen. When you were working in the stockroom and therefore happened to hear Mr Persimmon talking on the phone, did anything of what he said come over clearly to you?'

Julie, whose mother would have prefaced such a catechism with the observation that 'little pigs have big ears' and a blow on each just to prove it, thought how nice and understanding this big, yellow-haired policeman was. She closed her eyes and rummaged conscientiously through the little rag-bag of her memory.

'He said,' she announced at last, nodding slightly at each word in warranty of its truth, 'that he couldn't make it that night and that whoever it was he was talking to should be sure to let Dilly know. I think he said that bit twice. And then there was another bit where he laughed and said well it was a bit of luck for whoever was at the other end of the phone because she'd get an extra turn.'

'She?' queried Purbright. 'Do you think it was a woman he was talking to, Julie?'

She frowned, confused by the complication.

'I don't know, really. He never called whoever it was by name. I just ...' Her thin shoulders rose and subsided.

Purbright hastened to say, never mind, she'd got a jolly good memory and the odds were that her first impression was probably the right one.

'Did you like Mr Persimmon?' he asked casually.

'He was all right. I'm sorry about what's happened to him.' Julie's mouth trembled. Purbright thought she was chiefly upset by the looming so near of the fearsomeness of death, but there was some pity there too, some regret.

Of the four other girls who worked at the supermarket, only one was able, or inclined, to say about her late employer anything that might be a clue to the circumstances of his death. She was an eighteen-year-old cashier, Doris Periam, and she told the inspector of having seen Mr Persimmon's car being driven along Priorgate fairly late on the previous Wednesday night.

'How late?'

'It had gone twelve. A friend was taking me home. I live in Moss Road and it was half-past when I got in.'

'You know Mr Persimmon's car, do you?'

'Oh, yes. It's a big powder-blue thing.'

'Why did you notice it especially that night?'

'Well, there wasn't much about. And then, this car went by. It was going ever so fast. I thought it would turn over at that bend into Marshside Road. It just scraped round, though. And my friend said look at that something fool. And I said it can't be, yes it is, it's my boss. Because I could see the car and the colour and everything in the light of that lamp outside Morrison's. And my friend said he must be drunk, but I said no, not Mr Persimmon, he never touches it. I thought it was ever so funny, though, him driving like that.'

During the few minutes it took him to walk back to the police station in Fen Street, Purbright pondered the behaviour and the route of Persimmon. Haste was uncommon enough in Flaxborough to be noticed at once, even by a courting cashier, and Persimmon must have been in an uncharacteristically rash frame of mind that night to use Priorgate as a speedway. He certainly was not drunk at the time, if, as seemed likely, he had met his death within the next few hours. No trace of alcohol had been revealed at autopsy. So why the erratic driving?

There was no doubt of where he had been going. Marshside Road, the continuation of Priorgate, led only to Orchard Road. And there, presumably by arrangement, waited his mistress, Edna Hillyard, in the privacy of her little tree-screened car.

But even at that time there must have been people about. The folk-dancing affair had gone on 'pretty late' according to Mrs Gloss. Both Persimmon and Edna had always taken good care – unusual care, in her case – to keep their meetings secret. Why, then, choose for an assignation the grounds of a house where characters had been prancing around at large all evening? Persimmon's car, it seemed, was readily identifiable. And as a local store manager, he himself would be familiar to the sort of middle-aged, middle-class women likely to join a folklore society.

Then – and Purbright reproached himself for having accepted at first an explanation more convenient than convincing – there was the point about the girl's neatly stacked clothes. Had she really had the forethought to set out that evening equipped with a duplicate set of clothing to put on after the revels? And if so, what had she carried it in? There was no suitcase in the car – not even a box or wrapping.

Julie's evidence concerning the phone call, examined beside what little was certain about Persimmon's movements on that Wednesday, should have suggested some line of inquiry. It must, after all, have had relevance – perhaps vital relevance – to whatever course and commitments were to lead Persimmon to his death. And yet those overheard fragments of conversation remained, however diligently Purbright sorted and examined them in his mind, as unilluminating as they must have been to the girl who had recorded them.

' "Dilly",' the inspector said to Love the moment he encountered him emerging from the side entrance of the police station.

Love halted and looked politely attentive.

'Supposing,' Purbright said, 'you had heard somebody referred to as "Dilly", who would you think was meant?'

The sergeant pondered.

'I think I've heard young women called dillies. It's supposed to mean that they're a bit of all right.'

'No, I don't want the generic application, Sid. What about nicknames? Is it an abbreviation for something?'

'Ducks are dillies,' announced Love after further consideration. 'Somebody short in the leg, maybe?'

Purbright looked unimpressed. 'Never mind.'

Love, brightening as at the recollection of an agreeable piece of tidings temporarily eclipsed by duller matters, said: 'Harry Bird's had a spell put on him.'

Purbright closed his eyes for an instant.

'He's what?'

'It sounds like that parish church business over again. One of the newspaper people came in looking for you. He said somebody's cut a black cockerel in two and nailed both bits to Bird's front door. I was just going to drive over and have a dekko.'

'Which reporter told you this?'

'The one with fangs. I think he said he was from the *Daily Sketch*.'

'And how did *he* know what had been nailed to Bird's front door?'

'He said they'd had a tip-off.'

Purbright was silent for some moments. Then he motioned Love to follow him into the yard where his car was parked.

'I think I'll have a dekko myself while we're about it. Incidentally, Sid, have you noticed what a lot of tipping-off there's been lately? Anxiety to oblige is something I don't much care to see in this town. It's usually a sign of conspiracy.'

Sir Henry Bird was the head of a firm of agricultural machinery manufacturers. His knighthood had been conferred only the previous autumn. He thereupon had moved out of 14 Birtley Avenue and into a big double-fronted house with pink stucco walls and false turrets behind one of the high hedges bordering Oakland, a cul-de-sac that ran parallel to The Riding, off Partney Drive.

Purbright and Love got out of the police car just in time to see a kneeling woman in a flowered overall wring out a cloth and vigorously rub the central panel of the front door. The water in the bucket beside her was slightly stained. A few black waterlogged feathers revolved slowly.

The woman glanced over her shoulder and got up, laboriously.

'Not more of you, surely?'

'Is Sir Henry in?'

'He's not seeing anybody else.'

Purbright said that they were policemen and that he was sure Sir Henry would have no objection to their going in to see him.

'I thought you was from the papers,' the woman said, grudgingly converted. She picked up the bucket and trailed off round the side of the house.

A little puff of pride distended the cheek of mistaken-for-a-journalist Love. He stroked the case of the portable tape recorder that hung from his shoulder.

Purbright bent and examined the step. The woman had missed two or three spots of blood, now dry and glistening like black varnish.

The door opened.

'Mr Bird says you can come in. He's in the front room.'

The chairman of Autocult (Flaxborough) Limited amplified this instruction by calling out: 'In here, Purbright. In the lounge.' He made the word sound long and squeezy and expensive. Purbright was prepared for red plush and Renoir reproductions.

In fact, the atmosphere they entered was cool and at first seemed restfully dim. But soon the eyes tired of the kind of light diffused by the long yellow muslin curtains that were draped and looped and re-looped with fussy precision over the entire window area, light that after a while made everything in the room look to be made of butter.

'To what,' asked Sir Henry, 'do we owe the pleasure of a visit from the constabulary?'

The voice, affable and with a pronounced smoker's rasp, was in keeping with the florid well-fleshed face. What Purbright found unfailingly fascinating about the man, though, was his ears. They were very small – no bigger than dried apricots and of similar colour – and set so snugly within corresponding recesses that only at close quarters could they be discerned at all.

Purbright explained that a report of damage to Sir Henry's property had reached him. 'Or defacement,' he qualified.

'Aren't there more serious matters to keep you people busy just now?'

Sir Henry's eyebrows, whose conspicuousness more than made up for his curious auricular deficiency, hunched like combatant caterpillars, challenging each other across the bridge of his nose.

'Serious, yes, sir. But not necessarily unrelated.'

Bird watched without comment the adjustments that Love was making to the tape recorder, which now was switched on.

'This defacement, as you call it. You know what happened, do you?'

'According to what little information I have, a mutilated chicken was left hanging on your front door.'

'A cockerel, Purbright. The distinction does matter, you know. A black cockerel.'

'Exactly, sir.'

'You sound as if you know something about black cockerels.'

'By repute, yes.'

'Ah, by repute, Purbright. Tell me, now, what is your understanding of this matter of black cockerels?'

The caterpillar-brows of Sir Henry reared to denote a sort of fierce interrogatory amusement. The inspector saw that 'Knocker' Bird, as he once had been known in the town, and still was by some of his contemporaries, was in a mood to make him feel small. The press, no doubt, had been troublesome. Purbright resolved to make allowances.

'It isn't a subject I know much about, sir,' he replied, 'apart from stories of black magic and that sort of thing.'

'Voodoo,' prompted Love, with a surreptitious nudge.

'You don't seem all that impressed, inspector. I did wonder when I read some of the Sunday newspapers. They depicted you as tolerant to the point of indifference.'

'Indeed, sir?'

'What are you proposing to do about this bit of foolery at my front door?'

'In the first place – and with your help, I hope, sir – to establish whether it was just foolery or something more serious.'

'You didn't *have* to come traipsing over here, you know, Purbright. I didn't send for you. Now why don't you be a good fellow and run along. The mess is cleaned up. If the papers want to make a silly song and dance about it, that's their business. So far as I'm concerned, the incident is over.'

'That is what you told the press, is it, sir?'

Sir Henry laughed. 'Yes, but in much more forthright terms, believe me.'

It was the laugh – a controlled, fruity chuckle which suddenly skidded into falsetto – that confirmed Purbright's suspicion. Bird had been frightened, and quite badly. Was it by the sudden prospect of publicity? As deputy chairman of the Bench, he had suffered, or enjoyed more likely, enough newspaper quotes to have broken his coyness in that respect. In any case, his reputation both in business and more recently in public life was that of an extrovert, a pusher.

'Well, we'll leave that for the moment, Sir Henry. It wasn't the only reason for my coming to see you. I've been wanting to ask you about a certain charity organization.'

Bird stared. He half rose from his chair.

'Now, look, Purbright, I realize you're not a chap who rushes round with a harassed expression all the time, but aren't you supposed to be in charge of this Persimmon business?'

'That is so, sir.'

'Yet you have time to trot over here to investigate a mutilated chicken – no, your words, Purbright – mutilated chicken – and when I laugh off that one, as you should have done in the first place, you start chatting about charities.'

'Perhaps I chose an inapt phrase,' Purbright conceded patiently. 'It was what I judged to have been meant by Mrs Persimmon when she spoke of her late husband's "samaritan nights". She named you, Sir Henry, as one of his associates on these occasions.'

Bird said nothing for a while. He gazed unseeingly towards an alabaster nude preening herself on the big, white-painted overmantel. A sheet of cellophane, strapped round the figure to protect it from dust, glistened wetly in the room's ochre twilight.

'Have you had words with the vicar?'

The quality of Bird's voice had undergone a radical change. It was quiet and earnest and free of the half-mocking, half-accusing tone he had employed before.

'Not on this subject specifically, no, sir. He did call to see me on Friday, but about something else.'

'About what he'd found in the church, you mean.'

'Yes.'

'That,' Bird said gravely, 'wasn't "something else", Purbright. All these events have a common cause, as I think you are beginning to realize. There are forces at work in this town – highly dangerous forces – which can't simply be arrested and locked up. They have been operating under the surface for a long time.'

Bird got up and crossed to the window. He stood staring out through the muslin folds. In profile, the chin was virtually non-existent. His head at that moment seemed to Purbright to be a round, yellow globe, featureless as a turnip.

'You say you've not mentioned the watchnights to the vicar.'

Bird turned and the turnip had a mouth again, and a nose, and eyes caved beneath those anxiously contracted bundles of hair.

'Watchnights? I'm sorry, I don't think I know what you mean, sir.'

Bird made an abrupt, dismissive gesture. 'No, never mind. I'll explain. You'll have to know, obviously. But not until I've spoken to Grewyear. That would be quite wrong.'

He left the room at once, closing the door behind him. The policemen heard the sharp ting that signalled the lifting of a phone.

On his return, Bird made no reference to his conversation with the Vicar but his manner suggested that Grewyear had sanctioned whatever he was about to say.

'About a year or eighteen months ago,' began Bird, 'some rather queer reports started to come in to a little social welfare set-up that a couple of friends and I had been running in our spare time. It was a sort of moral advice thing – you know what I mean? Quite unofficial, but with connections. Cropper, for instance – he's in the right job to know about problem families and so on. I'm on the

Bench and a few committees. Grewyear – well, his value is obvious. And poor old Persimmon had his Boy Scout and Home Mission contacts.

'The first strange story that came to us was told by a woman who claimed that an animal of some kind kept clattering about on the roof at night and pawing at the tiles just above her bed. When she looked up from the street, there was nothing there. She was a widow and lived alone. One morning, she woke up parched with thirst and hardly able to breathe. The space in the bed beside her was hot, she said – not just warm but hot – and she saw hairs on the sheet, rough and wiry, like a goat's hairs. Know what I mean?

'Then a young girl brought us something she said she kept finding on the floor in various rooms at home, no matter how often she threw it away outside or even burned it on the kitchen fire. It was a rough figure made out of straw. We knew what it was, but we didn't tell her. It was a Hugger-doll. The tale goes that if this thing isn't discovered during daylight, its maker will be able to take its place after dark and do what he wants – you know what I'm getting at, don't you? – to anyone in that house – kill them, even – without fear of discovery.

'I could go on, but those two first cases were fairly typical. Some of the people who came to us were absolutely frantic. They thought they'd seen the devil, or were dying of some illness their doctors couldn't discover, or had been possessed – and I mean *physically* possessed, you understand, in the sense of being ravished, coupled with, inseminated – you know what I mean? – by creatures not human. There were others who complained of mysterious infestation of their houses or their bodies – particularly their secret parts – you know what I mean? – by hordes of strange insects that disappeared when doctors or health inspectors were called.'

Bird had been leaning further and further forward in his chair as his story progressed. Now he paused and sat back.

'You see what we were up against, don't you? Oh, we didn't believe it at first, any more than you would have done. Or a doctor. Or a lawyer. Of course, Grewyear had to pretend to. Not that he actually did any interviewing of these people himself. It was understood from the beginning that the rest of us would constitute a sort of auxiliary – you know what I mean? – to leave him free to get on with his regular parish duties. We passed on the details, though, so that he could advise. And in the end, none of us had any doubts at all any more.

'Do you know what we were doing? We were fighting a battle, Purbright, a battle with evil. Right here in this town. Make no mistake about that.

'Forces had gained hold in Flaxborough that would have corrupted and then devoured it. You think that's a melodramatic way for an experienced business man and a magistrate to talk, don't you? All right. But I tell you this. If there's such a thing as the mark of the devil, I've certainly seen it in Flaxborough. And not just once or twice.'

Chapter Twelve

LUCY-PROBATIONER BARBARA 'BUBBLES' WESTMACOTT was feeling inspired and ambitious. She had been permitted, together with four other junior members of the team, to watch some of the re-making of the Lucillite campaign film and so splendidly had the occasion gone off – with lots of absolutely spontaneous Ooo's from the washwives, quips and grins galore from Hughie, and a spell-binding imitation by boatmen Heath of Long John Silver – that she had set herself to convert eleven households (eleven was her lucky number) to whiter, and therefore more joyous, living that very day.

'If Lucillite is in your home, I've brought good news from Dixon-Frome.'

Miss Westmacott, spruce and plump and engaging in her fractionally too tight uniform, smiled confidently at the old lady who had opened the door of the pretty little bungalow.

'Eh?'

Miss Westmacott repeated her incantation.

Nutcracker jaws champed four or five times while the white plastic tunic was submitted to slow and dubious scrutiny by eyes like mildewed bilberries.

'You from the chiroppy?'

'I beg your pardon?'

'Come to do me feet, 'ave yer?'

'Oh, no, I'm not a chiropodist. I am here to show you how to get a white wash.'

With speed almost incredible in one so frail, the old lady snaked back behind the shelter of the door and slammed it shut.

'There's a Gift!' cried Miss Westmacott, as mellifluously as she could manage in the discouraging circumstances.

From behind the door came an angry and very brusque retort. It sounded, curiously enough, like Russian. Then, in English, the girl heard that she was to tell them dratted council lot to bloody well get a bath themselves and stop bloody pesterin'.

Barbara sighed and conscientiously put a cross on her progress analysis chart in one of the squares marked 'consumer resistance'.

She went up the path between the lawns of bright green not-to-be-walked-on turf, and rang the bell of the next bungalow.

After some delay, it was opened generously and suddenly by a woman five feet tall and two feet thick all the way down. The hat of her butcher-blue uniform looked like a chopping block with a brim. Sticking out at one side of the hat was a big amber bead. Diametrically opposite there emerged an inch of steel point. Barbara tried with some bewilderment to decide whether the woman had an uncommonly flat head or a cranium insensitive to the passage of hat pins. 'Yes?'

'If Lucillite is . . .'

The girl faltered, having grasped belatedly that the woman was a visiting nurse and not the householder.

'It's all right,' she said, turning away.

'Here, I hope you're not selling things,' said the woman, sternly. 'Not in Twilight Close.'

'No. Oh, no.'

Barbara gave the next bungalow a miss, just in case the nurse was still watching. She turned a corner past a row of symmetrical tame-looking almond trees, and walked up the path to a dwelling similar to all the others except that there came from its half-open door waves of pop music from a turned high radio.

The girl felt encouraged. She let her shoulders and hips rock gently in time with the pop and drummed her fingers on the white plastic satchel while she awaited a response to her ring.

It was not long in coming.

The prolonged stare of astonishment melting into delight that the girl received from Mr Herbert Stamper, one-time farmer of Flaxborough Fen, would have warned a more worldly caller to make some quick excuse and depart.

But Miss Westmacott's head was too tightly packed with her dream of the Dixon-Frome Golden Merit Medal to notice, let alone interpret, a look that in its time had made even goats bolt for cover.

'If Lucillite is in your home, I've brought good news from Dixon-Frome!'

''Ave ye, be-Christ!' gruffled Mr Stamper, his regard ranging appreciatively from hock to haunch.

The Lucy accepted this as a token of understanding.

'Do you have the three packets, then?' she inquired. 'They can be empty or full – it doesn't matter.'

Mr Stamper scratched one ear (Barbara decided, on thinking about it later, that it was the only time she had actually *heard* anyone do this) and made a remark about 'three bags full' at which he shuddered with merriment for more than half a minute.

Then, abruptly, he indicated with a jerk of his head the interior of his bungalow.

What vestige of self-preservative instinct had survived a Dixon-Frome Product Loyalty Course prompted the girl to hesitate.

'Your wife ... shall I find her in the kitchen?'

Mr Stamper made a noise she took to signify assent.

She walked primly past him into a passage-way that smelled of paraffin and raspberry jam. He left the front door open long enough to admit daylight while he admired Miss Westmacott's hind quarters and calculated the best approach for a serving throw.

*

Sir Henry Bird had suspended his narrative while he fetched whisky for Purbright and himself, and on the sergeant's insistence that he would prefer it, a glass of orange cordial for Love.

'Am I right,' Purbright asked, 'in thinking that this small group that had been formed eventually became concerned solely with – what shall I say? – with apparently supernatural occurrences?'

Bird stared into his glass and pouted. 'I'd just like to qualify that a little,' he said. 'You make it sound as if we were investigators. There was nothing detached about our attitude. To help these people – to rescue them, if we could – that was our object.

'Of course, we didn't pretend to have any scientific training. But we discussed and we read and we kept our eyes open. And by the end of our first year's working we had noticed something very peculiar. Do you know what it was? I'll tell you. It was something to do with dates.

'We noticed that nearly all the most horrible incidents that people described to us had taken place about the same time – or at least during the same period. There would be a whole crop of these happenings, all within a few hours, all during darkness. Then nothing – nothing serious, anyway – for weeks. And then, off it would go again. Another night of poor creatures being tormented in the most dreadful, filthy ways. You know what I mean?'

'Not precisely, sir,' said the inspector.

'Beastliness, Purbright. Beastliness. Quite indescribable.'

'Yes, sir. And these dates?'

Bird looked him in the eye. 'The second of February, the last day of April, August the first, and the thirty-first of October.'

Purbright considered. He shook his head.

'You don't recognize them?'

'I can't say that I grasp their special significance.' Purbright turned to Love. 'Do you, sergeant?'

'One's Mischief Night,' Love declared. 'I know that.'

For the first time Bird's face registered a flicker of amusement.

'That is what children call it. A much older name is the Eve of Hallowtide. Last day of October. Let me identify the others. February the second, Candlemas. The first of August, Lammas. And perhaps the most sinister of all – the thirtieth day of April.

That's May Day Eve.

'Now then, inspector, you see what I'm getting at, don't you?'

'I think so, sir. You mean that these dates are all associated with a belief in magic.'

Bird regarded him for several seconds.

'No, Purbright, I mean a lot more than that. I mean that the times of the year when evil is let loose upon this town in a very special and terrifying way are the ancient festivals of witchcraft. They are the nights of the great Sabbaths.'

There was a long pause.

'Do you believe in witchcraft, sir?'

Another silence, but shorter.

'Let me put it this way. I believe in the *belief* in witchcraft. And I believe in the effects it has had. Because' – Bird's normally rich-toned voice rose, as it was apt to do either when he was nervous or when he asserted something with special emphasis, to a momentary treble – 'I have *seen* them. We have all seen them, all three of us on this little vigilante committee of ours. Do you suppose me gullible? Or Dr Cropper? An important council official? Or a businessman like poor old Persimmon? I tell you we acted on evidence, Purbright, not on superstition.'

'I accept that, of course, sir. But I cannot yet quite see in what way you and your colleagues were able to help these people. I would have thought that exorcism or something in that line was indicated.'

'It is, sometimes. There is nothing wrong with incantation, Purbright, provided it works.

'Be that as it may, though, the first thing you have to do if you want to help people in trouble is to be *available*. You see what I mean? So this is what we did. Grewyear let us have a little room at the back of the church hall. We had the phone put in and we gave the number of that phone to everyone who knew about our work and might hear of cases. Cases – that's what we called them, you see? In the Middle Ages, they would have been described simply as "bewitched", of course, but that won't do now.

'So . . .' Sir Henry shrugged, spread his hands, and directed a look of hospitable inquiry at the policemen's drinks. 'There you have the truth about what Mary Persimmon called poor Bertram's "samaritan" nights. Watchnights are what they were, Purbright. Or vigils, if you like.'

The inspector declined a whisky refill, but remained sitting silent as if in expectation of the climax to the story.

Bird seemed to have nothing more to say.

Purbright prompted him.

'The dates of these watchnights ...'

'I told you, inspector. Your man can produce them again on his machine, can't he?'

'I know *those* dates,' said Purbright. 'But I presume there were others.'

'Certainly. Those were the vital ones, though, the productive ones. We met on other occasions, of course, but not to remain on call throughout the night.'

'Is that what you did – all three of you – on what you called the Sabbath nights?'

'Invariably.'

'And if there was a call, sir?'

'We gave what reassurance or advice we could. It seemed sufficient in some cases. Not in all. Whenever we believed the caller to be in real and immediate danger, one of us went over at once.'

'Last Wednesday night, sir ...'

Bird looked up, attentive. 'Yes?'

'It was the thirtieth of April. What you called May Day Eve.'

'It was, yes.'

'Did you and the other gentlemen undertake your stand-by duties at the Church Hall that night?'

'Certainly we did. And I'm well aware of what you're going to ask next, Purbright.'

Bird busied himself with the flat silver cigarette box on the little table by his chair. The lighter he used was yellow, presumably gold-plated. As an afterthought, he pushed the box towards the inspector, who shook his head.

'Sir Henry, surely, as a magistrate ...'

Bird held up his hand. 'All right. I know. Bert's death. You think I should have got in touch with you earlier. I did consider having a word with Chubb, as a matter of fact, but the situation's so delicate. Quite frankly, I didn't think he'd understand.'

'Why, sir?'

'Well, good heavens – witchcraft! Can you imagine your chief constable's reaction to that sort of suggestion?'

Love, who could, turned his face aside and smirked.

'Perhaps,' Purbright said coolly, 'we'd better try now to make up for lost time, sir. First of all, how long did Mr Persimmon remain with you and Dr Cropper?'

'From about nine o'clock until, oh, shortly after midnight.'

'You were together in the room in the church hall.'

'That's so.'

'Were there any telephone calls?'

Bird thought. 'Three. And then this one just about midnight.'

'Would you care to tell me the names of the first three callers, sir?'

'I'm sorry, that's quite impossible.'

'You don't know them?'

'I cannot divulge them. They were people in distress who had been promised secrecy. You must see that I am in exactly the same position as a doctor or a priest.'

'Can you tell me what *kind* of trouble the calls referred to? Was Mr Persimmon involved in any way?'

'They had nothing to do with him. He didn't even take one. Cropper and I dealt with all three. As I remember, they were similar. Mild cases of possession. A lot of sex mixed in, of course. You know what I mean?'

'People you knew, sir?'

'*Cases* I knew, Purbright.'

The inspector nodded, as if satisfied.

'Now maybe you'd be good enough to tell me the call that Mr Persimmon *did* take, sir.'

'I can't tell you anything about it. I don't know anything.'

'Look, sir, I'm sorry, but this time I must insist.'

'Insist all you like. I just cannot help you. And this time it is not a case of respecting confidences. The phone rang – at about midnight, as I told you – and Persimmon answered it. He listened, not saying a word himself, and then slammed the phone down and rushed out straight away. We both heard his car start off and that was that. He didn't come back.'

'Did he say nothing when he was leaving? Nothing at all?'

'Not a word.'

'Presumably he knew who the caller was?'

'I suppose so.'

'Was it a man or woman, sir?'

'I've no idea.'

'But it would be fairly quiet at that time. And one can generally catch the tone, at least, of somebody's voice coming over a phone in the same room.'

'Not when Bert was listening, poor devil,' Bird said. 'He had an odd habit of holding a telephone tight against his ear.'

'A secretive man?'

'In some way, yes, decidedly.'

'But not, would you say, sir, a guilt-ridden one?'

Bird took some seconds to reply.

'I have,' he said hesitantly, 'wondered sometimes about that. Only wondered, mind you.' He quickly finished his drink and set down the glass. 'You know what I mean?'

The Lucy-probationer who, in her enthusiasm, had strayed off scheduled territory into the municipal bungalow settlement of Twilight Close, made two discoveries in quick succession.

The first was that if Mr Stamper had a wife he kept her neither in his kitchen nor anywhere else within calling distance. The second and much more welcome discovery was of the remarkable elusiveness of her plastic costume in the grip of a Senior Citizen.

Miss Westmacott backed into a recess between the sink and the refrigerator. Her hands were behind her, against the wall.

'Whoaa . . . come up, there!' cried Mr Stamper. He made a grab for her withers. She bobbed down and at the same time thrust herself away from the wall. Her head collided with Mr Stamper's stomach.

When he had recovered breath, he clicked his teeth good-naturedly and followed her into the passage. She was trying to open the front door.

Mr Stamper copiously licked both hands, rubbed them on the seams of his trousers, and lumbered towards her.

She turned and swung her satchel at the same time.

Against the side of Mr Stamper's head there landed the combined weight of 450 forms of entry to the Lucillite 'Win-a-Paradise-Island' competition and three one-gross packs of Scintillometers.

For a moment he remained inert, one glazed eye only six inches from Miss Westmacott's coveted forequarters. Then he began to slide down the wall – quite happily, as she judged from his smile – and subsided in folds upon the floor. She stepped over him carefully and hurried back to the kitchen.

The key was in the farther door. She turned it.

From the passage came a grunt, then a chuckle. She glanced back. Already Mr Stamper was hauling himself upright. He waved cheerily and made groom-like noises of enticement.

The girl pulled open the door and ran into the garden beyond.

'Whooaa there!' cried Mr Stamper. 'Coom 'ere and git mounted, theer's a good gel!'

Miss Westmacott looked about her. The garden was flanked on two sides by a high fence of woven osiers. At the bottom of the garden was a wall. The only way of reaching the road by which she had arrived was to go back through the house.

'Whooaa-back, gel!'

She sprinted over the patch of lawn and across vegetable beds neatly staked and strung to keep birds off their rows of sprouting seeds, plunged through a tangle of spear-grass and dead thistle, and with a leap and a scramble reached the top of the wall.

The wall continued for some distance in each direction, forming part of the boundary to the Close. Below her lay concrete, cracked and ruptured by weeds growing through it. The concrete extended for fifty yards or more, as far as a second wall. There were two buildings within this silent and seemingly derelict area.

The girl gave a backward glance at her thwarted pursuer and jumped lightly down.

She walked towards the nearer building.

It was tall but of only one storey, made of cement-faced brick and quite plain in design. At one corner a plant with long leaves and little red flowers had sprouted from the edge of the flat roof. Most of the panes in the big steel-framed windows had been smashed.

Barbara raised herself on tip-toes and looked in. It was like peeping into a den filled with petrified mammoths. She glimpsed vast jaws and beaks of steel, dulling over with rust. The place was a store for snow-clearing machinery.

As the girl turned away, there registered on the very edge of her consciousness a slight movement. She looked at once towards where she could not help fancying that something odd, something out of place, had happened while her attention had been on the ploughs and bulldozer blades.

All she could see was the grey wall of the other building in the depot, blank save for green and brown streaks of moss and lichen and a small blind-looking window about twenty feet above the ground.

Towards this window she gave an occasional glance while she made her way to a gate in the depot wall that rounding the plough store had revealed.

The gate was padlocked. The wall on either side was a good foot taller than the one she had climbed to escape from Twilight Close. From the farther side came the sound of a passing car.

She tugged and rattled the padlock, then brushed her hands with her handkerchief and patiently turned away. There would, no doubt, be another way out.

The window, though. Something was hanging from it. That must be what she had glimpsed before. A white arm, listlessly swinging from the elbow. Just the arm – forearm, rather – hand and forearm – swinging limply.

But how extraordinarily white it was.

Impelled partly by a practical intention to ask advice in her predicament, but chiefly by curiosity tinged with unease, Barbara crossed the yard and stood beneath the window. She looked up.

'Excuse me,' she called, and waited.

There came no sign that she had been heard. The hand above her continued to hang motionless.

Half a minute went by.

'I say!'

The sound echoed from wall to wall. Watching – anxiously now – Barbara thought she saw the chalk-white fingers twitch.

She called again.

'I say – are you all right?'

This time the hand moved perceptibly. But its motion was aimless, weary.

Barbara shouted. She hurried round to the second side of the building.

Almost its entire width was filled by a set of corrugated shutters. They looked the kind that could be unlocked at the bottom and rolled up to disclose a garage. The girl stopped only to pound on them with her fists. Then she ran on, grasping the next corner to swing herself round.

Level with her head was a window, or at least the rusting steel latticework that once had held twenty or thirty panes of glass. Fragments of glass, thickly begrimed, lay amongst rubble on the ground. They crunched under her feet.

She looked through the lattice and saw that this end of the ground floor of the building was, as she had supposed, a garage. What she had not expected to see, though, was the big, blue, new-looking car that it contained.

The building's only door was at the top of a flight of five concrete steps. It was a plain door, painted dark green, and it had no handle, just a keyhole.

The girl had only to look at it to know that it was locked and that nothing she was capable of doing would open it, but she pushed and kicked it nevertheless.

Then she ran as fast as she could towards a part of the border wall of Twilight Close that she judged to be well clear of Mr Stamper's territory.

Inspector Purbright had only just returned to his office when a message was relayed to him from Constable Palethorp, the driver of the patrol car which had been sent in response to Miss West-macott's 999 call.

He left again at once.

Joining the sluggish tide of traffic along East Street, he drove into the Market Place, over the Town Bridge, and diagonally across Burton Place into Leicester Avenue, at the far end of which was the old Corporation depot.

The journey took him exactly eighteen minutes, which was not bad going. Patience had paid off, as usual. No Flaxborough police-man ever dreamed of using a siren: he knew it would simply dam up the road ahead with inquisitive citizenry.

The depot gate stood open, its padlock having been levered off by Constable Palethorp.

With the aid of an ambulance man, he had also breached the green door that had defeated Miss Westmacott.

Purbright climbed the straight wooden staircase that led from the room behind the garage – it appeared to have been a workshop at one time – to the upper floor.

Palethorp awaited him in a bare loft-like chamber, at the far end of which was a low doorway. Palethorp stooped and went through. The inspector followed.

There was barely room for the two men in the tiny enclosure. The air was hot and foetid above the floor. Paper sacks were strewn over the boards. Some were streaked with what Purbright surmised to be dried vomit. A thick glass tumbler had rolled away into a corner.

Purbright spoke very quietly, as if he was anxious not to be overheard.

'How do you think she'll make out?'

Palethorp shrugged, saying nothing.

'What did she look like?'

'Bloody terrible, sir.'

'She hadn't been attacked, though, had she?'

'No, I don't think so. Not in any obvious way, that is.'

Purbright looked about the compartment, taking care to avoid disturbing what little it contained.

'I'll get over to the hospital. You can leave as soon as Harper and the others arrive with their stuff.'

Down in the yard, Purbright glanced through the window at the garaged car before getting into his own.

'Thank you,' he said to Palethorp as he drove off.

Palethorp, watching his departure, looked faintly puzzled.

Against the white linen of the hospital pillow, Edna Hillyard's face showed up as yellowish grey. The skin shone with a thin dew of sweat.

Dr Palmaj, house physician, caressed the girl's wrist experimentally, one lean finger seeking the pulse.

'We are fortunate that this is a strong woman. It is her good fortune, too, of course.'

Purbright said, 'She looks very ill.'

'Not fatally, I am sure, inspector. Unless a pneumonia develops, she should recover in a week or two.'

'Are you able yet to say what is wrong with her?'

Dr Palmaj gently released the girl's hand and straightened the coverlet. The letters F G H were embroidered on its edge in red cotton.

'Exposure effects, mainly.' He looked up at Purbright. 'She was quite naked, you know, when that policeman found her. Did you know that?'

'Yes. Although in fact there was a blanket there, I understand. A travelling rug, rather. He put it round her.'

There was a pause. Then Purbright asked: 'What had she been given?'

'That is hard to say, inspector. Barbiturates, I should imagine. And in quite big quantities. Stupid quantities.'

'By mouth?'

'Oh yes. There is no sign of injection.'

'There would have had to be persuasion, then. It is very difficult to force anyone to swallow things, isn't it, doctor?'

'That is true. But a person who is confused or sleepy or very, very unhappy seldom offers much resistance.'

'Not even when the object is murder?'

The houseman looked startled.

'So that is what you believe? Oh, but surely, inspector ...'

'You didn't suppose she had been taking drugs herself, did you?'

'Taking them herself – well, perhaps. But not *by* herself. I spoke just now of stupid quantities, did I not. I was thinking in terms of drug taking for self-gratification. In seclusion naturally, but in company. The sexual element, you understand – always that. In my experience. But such people handle these things absolutely without a normal sense of caution. You will yourself know how common is the overdose in such cases.'

They had been moving slowly away from the bed in the small white room with its glass-panelled walls. At the door, Purbright asked:

'Has she said anything that made sense to you?'

'No, no. Words – half words – quite unintelligible.'

'A policewoman is coming over. You would have no objection to her sitting here?'

'Certainly not. But I think it rather unlikely that this woman will have much to tell. Her remembering may be much damaged.'

Dr Palmaj turned the handle of the door and stood aside in readiness for the inspector to leave in front of him. Then, suddenly, he took away his hand and patted his forehead in self-reproof.

'My remembering, too, is not what it ought to be, inspector. Come.'

He stepped back to the foot of the bed.

'Something very strange is here. I shall be most interested to know what you think about it.'

Purbright watched the doctor deftly untuck blankets and sheet and raise them just sufficiently to disclose the feet of the unconscious girl.

Tatooed in blueish-black on the sole of the left foot was a carefully-executed cross.

Chapter Thirteen

IN AN IDEAL WORLD, IT WOULD HAVE BEEN ENOUGH FOR Purbright to set a couple of men in secret occupation of the building in which Edna Hillyard had been found, in order to intercept a return visit by her abductor, who, it seemed reasonable to suppose, was also the murderer of Bertram Persimmon, and thus to bring him to justice.

But the success of so simple a plan would have depended on the continued ignorance of the population at large, murderer included, of the fact that Miss Hillyard was safely tucked up in a bed of Flaxborough General Hospital.

And on that Purbright knew better than to place any reliance whatsoever.

Feeling a little like Macbeth, he called upon the secretary of the Edith Cavell Psychical Research Foundation.

Miss Teatime welcomed him warmly and said what a long time it seemed since their last meeting. The loss, Purbright assured her, had been his entirely.

With which pleasantries they ascended the little staircase in Church Close and entered Miss Teatime's sitting room.

'I have come to seek your expert opinion,' said Purbright. He stretched back in the chair facing the window and gazed appreciatively at the view of St Lawrence's.

'How very nice of you.' Miss Teatime dexterously transposed a bottle of whisky from the mantelpiece into a Victorian workbasket.

'What does it mean when somebody has a cross tattooed on the sole of his foot?'

Miss Teatime paused in the action of bringing forward a cushioned cane chair and glanced sharply at the inspector.

'Dear me . . .' She sat down. 'You *have* been moving in peculiar circles, Mr Purbright.'

'So it seems.'

'Tell me, what kind of a cross do you have in mind? Can you describe its shape?'

'An ordinary, straight-forward cross, I suppose. Not the sort one votes with. Certainly not a swastika, either. Here ...' He made a quick sketch on an envelope.

'That,' Miss Teatime informed him, 'is what is known as a Latin cross. It is the ecclesiastical variety and if you have found it upon the sole of someone's foot the probability is that he or she is a practitioner of black magic. Or, more likely, a would-be practitioner.'

'I take it that you are sceptical on the subject.'

'Witchcraft is terribly unscientific, inspector. And very messy. But simply to dismiss it as superstition is to evade an important question. What is the nature of the Force that some dabblers in the so-called black arts have undoubtedly encountered and afterwards – quite spuriously, let me say – claimed credit for unleashing?'

'Do *you* know, Miss Teatime?'

She gave a smile of quiet reserve. 'You did not come here, I am sure, inspector, for a lecture on psycho-thermal kinetics.'

'This cross ...'

'Ah, yes. The cross. Let me see if I can tell you more. This is part of what I term the messy side of witchcraft. The fart-in-the-font department, I regret my old anthropology professor used to call it. To walk constantly upon a religious symbol, you see, is supposed to be very daring and diabolical. Only really dedicated devil-worshippers have the operation done. Well, it must tickle unbearably.'

Purbright smiled. He was silent for a moment, then asked:

'Has your research led you to the discovery of any specific instances of this kind of thing in Flaxborough? I don't need to tell you that the press has been almost embarrassingly successful in turning the town into another Salem.'

'Yes, I had noticed,' Miss Teatime said acidly.

Almost at once her helpful manner returned.

'As for investigation, it is like everything else – a matter of funds. Some research bodies are fortunate in being retained in an advisory capacity by public authorities.'

'Indeed?'

There was a slight pause.

'Others, of course, have been able to help on the understanding that the expense entailed would not need to be met out of their own funds.'

The inspector pursed his lips. 'Not an unreasonable arrangement, I should have thought.'

Miss Teatime's prim but friendly smile signalled him to speak his mind.

'My interest,' he began, 'is centred upon what you have called the messy side of witchcraft and the people in this town who go in for it. I see no point in trying to conceal from your – what is the phrase? – extra-sensory perception? – the fact that there is a distinctly black magic smell about the death of this supermarket manager ...'

'Ah, yes. Poor Mr Persimmon.'

Purbright raised his brow. 'You knew him?'

'Not in any very personal sense. Our little organization was able to help him on one occasion when his store was being subjected to paranormal activity of quite high polterage. But please go on, inspector.'

'Another thing you might as well know, although I must ask you to keep it strictly to yourself at this stage, concerns the cross I questioned you about earlier. The person who wears it – if that's the appropriate verb – is the young woman who disappeared last Wednesday and who has now been found.'

'Alive?' The question was urged, rather than asked.

'Oh, yes. Alive.'

Miss Teatime nodded. She looked relieved.

'Furthermore,' Purbright went on, 'the story is now being told us, and not by hysterical or credulous people but by certain pretty solid citizens, that cases of diabolism were getting so serious a problem some time ago that a sort of body and soul rescue service was set up. Did you know that?'

'No, but I am not altogether surprised. Amateurism does tend to flourish in a place like this.'

'I should rather like to know, Miss Teatime, the names of some of our amateur satanists. In the strictist confidence, needless to say.'

Dreamily, Miss Teatime regarded the ancient stone of the parish church.

'You would be well advised, I think, inspector,' she said, 'to observe the distinction that was so properly drawn in *The Wizard of Oz*. "Are you a good witch or a bad witch?" Remember the line? In other words, you will save a good deal of time if you leave the merely folksy out of your calculations and concentrate on those whom that nice sergeant of yours would call the nutters.'

'Are there many of them?'

'Oh, no – remarkably few, considering how fascinating pagan licentiousness must appear to ladies whose idea of ultimate degradation is being trapped in their hostess's lavatory with an unsinkable turd.'

The inspector looked a little startled, but at once recovered composure.

'By "merely folksy", would you be referring to the membership of the Flaxborough Folklore Society?' he asked.

'In general, yes.'

He took from his pocket a folded sheet of paper.

'I've a list here of the people who belong to it. All those who turned up at the meeting last Wednesday night – the one from which Edna Hillyard disappeared – have been questioned. I haven't seen reports of all the interviews yet, but I do know that they tally in most particulars and that they contain no suggestion of what might have happened to Miss Hillyard.'

'Do you believe them, inspector?'

'No.'

Miss Teatime leaned forward. 'May I?' She took the list from the inspector's hand.

After a brief scrutiny, she said: 'All very respectable people, Mr Purbright.'

'Yes, indeed.'

'But you suspect, do you not, that a trained psychical investigator, with proper equipment, might detect a sepulchre or two beneath all this whiteness.'

'I have an open mind on the subject, Miss Teatime.'

'How refreshing to encounter an unprejudiced policeman. You have no idea what a *rara avis* you are, Mr Purbright.'

She rose.

'If you will make yourself comfortable for a few moments, I shall see what comes of submitting this list to a few preliminary psychometrical tests.'

Half-way to the door, she stopped and came back to pick up the workbasket.

'What is that for?' Purbright asked.

'It contains my resonating orgonoscope,' explained Miss Teatime.

In her bedroom, she relaxed against stacked-up pillows after pouring half a tumbler of whisky and lighting one of her little chocolate-coloured cigars. She read again through Purbright's list and underlined in pencil the names of Mrs Gloss, Mrs Pentatuke, Mrs Gooding and Paracelsus Parkin.

Rejoining Purbright a quarter of an hour later, she handed him the list.

'Your consort of viles,' she announced.

'You *have* been quick.'

'Ah, we do not depend upon things like the old Ouija board nowadays, inspector. With a modern orgonoscope, it is possible to pre-set the vibrations. Then all one has to do is read off the radionic dials. Would you care for a cup of tea?'

'That is kind of you, but I think not.' He put the sheet of paper in his pocket.

'To be quite fair,' said Miss Teatime, 'there are other names there which produced some reaction on the multi-oscillator unit. However, I thought you would wish me to keep the field as narrow as possible. Those I have indicated are the real off-the-scale ding-dongers.'

Purbright thanked her and prepared to leave.

'Oh, by the way ...' She pointed to the pocket in which he had slipped the list of folklorists. 'Had you noticed something rather interesting about the holders of office in that organization?'

He frowned. 'No, I don't think so.'

'It seemingly has no president.'

'But there is a chairman. Mrs whatsername – Framlington. Not all these societies have presidents.'

'If you will look in the current issue of the local paper,' said Miss Teatime, patiently, 'you will find in the report of the quarterly Revel, as they call it, a reference to Miss Hillyard's having been the winner of a prize. The name of the prize was the President's Maypole Trophy.'

Purbright gazed at her admiringly.

'You are being very perceptive today, Miss Teatime.'

She laid a finger delicately against the side of her small and nicely shaped nose.

'*Re*ceptive, Mr Purbright,' she corrected. 'It is the spirits that should be given credit, not ourselves.'

'KILLER CURSE PUT ON HEALTH CHIEF IN VOODOO TOWN.'

Purbright looked with disbelief at the identity of the paper Love had just handed him. It was none of the national news organs, but the usually prosaic *Eastern Evening Advertiser* from the next county, an early edition of which reached Flaxborough in mid-afternoon.

'Not more poultry, surely,' murmured the inspector, beginning to tackle the main text of the story.

'No,' Love said. 'Sage.'

Purbright scowled at the page before him. 'Jokes, Sid, we can do without just now.'

'It's not a joke. Read on a bit. You'll see.'

According to the *Evening Advertiser* report, a cleaner in the department of the Flaxborough Medical Officer of Health had come across what appeared to be a sort of wreath propped against the door of Dr Cropper's private office. Attached to the wreath was a white card with his name on it. Supposing it to be something agricultural that had been left for analysis, she laid it on a sheet of paper on the doctor's desk.

Only then did the cleaner notice an object twisted amongst the twigs and leaves that made up the wreath. It was a snake. She ran screaming out of the office and locked it behind her.

When the department staff arrived, two of the men – a clerk and a health inspector – went into the office prepared to deal with the snake. They found it was a grass snake or 'slow-worm', as people in the locality would have called it. It was dead.

There were interviews with the cleaner and the clerk, a man called Hodgson. Hodgson it was who had identified the snake. He thought he knew what the wreath had been made from, too, although it was half rotten and looked as if it had been buried for some time. Sage, diagnosed Mr Hodgson.

'I beg your pardon, Sid,' said Purbright, and read on.

The paper recapitulated some of the allegedly occult goings-on which had given Flaxborough recent notoriety; then spread itself on an interview by telephone with Denise Cornelius, demonologist and author.

'Common or garden sage,' Miss Cornelius had revealed to the *Advertiser*, 'was once considered a very powerful harm-dealing magic when it had been kept in the ground for a certain period and dug up with prescribed ceremony. English witches valued its malignant properties highly. The most terrible use of "sage-rot" was in conjunction with a reptile-type charm. The purpose of that combination invariably was to kill. And I have no doubt that it worked.'

The Russians, added Miss Cornelius, were known to have organized the re-establishment of witch covens in England and America. Their recruitment of evil powers was far advanced.

'It might well be that Flaxborough's present ordeal is but a rehearsal for an unimaginably more horrible onslaught upon the Christian world in the not far distant future,' Miss Cornelius declared.

In a small final paragraph, the paper noted that the Medical Officer had not been available for comment.

'I wonder if he's available now,' remarked Purbright. 'Come on, Sid.'

Sergeant Love's second appearance at the Municipal Offices was acknowledged by excited whispering amongst the totties, surreptitious stares, and even – to his almost unbearable gratification – a slow and sultry wink from Miss O'Conlon. Patriarch Purbright, naturally, was ignored.

House, the chief clerk, hastily put himself between the policemen and his girls. He was a fussy, dusty, ink-stained man, with creases of chronic suspiciousness about his eyes.

Purbright asked if it would be convenient to see Dr Cropper.

House pouted dubiously and crept to a big oak-panelled door marked Private. He touched it delicately with one knuckle, listened for ten whole seconds, and went in.

Like opening a safe, Love reflected.

When House re-emerged, his chief could be seen immediately behind him, one open hand already thrust forward.

'Lovely to see you, inspector!'

There was a vigorous handshake for each of them, an extended chair, a wave towards a box of cigarettes, a nod of genial professional approval when they declined. Then the big man with the pink, handsome face strode back behind his desk and sat, straight as a company director on audit day.

'And what can I do for you, gentlemen?'

The tiny click of the switch of Love's recording gear brought Cropper's eyes round at once.

'Aha!' he said, roguishly, on seeing the sergeant unwind the microphone flex. 'Bugged, eh?'

'I hope you've no objection, sir,' the inspector said. 'The more conventional kind of note-taking does tend to hold things up rather.'

For a few moments more, Cropper continued to watch the recorder with amused interest. Then he returned his attention to the inspector.

'I'm sure you will be aware, doctor,' Purbright began, 'that an investigation is in progress into the death of the Bride Street supermarket manager, Mr Bertram Persimmon ...'

'Aware?' interrupted Cropper, suddenly grave-faced. 'I am very deeply aware, inspector. He was a friend. In a sense, a colleague. But you must know this, surely? Sir Henry ...' He waited, his head slightly forward, inviting Purbright to adopt a franker approach.

'Sir Henry has been in touch with you, has he, sir?'

'But of course. He is as concerned as I am to learn the truth of this terrible affair. I trust I have not broken a confidence of some kind?'

'Certainly not, sir. I am glad to think that you'll be better prepared to answer some of the questions I shall be putting to you. For the moment, though I'm rather interested in the incident which the *Evening Advertiser* describes so graphically.'

Purbright began to unfold the newspaper that he had taken from his pocket.

Dr Cropper waved it aside.

'Don't bother. I've seen it. And really, inspector, of all the nonsensical fuss ...'

'Is the account not accurate?'

'As far as it goes, yes. But, good God, "killer curse" – "voodoo town" – I ask you! Are you aware, my dear inspector, of the amount of offensive rubbish dumped by crack-brained members of the public at this office during the year? We get rotting fish, underweight sausages, beer with tadpoles in it ... Listen, somebody once actually managed to get in and tether a sheep to the door handle. Don't ask me why. One gets used to it.'

'I appreciate that, doctor. But it seems to me that what was left here this morning was intended to convey a threat – a threat to you personally.'

Cropper grinned beamishly. 'Oh, I fancy I'm able to look after myself, inspector.'

'Mr Persimmon wasn't, though, was he?'

The grin was switched off.

'I don't think I quite understand.'

'Look sir, four of you gentlemen have been associated in what I gather is a kind of vigilante committee. Sir Henry Bird has explained its purpose. And if this reading of the situation is correct, you all have been running certain risks.'

'But very willingly, inspector. Remember that.'

'I don't doubt it. At the same time, I have to remind you that it is the job of the police to run risks, not the ordinary citizen's, however public-spirited.'

Cropper leaned forward and spoke very quietly.

'You cannot put handcuffs on Satan, my friend.'

'Perhaps not, sir. But do you contend that it was Satan who murdered Persimmon?'

'Indirectly. Yes, I do.'

'And then made threats of what I can only call a particularly vicious and dangerous kind to each in turn of Persimmon's collaborators?'

'Through some human agency. Again, yes.'

'You don't dispute that they *were* threats, then, doctor – including the so-called spell addressed to you?'

Cropper shrugged. 'No, of course I don't. Perhaps I should not have tried to impress you with my indifference, but for anyone in a job like mine publicity is an extremely unwelcome thing. You must see that.'

'Oh, I do. But I am not a journalist, Dr Cropper. What goes into that little box the sergeant is holding does not come out again for public consumption.'

'The press arrived here remarkably promptly this morning. I find that rather puzzling.'

'Reporters are around in some strength at the moment, sir. I expect they've established their own intelligence system. Would there, though, be anyone you can think of who might have let them know?'

'No one in the department, certainly.'

'Talking of the department, doctor, do you happen to have any idea of Miss Edna Hillyard's choice of friends?'

There was a pause.

'Inspector . . .'

Cropper was regarding Purbright with an expression that was at once respectful, wily and reproving.

'Sir?'

'You are trying to trap me into pretending that I occupy far too elevated a position here to be aware of what mere clerks get up to.'

'And what *do* they get up to, sir?'

Cropper smiled and shook his head.

'I know perfectly well, Mr Purbright, that Miss Hillyard

associated – that is the word, I believe – with Bertie Persimmon.'

The inspector put another question at once. 'Do you know who made the call last Wednesday night that resulted in Persimmon going out?'

'I have no idea.'

'What is your recollection of that call, doctor?'

'None, naturally. I didn't take it.'

'Persimmon did?'

'Yes. We'd had one or two earlier, but they were – well, relatively trivial. Then this one came through about midnight.'

'Did he not say anything that might suggest who the caller was?'

'Not a single word. He scarcely looked at me. Just slammed the receiver down and went straight out. Then I heard his car start up.'

'That was the last you ever saw of him, in fact?'

Dr Cropper spread the fingers of his right hand on the desk before him and scrutinized them sadly.

'As things turned out – yes, I'm afraid it was.'

Chapter Fourteen

THE BOOT, OR TRUNK, OF THE LATE MR PERSIMMON'S car had been crafted with special care to solve for the family man all those holiday luggage problems; to provide the modern business executive with space equivalent to a second officer; and to give the sportsman the big, BIG, B-I-G-G-E-S-T rod, gun or clubs locker he had ever dreamed of.

It was now known to have served a fourth, unscheduled, purpose – the posthumous transportation of its owner.

The fact had been established quite simply and quickly in a Nottingham police laboratory by analysis of blood samples and by comparing fibres recovered from the boot with others taken from clothing on the corpse.

Of the significance of fragments of hard varnish and aged, brittle, animal hair, also found in the boot, the forensic scientists had offered no opinion.

Purbright treated Love to his own confident interpretation.

'They must have chucked that bull's head mask in with the body and then dumped them both in the river.'

The sergeant thought about this for a moment. Then, 'Who's "they"?' he asked.

'One, the man who killed Persimmon, whoever he is. Two – and I'm afraid there seems to be no doubt about this – the Hillyard girl.'

'You mean she *helped* him?'

'There are her prints all over the car. Those inside and round about the boot are bloody. And their position indicates that she must have been helping to lift. That's what the report says, anyway.'

'Perhaps he forced her to.'

'Perhaps.'

'And abducted her afterwards.'

Purbright sighed. 'You have a chivalrous disposition Sid.'

He looked at his watch.

'In twenty minutes from now, our colleagues will be paying simultaneous calls upon three of the folklore enthusiasts we discussed earlier. I want you at the same time to take four county men and give Mrs Gloss's grounds a thorough going over. What story-fixing there's been up to now between these people can't be helped, but at least we can deny them a chance to tip one another off today.'

Leaving Love to marshal his squad from the men lent by County Chief Constable Hessledine, Purbright entered the office of his own superior, Mr Harcourt Chubb.

'This warrant, Mr Purbright – I'm not altogether happy about it, you know. Mrs Gloss is not a poor woman. She has the means to make things awkward for us if it turns out that you've acted hastily.'

'On the contrary, sir. Persimmon was murdered last Wednesday. I think you can claim to have acted with great restraint in waiting so long before ordering a search of the grounds where he almost certainly met his death.'

'But is it your contention that Mrs Gloss was involved in the crime? I mean, this is just what people are going to think when they see policemen on the place. You're using some of the county fellows, I understand,' added Mr Chubb, with the slightest wrinkle of distaste.

'I wouldn't go so far as to . . .'

'Sit down, my dear chap, do.'

Mr Chubb made no move towards a chair himself but remained standing by the mantelpiece, on which he supported one elegantly-extended arm.

'I would not go so far,' repeated the inspector, 'as to accuse Mrs Gloss of actually having a hand in what happened to Persimmon. But I certainly do believe that she and some of her friends were aware of it soon afterwards and came to an agreement among themselves to keep quiet.'

'And why should they do that?'

'Because they did not wish the police, or anyone else for that matter, to find out what *they* had been up to that night.'

'You are talking about this folk-singing carry-on, are you?'

The chief constable sounded disparaging yet intrigued.

'It was something rather more sinister than that, sir.'

Mr Chubb slightly widened his regard of the inspector, but said nothing. Purbright explained.

'The ground behind Mrs Gloss's home was being used for black magic rites of some kind. Possibly fairly harmless. Possibly not. It rather depends on one's point of view. But erotic – that, I fancy, we can safely bet on.

'We don't know yet how long these things have been going on, nor at what point did a society genuinely devoted to local folklore become dominated by its witchcraft lobby. The newspaper stories are not only extremely unreliable in detail; they have been deliberately inspired by somebody who knows about the black magic activities and for some private reason wants to embarrass their organizers.'

'They've certainly embarrassed *me*,' said Mr Chubb, with feeling. 'That fellow Hessledine was on the phone yesterday, making what I suppose he thought were jokes about magic spells. I had to be rather short with him. Never mind about that, though. What I can't understand is how a decent sort of chap like Persimmon got mixed up in all this nastiness.'

'You don't know, sir?'

'Of course not. Why, do you?'

Purbright pondered how favourably he could present the manner of the passing of a vice-chairman of the Conservative Club.

'He was a member of a small but very public-spirited group of citizens – something on the lines of Rotary, I gather – formed to try and counteract the influence of the black magic cult. They had what I believe self-dramatizing politicians like to call a "hot-line". A number that can be rung in an emergency.'

'It sounds rather far-fetched,' observed Mr Chubb.

'So I thought, sir, when I heard about it. But someone called that number on Wednesday night, and it was Persimmon who went to the rescue.'

'Rescue of whom?'

'His mistress, actually.'

The chief constable took his arm from the mantelpiece.

'His *what*?'

'His mistress, sir. Miss Hillyard.'

Purbright waited, in case Chubb should wish to express shock or disbelief, but the chief constable silently motioned him to proceed.

'As soon as I learned about that call to Persimmon, other facts seemed to fit in. At first, I reasoned that the girl had gone to the affair at Mrs Gloss's out of curiosity or for a thrill and was then inveigled or even forced into taking part in the sexual shenannigins. When these became too violent or too bizarre for her taste, she took fright and managed to persuade one of the other women to get out to a telephone and send for help.'

'How would the Hillyard girl have known the number of this "hot line", as you call it?'

'Persimmon would have told her. He and his friends unquestionably took this self-appointed task of theirs very seriously. Actually, knowing something of Miss Hillyard's reputation, I wouldn't be surprised if the evangelistic attitude of her lover had put the idea of going to Aleister Lodge into her head in the first place.'

'Morally unstable, I suppose.'

'That is one way of putting it, sir.'

'And you say Bertram Persimmon took up with her. There are some strange depths in people, you know, Mr Purbright.'

'Yes, sir. I was saying, though, that the idea of Edna Hillyard's taking fright and sending for help was my *first* interpretation. I now think quite differently.

'For one thing, it was naïve of me to assume that the clothes in her car were evidence of her having changed into others. She was naked when found and clearly had stripped that evening without any compulsion. Which suggests a good deal more than mere curiosity.

'It is probable also that the girl lost no time in priming herself with the liquor that undoubtedly was available. I suspect that modern witches are no different from ancient ones in having to use potions to get them off the ground.

'Then there is the matter of her complicity in shifting Persimmon's body. Forensic are quite convinced of that because of the grouping of her prints on the car.

'Lastly – and this could be the most significant circumstance of all – we find that the place chosen as a temporary hiding-place for the car is a Corporation depot. It is largely derelict, certainly, and unlikely to be entered by workmen or anybody until the ploughs are wanted again for snow-clearing, but normally it is kept locked and the keys hung with others on a board in the Public Health Department.'

Purbright paused.

'You see the implications, sir.'

'I can see a connection,' said Mr Chubb. 'The girl worked in that department, if I remember rightly.'

'Exactly, sir. She had access to those keys. But not in the middle of the night. So if she took them – and I can think of no one more likely – she must have done so in advance and presumably with full knowledge of what they would be needed for.'

'In other words, Mr Purbright, the woman was a partner in a

murder conspiracy. Is that what you are saying?'

'It is extremely difficult to put any other construction on the facts as we know them, sir.'

'But there are facts that we do *not* know, surely. If that crime was premeditated, there must have been a motive. What was it?'

Purbright shrugged regretfully. 'That remains to be established, sir. But I should not expect anything conventional. There is more than a little madness about this case.'

'Another point bothers me,' said Mr Chubb. 'To lure that poor chap off in the dark to a remote part of the town – yes, I understand the cunning of that. But what about all those characters cavorting about on broomsticks or whatever you say they were doing? Potential witnesses. Very risky.'

'By that time, most of them would have been mutually preoccupied, I think, sir. And we should remember that they were much too heavily compromised to be keen on giving evidence.'

'Do you know the names of the people who were there?'

'Oh, there's no secret about that, sir. They're in the local paper. Or some of them are. I think the bogus publicity must be felt to add to the thrill. They actually have a press secretary, a chap called Parkin.'

'Good gracious,' said Mr Chubb, much disgusted.

'Naturally, I am having them very closely questioned,' Purbright added. 'As the girl will be, as soon as she's considered fit enough.'

'By the medical staff, presumably.'

'Yes, sir. They're rather apprehensive of brain damage, actually. She had barbituric poisoning.'

'You did mention the possibility when you rang from the hospital. It's confirmed, is it?'

'They're pretty sure.'

Purbright thought for a moment.

'Which leads, I'm afraid, to another question I can't answer. Why was the wretched girl doped to the eyes and left lying in that place? It seems an odd way to treat a collaborator.'

'As I understand it,' said the chief constable, 'people of that sort pass dangerous drugs around as you or I might hand out peppermint lozenges. Hippies. All that.' He wagged his head gloomily.

Purbright was wondering if Mr Chubb would appreciate his pointing out the contradiction between a love-in and a black mass when the telephone rang.

Mr Chubb walked to his desk and picked up the receiver with cold fastidiousness.

'Sergeant, I did tell you that I would be engaged in conference for at least half an hour. That half an hour has not yet elapsed.'

He seemed about to replace the phone, then to change his mind. The lean, ascetic features sharpened to attention. One slim hand slipped half-way into the side pocket of his jacket and rested there delicately.

'Good afternoon, councillor,' said Mr Chubb into the telephone.

It was a brief and mainly one-sided conversation. The chief constable made occasional noises of judicious concern and said that he would certainly ... Also that he quite ... And finally that he would be glad to see if ...

Purbright meanwhile looked impassively out of the window.

'Hideaway,' said the chief constable after he had put down the phone. His face was stony. Purbright could sense behind it the black swirl of private opinion.

'He is the brother-in-law, it seems, of Mrs Persimmon,' said Mr Chubb.

Ernest Hideaway, estate agent and humorist, was possessed of a tidy fortune that had been his reward for compounding the felonies of local jerrybuilders over the years. He was a member of Flaxborough Town Council and a diligent giver of advice.

'Hideaway says,' Mr Chubb went on, 'that Mrs Persimmon is very upset indeed, and if what the man alleges is true, she has some justification. You will have to look into it, I'm afraid, Mr Purbright.'

'If you'll tell me what the complaint is, sir ...'

'Well of course I'll tell you,' Mr Chubb retorted irritably. 'That's what I'm doing now. It's about the man's body, actually. Very distasteful. You'll remember that after the post-mortem and the adjournment of the inquest the coroner issued a burial certificate.'

'Yes, sir.'

'Yes, well the family fixed the funeral for tomorrow. All the arrangements were made. The undertaker collected the body. Everything normal, everybody happy. And then, dash me if the blessed woman doesn't ask to see the corpse.'

The chief constable shook his head.

'Very ill-advised. Just morbidity, you know, but there you are. They let her.

'And straight away she played Holy Harry. Wanted to know what business the hospital had to stamp her husband like something going through the customs. The hospital people said postmortems were the business of the police and nothing to do with them, so she went along to her brother-in-law.

'He confirms what the woman says. Somebody, at some time, has stamped a black cross on the bottom of her husband's foot. And it won't come off.'

Chapter Fifteen

SERGEANT LOVE AND HIS POSSE SWEPT UP TO THE DOOR of Aleister Lodge with something of the panache of a car full of bootleggers in a mid-1930s film. Mrs Gloss, alarmed and annoyed by the noise of the displacement of gravel, hurried from the house. She was in time to see the sergeant glance back with bland interest at the furrows in the drive while he fished a paper from his inside pocket.

The search of the grounds was lengthy, thorough, and, in the subsequently expressed opinion of Inspector Purbright, undeservedly fruitful.

The finds were distributed mainly in and around the grove of ash trees which earlier had attracted the attention of Constable Palethorp.

They included six empty wrappings representative between

them of four different brands of prophylactic. Two of the packs were so worn and dirty as to be only just identifiable. Of the rest, one was almost new. It lay behind a tuft of grass in the lee of one of the four short pillars that supported a stone slab about eight feet long by two wide.

This slab was damp and green. It looked very old. The supports had sunk into the ground irregularly, and the slab leaned a little to one side.

Several dark brown splashes were discernible on the stone, a group of them at its higher end. A policeman noticed that dead leaves had been strewn about on the ground near by. He brushed them aside. Quite a lot of blood had soaked into the earth.

The policeman scrutinized this area inch by inch. Eventually he discovered a sliver of ruby glass. Nothing else.

A few yards away, just clear of the trees, one of his colleagues was busy with cast-making materials. He had seen in a bald patch of soft ground the impression of a tyre tread. It seemed identical in pattern with the tread of one of Persimmon's tyres, blown-up photographs of which he had been using as a guide.

Constables three and four took turns with notebooks and tape-measures. Painstakingly they charted from heelmarks and from crushed and stained grass the short haul of a body.

Farther away, incidental finds were made, less dramatic, but significant in context.

Two bottles, overlooked by a Folklore Society cleaning-up detachment the previous Thursday morning, contained still the potent lees of pumpkin champagne laced with rum.

A policeman who zealously, but with misgivings, investigated a small parcel he had found in the summerhouse censer, jumped when there fell out the shrivelled corpse of a bat. The creature's shroud was a page of the Baptist Bugle embellished with a photograph of the Rev. William Harniss.

Lastly, high in the branches of a fine yew tree near the house, the searchers descried what at first appeared to be a great roosting bird of prey. It proved on closer examination to be a black corset.

Sergeant Love himself made it his business to see that Mrs Gloss was given no opportunity to use the telephone.

He tried to offset the irritation his persistent presence obviously caused her by making a fuss of the big sleek cat which had appeared from the kitchen.

The cat walked round him three times, unhurriedly bit him on the calf, and strolled out.

Mrs Gloss told Love that if she ever saw him ill-treat an animal again she would have him removed from the Force.

At the home of the Goodings, Constable Brevitt did his best to cope with fauna of a different kind.

Out in the garden an enormous black dog paced up and down, baying, while a pair of macaws in a cage high in a corner of the living room were carrying on a dialogue that sounded like a continuous rail disaster.

Mrs Gooding appeared to find the uproar not only tolerable but enlightening. She smiled knowingly and every now and again glanced at Brevitt's face as if to confirm some particularly unpleasant characteristic that the birds had just pointed out to her.

Questioning Mrs Gooding in such circumstances was not easy. Doggedly and without much imagination, Brevitt followed his brief.

Had she, on the night of the Folklore Society's Revel, seen anything of a man called Bertram Persimmon? No. Or a Miss Edna Hillyard? Yes. With whom? Lots of different people. Did she know a Mr Persimmon? No. Had there been a fight at the Revel? No. Any unnatural practices? What an idea! Who had dressed up as a bull? She didn't know what he was talking about. Who had put offensive articles in the parish church? Ask somebody else. On the door of Sir Henry Bird? How would she know. In the office of the Medical Officer of Health? Likewise.

Brevitt looked grim. He sighed through clenched teeth.

'If my George was here,' Mrs Gooding said, suddenly removing her regard from birds and ferociously swinging her big, knobbly face close to Brevitt's, 'd'you know what we'd do?'

The policeman involuntarily reared back.

Again Mrs Gooding's features were thrust up to his.

'We'd pray for you,' she growled.

One of the imported officers, a Brocklestone plain-clothes man called Miller, had been assigned to call on Press Secretary Parkin.

Parkin was not at home. Nor was his sister, Amy. Miller learned from the woman next door that Miss Parkin did not normally return from school until nearly five o'clock.

'And Mr Parkin?'

'Isn't he at the shop, then?'

'What shop?'

A chemist's shop. Dispensing. Well, no, he'd not know, not if he was a stranger to Flax. But that's where Mr Parkin would be. Amis and Jeffrey, in Eastgate.

Miller asked if the Parkins kept chickens.

The neighbour said that was a funny sort of question and who was *he*, anyway?

A buyer of cockerels, replied Miller, with spontaneous cunning. Black cockerels he was especially interested in.

The neighbour looked him up and down and said:

'That wouldn't surprise me, either.'

And she shut the door.

Number 33 Partney Avenue was a semi-detached villa with a bay window, behind one of the five panes of which was displayed a pink poster advertising the forthcoming performance of 'The Gondoliers' by the Flaxborough Amateur Operatic Society.

A precisely circular flowerbed had been cut in the centre of the few square yards of closely-mown lawn. It contained eight wallflower plants and one standard rose bush.

The concrete approach to the built-on garage was marked in imitation of crazy-paving. On the garden gate was an enamelled notice. NO CANVASSERS.

A man and a woman who had entered Partney Avenue from Arnhem Crescent stopped before the gate and read the notice. They looked at each other and the man gave a very thin smile. He opened the gate.

The man and woman stood side by side before the front door, awaiting response to the man's double ring. They looked patient, disciplined, impermeable – a pair of Jehovah's Witnesses, perhaps, anticipating with flinty pleasure an hour or two of apocalyptic interpretation upon Mrs Pentatuke's doorstep.

Suddenly the door was open and Mrs Pentatuke was revealed, more than a little Jehovah-like herself.

She looked imperiously from one to the other.

'Well?'

The man said: 'We are police officers, ma'am. My name is Harper, and this is Policewoman Bellweather. May we come in?'

Mrs Pentatuke's frown deepened.

'I haven't sent for the police.'

'No, ma'am. We've called. We think you might be able to help us in our inquiries into certain matters.'

Fill his bowels with books, prayed Mrs Pentatuke. *O Belial, make her miscarry in a Woolworths'*.

Aloud, she demanded to see documents of authorization.

They were produced.

Coldly, Mrs Pentatuke ushered her visitors into the room containing the Gondoliers poster. It was not a large room. The settee and its matching pair of armchairs in mustard-coloured miracle Carfelon had the appearance of having arrived the previous day, on approval. The fitted carpet, super tough yet fibre-groomed to give the caress of real lambswool, also had an unused look. There was one picture, a reproduction of a portrait of Winston Churchill. It hung above the fireplace, which had been sealed with a laminated plastic panel before which stood a chrome-plated, two-bar electric heater. This was not, and possibly never had been, switched on.

'It will save time, if you agree,' Harper said to Mrs Pentatuke, 'for my colleague to take a quick look round the house while I put a few questions to you here. Of course, you may accompany her if you would rather.'

'And if I forbid her to do anything of the kind?'

Harper looked regretful.

'Ah, as to that, madam, I'm afraid there's the matter of the warrant. We don't as a rule expect any trouble over these things. Not in a nice neighbourhood like this.'

Mrs Pentatuke compressed her lips in angry resignation. *O Astoreth, lead her great cow foot into the hair oil that Lionel spilled on the bathroom floor this morning. Let her horrid head be wedged down the poo-box.*

Policewoman Bellweather gave her a nervous little smile, bobbed apologetically, and went out of the room.

A long pause having failed to win Harper an invitation to sit down, he lowered himself to a chair-edge perch on miracle Carfelon and started to put his questions.

A quarter of an hour later, he had secured not a single admission from Mrs Pentatuke that promised to have relevance to the Persimmon murder, the abduction of Edna Hillyard, or the persecution of members of the anti-witchcraft committee. Her answers were curt – often a simple yes or no – but never evasive in a way that Harper could challenge. And she took so little time to deliver them that Harper was constantly being left unprepared with another question and had to look into his notebook like a schoolboy at a crib.

He was greatly relieved when Policewoman Bellweather came back into the room. She was holding a large translucent plastic box fitted with a lid. The box was thinly encrusted with crystals. It was steaming slightly.

Sadie Bellweather addressed Harper.

'I found this in the deep freeze cabinet in the kitchen,' she told him. She did not look at Mrs Pentatuke.

'Is that your property, madam?' Harper asked, trying to appear stern but at the same time scrupulously open-minded.

'And what in hell's name,' retorted Mrs Pentatuke, 'has that got to do with you?'

Harper signalled the policewoman to proceed.

She clutched the box to her bosom with one arm and levered off the lid. Out of the box she drew a bird, stiff as a Roman eagle but black-feathered and unmistakably domestic in origin.

'That your chicken, ma'am?' (In for a penny, in for a pound, reflected Harper, secretly nervous.)

'Of course it's my chicken, you idiot.' Mrs Pentatuke made a grab for it.

'Cockerel,' corrected Policewoman Bellweather, who had been brought up on a farm.

'It's for a dinner party tomorrow night,' said Mrs Pentatuke, 'and I'll thank you not to maul it about.'

Policewoman Bellweather carefully replaced the fowl, which she had been holding upright by the feet, like a feathered club. Next, she produced a small metal tray and handed it to Harper.

Harper gave a start, then peered cautiously at the tray's contents before holding them out for Mrs Pentatuke's inspection.

'These for dinner as well, are they? Starters, like?'

Mrs Pentatuke gazed, tight-lipped, at the frozen corpses of a shrew, two frogs, a mouse and another small creature less easy to identify because of its somewhat chewed condition.

'The cat brings them in from time to time,' she said, after consideration.

'Would you care to give me an explanation of why you have put these things into the refrigerator?' Harper asked. He ignored the policewoman's whispered 'deep freeze' and waited for Mrs Pentatuke to think up something convincing.

'I don't consider I need give you anything of the kind.'

'As you wish, madam,' said Harper, handing back the miniature mortuary to Sadie Bellweather.

The third and last production from the box was a tiny notebook. The policewoman held it up between finger and thumb. It measured about two inches by an inch-and-a-half. Harper reached across and she put it in his hand.

Again the monotonously delivered question.

'This your property, madam?'

Mrs Pentatuke affected silent contempt, but her face had paled noticeably.

Harper slowly turned the pages of the notebook. After a while, he raised his eyes.

'Do you wish to offer an explanation of why you keep a memoranda book in the ...' He sent an inquiring glance to the policewoman.

'It was taped behind a sort of dividing panel in the freezer.'

'... in the position my colleague has described?'

'I intend to say nothing more to you,' declared Mrs Pentatuke. 'Your presence here is preposterous and your behaviour unspeakable. What your object is, I have no idea, but I warn you both that unless you can be shown to have had some very good reason for bursting in on my privacy you and your superior officers will find yourselves in the most serious trouble.'

Harper waited patiently for this speech to end. Then he returned the notebook to Policewoman Bellweather, motioned her to hang on to the box and its contents, and said to Mrs Pentatuke:

'I have to tell you that I propose now to take to police headquarters, Flaxborough, the articles which I have shown to you and which I believe to be your property. I shall give you a signed receipt for these articles, and they will be treated with all reasonable care. Do you wish to make objection to my removing them?'

But Mrs Pentatuke's vow of silence seemed to have been put already into operation. The faint stirring of her lips conveyed nothing to Harper. Which was just as well, because she was then placing upon him in yellow, dun and black degrees, the miring malediction of Saint Gringoire.

Love and Miller nearly collided with each other in the corridor outside the CID room. Both were in a hurry.

'Conference,' said Miller. 'You did know, didn't you?'

'Twenty minutes yet,' Love said. He dodged into a file closet and started pulling out drawers. 'Tell Harper when you see him. Oh, and Brevitt, too.'

Purbright appeared at the end of the corridor, then turned and was gone again. Love heard the clanking of an iron staircase.

When Harper and Sadie Bellweather came in from the transport yard, it was Harper who was carrying Mrs Pentatuke's deep freeze container. Encountering the bulky obstacle of Sergeant Mally, Harper halted and invited the coroner's officer to take a look.

'Christ, we're not having inquests on bloody frogs now, are we?'

'Where's the inspector?'

'Upstairs.'

They squeezed past each other.

Harper was hailed by Love and told about the conference. Proudly, he displayed his collection. Love picked up the mouse by its tail, which had become limp in the warm air, and pretended to set off in search of Policewoman Bellweather. 'No, don't piss about,' Harper told him, grabbing back the mouse.

The face of Constable Palethorp appeared round the door.

'Tapes,' he said to Love. 'The inspector says don't forget the interview tapes. And can you come up straight away, he says.'

'Righty-ho,' said Love.

Palethorp moved closer. 'Hey,' he said softly, 'they reckon old Purby's going to knock off the vicar for that Persimmon business. Has he said anything to you?'

Love slipped two cassettes in his pocket and started to leave. He looked happy but said nothing.

Closeted in one of the two small interview rooms with a Mr George Tozer, Detective-Constable Pook frowned peevishly at the noise of all the comings and goings in the corridor. He had been hearing from Mr Tozer – a man of slow speech and gesture with black cavernous eye-sockets and hairy nostrils – about certain strange tribulations suffered lately by members of Flaxborough Chamber of Trade, whose current secretary and spokesman Mr Tozer was.

'I shall pass on these people's complaints, sir,' Pook assured him. 'It isn't nice for that sort of thing to be happening. Especially in food shops.'

He was ushering his informant out when Sadie Bellweather, clutching a new notebook and two shiny red pencils, patted his arm as she bounded by.

'Conference. Now. They asked me to tell you.'

Love reappeared, waving his hand like a shipyard foreman trying to stop a launch.

'Sorry, slight delay,' he called along the corridor. 'Not to panic, though.'

Purbright, slightly out of breath, joined him. The inspector was putting on his raincoat. He paused to beckon the two nearest men. They were Harper and Palethorp. All four hurried towards the transport yard.

'Quickest way would be by St Anne's Place and Spindle Lane, wouldn't you say, sergeant? Save going through the Market Place.'

Purbright took the wheel.

At the East Street junction, Palethorp got out, audaciously held up the cross traffic despite his being in plain clothes, and climbed back into the car.

'Who rang in?' Love asked the inspector.

'Grewyear. I'd asked him to keep an eye on the place until someone could be spared to make a search.'

The car travelled two-thirds of the length of Spoongate, turned sharply left between two stone gate pillars, and drew up in the lee of a big beige Daimler in the courtyard that separated the Vicarage from the Church Hall.

Two men were coming out of the hall's back door.

They carried between them what appeared to be a small flexible raft. Not until they were within a few feet of the open boot of the Daimler did they notice the police car.

Purbright got out and strolled towards them.

'Do you need any help, gentlemen?'

Neither Sir Henry Bird nor Dr Cropper appeared to be in the slightest degree disconcerted.

'That's extremely obliging of you, inspector,' said Bird, 'but I think we can manage.'

'Unless,' remarked Dr Cropper, 'you or one of your colleagues would be good enough to bring that old box across for us.'

He indicated with a nod something large and brown and cylindrical that had been left standing beside the hall door.

'It would save us making another journey.'

Purbright made a sign to Palethorp, who set off across the courtyard.

Love and Harper had moved quietly round the front of the Daimler. Love stood close to the door on the driver's side.

Bird and Cropper lowered their burden into the Daimler boot. It could be seen now to be a narrow mattress, about six feet long.

Purbright felt it. It was resilient, made probably of foam rubber. The canvas cover was stained brown here and there. He bent the mattress over, to examine the other side. Streaks of green. He touched the streaks with a finger tip and looked inquiringly at Bird, then at Cropper, but was careful not to put a question in words.

'Paint,' said Bird. 'It's pretty messy in that hall.' He reached across as if with the intention of lowering the boot lid.

Purbright stopped him and indicated Palethorp, approaching with the cylindrical object. It was a huge old-fashioned hat box made of leather.

'Ah, yes,' said Sir Henry. He called: 'In here – there's a good chap.'

Again Purbright was ready to intercept. He told Palethorp to set the hat box down on the ground, then turned to Bird.

'I'd be obliged if you or Dr Cropper would open this, sir.'

'Now look here, Purbright, don't you think you're going a bit . . .'

'Of course,' Dr Cropper firmly and loudly declared, before Sir Henry could say any more. He stepped to the box and unfastened the strap that secured the lid.

'Odds and ends, you see, inspector. They've been kicking about in there for ages. We thought the Scouts might devise a use for them.'

One by one, Purbright removed and handed to Palethorp the objects in the box. The biggest was a megaphone about a foot long, with some kind of detachable reed or vibrator fitted into the mouthpiece. There were also two small flashlight batteries; a card that had held three crimson 'Santa-lite' electric bulbs, of which two remained; a pair of pliers; and a partially emptied Family Size pack of 'Safemate' condoms.

'And now, gentlemen, I must ask you to accompany me and the sergeant while we examine the room from which you have re-moved these things. The key, if one of you will be so kind . . .'

Sir Henry slowly withdrew his hand from his jacket pocket and dropped a key into Purbright's open palm. He was past the point at which indignation could still be conveyed in words. He tried instead to look contemptuously unconcerned. But his face was grey, blotched irregularly with nets of tiny inflamed veins.

Dr Cropper's manner, on the other hand, became increasingly cheerful, almost jocose. He bowed Purbright into the small, musty-smelling room with a remark about 'desirable business premises'.

The room contained a card table, three heavily old-fashioned dining-room chairs, and a leather-covered couch. There was a cupboard in one corner. A telephone stood on a shelf near by. Half the floor area was covered with carpet too badly worn to give any hint of its original colour or pattern.

The two policemen opened the cupboard, and surveyed what little it contained. They saw a few cups and saucers, a kettle, jars of instant coffee and dried milk and sugar, two part bottles of whisky, another of sherry, nearly full.

'Drink, inspector?' inquired Dr Cropper.

Purbright turned. He was not smiling. Love closed the cupboard door. With a sad, hardly noticeable tilt of his head, Purbright ushered them all out of the room.

They walked back along the short passage into the hall and picked their way between a case of hymn-books and some stacked chairs towards the door that led into the courtyard. Just before they reached it, Purbright stopped and spoke.

'Henry Loxley Bird and Halcyon Arthur Marshall Cropper, I am now taking you into custody. You will be charged, severally and jointly, that you did, on or about May the first, this year, at Flaxborough, unlawfully abduct Edna Hillyard and continue unlawfully to restrain and imprison the said Edna Hillyard. I have to tell you that you, Henry Loxley Bird, and you, Halcyon Arthur Marshall Cropper, need not say anything either now or when you are formally charged, but that what you do say will be taken down in writing and may be given in evidence. Does either of you wish to say anything at this stage?'

The ensuing silence was broken only by the click of Love's priming his retractable ball-point.

'I am now,' went on Purbright quietly, 'going to put another question to you, but this time without formality.'

He threw a side glance at Love, who pocketed his notebook.

'Which one of you actually did the killing of Bertram Persimmon?'

Chapter Sixteen

TWO WEEKS LATER, THERE PRESENTED HIMSELF AT FEN Street a gentleman wearing a black morning jacket, pin-striped trousers, highly polished black shoes over silk socks and the hardest-looking bowler hat that Flaxborough ever had seen. His furled umbrella was as slim as a wand, his briefcase supple and well matured.

'Who's the pox doctor's clerk?' Love inquired of Constable Braine, who had just escorted the visitor to Purbright's office.

'Solicitor from the D.P.P.' Brain's tone was airy; he liked an opportunity of scattering initials about.

'Come to tie it all up, has he?' Harper asked.

'Suppose so.'

Love wandered off, but not out of the building. He hoped that he would be sent for, and perhaps consulted, by the man in that super Old Bailey get-up: the representative, no less, of the Director of Public Prosecutions.

After all, Love reflected, if it hadn't been for his tapes, they'd probably be as far up the creek as ever in trying to decide between Bird and Cropper.

The summons came after only quarter of an hour.

Purbright introduced the man from the Director's office as Mr Spratt-Cornforth.

Love's hand was taken in a quick, cold grip and immediately released. Less brief was the stare of appraisal from grey eyes in a long, rather wooden face.

'We've heard about you, sergeant,' said the solicitor as he turned to resume his seat, 'and that keen ear of yours. Splendid.'

Love blushed. He fingered his keen ear. Purbright motioned him to a chair.

Spratt-Cornforth picked up the topmost clip of typescript from the pile before him.

'The forensic stuff is pretty straightforward. We rather approve of the forensic stuff. Can you see them shaking us on that, Purbright?'

'I don't think so, sir. The chain is clearly established. Hairs and varnish from the bull mask – found in car boot, hat box and altar mattress . . .'

'Strong belief in comfort in these parts,' interjected Spratt-Cornforth.

'It's a fairly high-class neighbourhood, sir.'

'Ye-e-e-s . . .' (It sounded like 'years', long drawn out.) The solicitor was glancing rapidly through one of the statements. He slapped it down on the table.

'This Pentatuke woman,' he said. 'She sounds to us a bit non compos. What do you think, inspector?'

'Odd, certainly. But only in this one particular.'

'The weird sister stuff.'

'Yes, sir. As with most of them, it's a sort of hobby.'

'We are thinking of her in the box, Purbright. We are not altogether happy. The defence would make short work of a witness who persisted in calling the accused Master of Darkness.'

'I do see what you mean. Actually, I have concluded a bargain with Mrs Pentatuke, who is more shrewd than might appear from the preliminary statement. In return for our dropping the sacrilege charge and promising not to mention her sexual relationship with the defendant, she has undertaken to make a lucid deposition about that phone call of hers that brought Persimmon to the Sabbath. That, after all, is the nub of her evidence so far as you are concerned.'

Three emphatic nods from Spratt-Cornforth.

'Precisely. And may we say how refreshing it is to find a police officer with a sense of *economy* in this matter of presenting a case. More prosecutions are weakened by too much evidence than by too little.'

Purbright modestly inclined his head.

'Incidentally,' added Spratt-Cornforth, 'we must hope that it will not occur to the defence to try and depict this woman as too jealous, and subsequently too vengeful, for her testimony to carry weight. It would not be difficult, you know.'

The inspector agreed.

'She certainly spared no effort to attract the maximum unwelcome publicity to the Coven and its Masters. We found a little notebook at her house. It had in it the telephone numbers of half the national newspapers. In addition, I suspect that she pestered the defendant himself a good deal by phone.'

'Yes, well, we shall keep clear of all that,' said the solicitor, selecting another sheaf of typescript. 'It would not do for a crown witness to appear to have known the murderer's identity all along.'

For a while he read in silence. Then, 'Ah.' He flicked the corner of the statement with long, white fingers.

'Our old friend. The blank memory. But well enough to go into court for us? Has she recovered that far?'

'She will have done by the time the case comes on at the Crown Court, I think, sir.'

'Lucky girl, Miss Hillyard, wouldn't you say?'

'To be still alive? Extremely.'

'The treatment of her shows ruthlessness. The jury won't like that. Good point for us. Provided, of course, the defence don't make a song and dance about her promiscuity. That always works the other way. Or is your society permissive in this county?'

'That is a question the press appeared to consider of enormous importance. Certainly, Harry Bird used to talk about it a good deal on the Bench when he was sentencing people.'

'Really?'

Purbright glanced to see if Love was showing signs of boredom, but he appeared to be lost in admiration of the London solicitor's rapid digestion and arrangement of their paperwork.

Spratt-Cornforth leaned back in his chair, tapped a thumbnail ruminatively against his lower teeth, and closed his eyes.

'Let us see,' he said, 'if we have a general picture of the case. Stop us at once if we go wrong.

'For some time past, a group of people living in Flaxborough and its surrounding area had indulged in what may loosely be termed Pagan religious practices under cover of a pretended interest in folklore. The central ceremony was a so-called Revel, held in the grounds of one of the members, witness Gertrude Gloss, four times a year on dates associated with the witches' Sabbaths of the Middle Ages.

'The climax of the Revel, or Sabbath, which involved dancing, drinking and probably a deal of licentiousness, was the appearance of the President, or Master. He was a sort of Minotaur figure, believed by some at least of the members to be the devil, and his prerogative was to summon the female of his choice from among the company and to possess her in an altar ritual.

'Whereas it was important for the ordinary members of the Coven, as we must call it, to shield their respectability behind the spurious title of Folklore Society; it was of double – indeed, of three-fold – importance to preserve the anonymity of the Master.'

Spratt-Cornforth opened one eye with which to regard Purbright.

'All right so far?'

'Absolutely.'

The eye closed again.

'We now know the clever and extremely confusing device whereby this was achieved. The Master of the Coven was not one person at all, but a triumvirate of lecherous worthies masquerading as – of all things – an anti-witchcraft action group that enjoyed the innocent patronage of the Vicar of Flaxborough. An Unholy Trinity, eh, sergeant?'

This quite unexpected acknowledgement of his continued presence left Love gratified but wordless.

The solicitor continued at once with his summary.

'There would appear, nevertheless, to have been some rudimentary sense of honour among these three. They observed a rota system, for example, as we may infer from the evidence of the witness Bollinger. It was she, was it not, who heard Persimmon say on the telephone that "he could not make it that night" and that someone "would get an extra turn".

'But that "someone" – and we may take it that Mrs Pentatuke was the woman referred to – did not get her turn, after all. The female Pearce will testify that it was Edna Hillyard's good fortune to be chosen.

'There followed the call to Persimmon, his furious drive – witnessed by ...'

Purbright waited a moment, then supplied the name. Spratt-Cornforth snapped his fingers.

'... Doris Periam. Of course. As we said, the furious drive, confrontation, attack. And murderous counter-attack by the man in that fearfully-armed mask. Then the loading of Persimmon's body into his own car and its disposal in the river less than quarter of a mile away. All conjecture, but supported by a certain amount of circumstantial evidence. We have known success in cases much more perforated than this one.'

The solicitor opened his eyes and hitched himself forward.

'One wonders,' he said, 'whether one might have some coffee. Nothing fancy. Lubrication is all.'

Purbright addressed Love immediately. 'Sergeant, would one fetch some, please?'

'Is there any hope,' Spratt-Cornforth asked, when Love had gone, 'of a voluntary statement from the defendant? It would make things easier for us, a lot easier.'

'Oh, I'm sure there is. His counsel is certain to advise him to rely on a plea of self-defence. For this to be convincing, he will have to explain what made Persimmon so violently jealous. A statement well in advance of the trial would help forestall suspicion of the story having been cooked up at the last minute.'

'Good. Encourage him, Purbright. We are not altogether happy that the authorship of this crime has been established beyond doubt. The only person we know to be able actually to *identify* the murderer is the Hillyard woman and she obviously will stick to her loss of memory, genuine or not, in her own interests.'

'In justice to the girl, I think she co-operated after killing only because she was terrified. The fact that she was heavily doped with barbiturate and locked up proves that they didn't trust her.'

'They?'

'Certainly. The two surviving members would collaborate for the sake of their mutual safety just as the original trio always had done to protect their respectability.'

'So the availability to Cropper, as a council health official, of both the keys and – we assume – the drugs, does not much help to incriminate him on the capital charge as such.'

'No, sir. Not specifically.'

'In that case . . .' – Spratt-Cornforth examined a typed list – '. . . I shall be interested to listen to these famous tapes of your Sergeant Love – numbers, what? – four and six – are we right?'

The door opened and Love entered with a tray. To commemorate the visitor's eminence he had brought cups instead of mugs and provided not only saucers in addition but the private sugar basin of the chief constable himself.

For the next ten minutes the case was set aside in favour of what Love considered a brilliant and daringly irreverent disquisition by Spratt-Cornforth on such matters as the state of Old Dicky Padstowe's chambers, Young Somebody Else's scrape with the Queen's Proctor, and the rumoured sitting stone dead for three hours of the learned judge in Number Two Court at the Bailey.

Then Purbright signalled the replacement of the tray with the Sergeant's recording machine.

They listened.

> *. . . fact, but the situation's so delicate. Quite frankly, I didn't think he'd understand. Why, sir? Well, good heav . . .*

Love raced the tape forward a little.

'Bird,' murmured Purbright for Spratt-Cornforth's benefit. The solicitor nodded.

> *. . . enough to tell me about the call that Mr Persimmon did take, sir. I can't tell you anything about it. I don't know anything. Look, sir, I'm sorry, but this time I must insist. Insist all you like. I just cannot help you. And this time it is not a case of respecting confidences. The phone rang – at about midnight, as I told you – and Persimmon answered it. He listened, not saying a word himself, and then slammed the phone down and rushed out straight away. We both heard his car start off and that was that. He didn't . . .*

Love switched off the machine and removed the cassette. He slipped another one in.

'This one's Cropper,' said Purbright.

... get up to, sir? *I know perfectly well, Mr Purbright, that Miss Hillyard associated – that is the word, I believe – with Bertie Persimmon.* Do you know who made the call last Wednesday night that resulted in Persimmon going out? *I have no idea.* What is your recollection of that call, doctor? *None, naturally. I didn't take it.* Persimmon did? *Yes. We'd had one or two earlier but they were – well, relatively trivial. Then this one came through about midnight.* Did he not say anything that might suggest who the caller was? *Not a single word. He scarcely looked at me. Just slammed the receiver down and went straight out. Then I heard his car start up.* That was the ...

Love pressed the 'off' key. He waited.

Spratt-Cornforth remained a while in thought. He shrugged.

'We seem to have missed it. Perhaps we are not at our brightest this morning.'

'In the first recording,' began Purbright, 'he ...'

'No, no.' The solicitor had raised his hand. 'Let the sergeant enlighten us. It was his discovery.'

Pink as a raspberry soda, Love looked at Purbright.

'Go on, then, Sid.'

'Well, sir ...' Love shuffled ecstatically in his seat. 'It's fairly simple, really. Just a couple of words. "We" in one recording. "I" in the other one. Bird said "We both heard his car start off". Cropper said "Then I heard his car start up". But once this bloke Persimmon had gone, there could have been only one left in the room, sir. So I reckoned that when Bird talked about "we" it was because he was being careful not to break that old alibi of theirs – the three-pals-together one.'

'Very succinctly put, sergeant,' said Spratt-Cornforth. 'We congratulate you. And of course we take your point. Bird was *imagining* the scene and so was fastidious about detail, Cropper, on the other hand, although equally concerned to thwart inquiry, was being prompted all the time by *actual memory*. Oh, yes, even a jury ought to be able to see the logic of that. What do you think, Purbright?'

'We must hope that you are right, sir,' the inspector said.

'Has one a date in mind for the committal proceedings?'

'I thought perhaps a week on Thursday, sir. If that is convenient to you.'

Spratt-Cornforth consulted a pocket diary and nodded. He looked at his watch.

'An adjournment, gentlemen, would now be appropriate. We have a luncheon appointment with your chief constable.'

For the briefest of moments, Love's mood of buoyancy tricked him into the dizzy supposition that he, too, was embraced within the solicitor's royal plural.

When the delusion had passed, and as soon as Spratt-Cornforth had briskly departed, running his rapier-like umbrella up and down in his gloved fist as if to wipe blood off it, the sergeant began to collect the cups.

'Thanks for the coffee, Sid,' Purbright said.

'Oh, and don't forget to put Mr Chubb's sugar basin back, will you?'

*Also available by Colin Watson
in Methuen Paperbacks*

The Flaxborough Novels

'Sharp and stylish and wickedly funny'
Literary Review

One Man's Meat

A dramatic death in the fairground is the harbinger
of a bizarre case for Detective Inspector Purbright.
Mysteries abound, including the precise truth
behind the initials RIP, the role of Happy Endings
Inc, and, not least, the exact contents of certain tins
of dog food.

The Naked Nuns

TWO NAKED NUNS AVAILABLE
PHILADELPHIA – it is the strangest cable ever to
come to Flaxborough. And Inspector Purbright,
who has coped with a few odd things in his time,
finds it opens a rich lode of skulduggery, deceit
and sudden death.

Lonelyheart 4122

'I'm afraid, sir, that another lady has disappeared . . .' Respectable ladies do not often vanish in
Flaxborough, and the loss of two sets Inspector
Purbright quite a poser. But much worse is yet to
be revealed. Trickery, blackmail, deception and
murder – none of it unconnected with the demure
arrival in Flaxborough of Miss Lucilla Teatime.

Hopjoy Was Here

When a secret agent disappears in highly suspicious circumstances connected with an acid bath, it is not long before two high-powered operatives arrive. But they find the Flaxborough citizenry even more inscrutable than the problems of international spying. It is Inspector Purbright who eventually comes up with the truth in a dénouement that is a masterpiece of plotting.

Bump in the Night

Connoisseurs of the English crime novel who thought Flaxborough epitomised mayhem behind lace curtains will discover Colin Watson's Chalmsbury with delight. For as Inspector Purbright discovers when he is loaned by the Flaxborough force to deal with a particularly odd and dangerous practical joker – Chalmsbury is every bit as rich in oddities, enmities and genteel assassination.

Methuen Modern Fiction

While every effort is made to keep prices low, it is sometimes necessary to increase prices at short notice. Methuen Paperbacks reserves the right to show new retail prices on covers which may differ from those previously advertised in the text or elsewhere.

The prices shown below were correct at the time of going to press.

☐	413 52310 1	**Silence Among the Weapons**	John Arden	£2.50
☐	413 52890 1	**Collected Short Stories**	Bertolt Brecht	£3.95
☐	413 53090 6	**Scenes From Provincial Life**	William Cooper	£2.95
☐	413 59970 1	**The Complete Stories**	Noël Coward	£4.50
☐	413 54660 8	**Londoners**	Maureen Duffy	£2.95
☐	413 41620 8	**Genesis**	Eduardo Galeano	£3.95
☐	413 42400 6	**Slow Homecoming**	Peter Handke	£3.95
☐	413 42250 X	**Mr Norris Changes Trains**	Christopher Isherwood	£3.50
☐	413 59630 3	**A Single Man**	Christopher Isherwood	£3.50
☐	413 56110 0	**Prater Violet**	Christopher Isherwood	£2.50
☐	413 41590 2	**Nothing Happens in Carmincross**	Benedict Kiely	£3.50
☐	413 58920 X	**The German Lesson**	Siegfried Lenz	£3.95
☐	413 60230 3	**Non-Combatants and Others**	Rose Macaulay	£3.95
☐	413 54210 6	**Entry Into Jerusalem**	Stanley Middleton	£2.95
☐	413 59230 8	**Linden Hills**	Gloria Naylor	£3.95
☐	413 55230 6	**The Wild Girl**	Michèle Roberts	£2.95
☐	413 57890 9	**Betsey Brown**	Ntozake Shange	£3.50
☐	413 51970 8	**Sassafrass, Cypress & Indigo**	Ntozake Shange	£2.95
☐	413 53360 3	**The Erl-King**	Michel Tournier	£4.50
☐	413 57600 0	**Gemini**	Michel Tournier	£4.50
☐	413 14710 X	**The Women's Decameron**	Julia Voznesenskaya	£3.95
☐	413 59720 2	**Revolutionary Road**	Richard Yates	£4.50

All these books are available at your bookshop or newsagent, or can be ordered direct from the publisher. Just tick the titles you want and fill in the form below.

Methuen Paperbacks, Cash Sales Department, PO Box 11, Falmouth, Cornwall TR10 109EN.

Please send cheque or postal order, no currency, for purchase price quoted and allow the following for postage and packing:

UK — 60p for the first book, 25p for the second book and 15p for each additional book ordered to a maximum charge of £1.90.

BFPO and Eire — 60p for the first book, 25p for the second book and 15p for each next seven books, thereafter 9p per book.

Overseas Customers — £1.25 for the first book, 75p for the second book and 28p for each subsequent title ordered.

NAME (Block Letters) ....

ADDRESS..

....